HE MAD_ _ _ _ _ _
TO_ _ _ _

Murdock grabbe_ _ _ _ _ _ _ _ _ _ _
chest and jerked o_ _ _ _ _ _ _ _ _ _ _
mouthpiece. The man flailed in panic. The Chinese
frogman desperately struggled to get at his knife.
Murdock pulled the weapon out of his scabbard and
dropped it. He forced the Chinese downward again,
and then Murdock wrapped his left arm around the
enemy's throat. The SEAL leader saw crazed eyes
through the dark water. Murdock's blade drove deeply
into the enemy's side. The blade sliced through
intestines and into one lung. Blood poured from the
wounded man's mouth.

The man's body contorted in one frantic effort.
Then his held-in air bubbled from his mouth and his
body went limp.

SEAL TEAM SEVEN
Firestorm

**Don't miss these other explosive
SEAL TEAM SEVEN missions:**

Seal Team Seven
Specter
Nucflash
Direct Action

By Keith Douglass

THE CARRIER SERIES:

CARRIER
VIPER STRIKE
ARMAGEDDON MODE
FLAME-OUT
MAELSTROM
COUNTDOWN

THE SEAL TEAM SEVEN SERIES:

SEAL TEAM SEVEN
SPECTER
NUCFLASH
DIRECT ACTION
FIRESTORM

SEAL TEAM SEVEN
FIRESTORM

KEITH DOUGLASS

BERKLEY BOOKS, NEW YORK

SEAL TEAM SEVEN: FIRESTORM

A Berkley Book / published by arrangement with the author

PRINTING HISTORY
Berkley edition / December 1997

The Putnam Berkley World Wide Web site address is
http://www.berkley.com

ISBN: 0-425-16139-0

With great respect and appreciation this book is dedicated to Jake Elwell, who made the whole project possible and who stem-wound the operation. Also to Cyndy Mobley, who made the connection and offered a writer's aid and comfort during the creative process.

SEAL TEAM SEVEN

THIRD PLATOON*
CORONADO, CALIFORNIA

PLATOON LEADER:

Lieutenant Blake Murdock.
WEAPON: H&K MP-5SD sub-machine gun.

FIRST SQUAD

David "Jaybird" Sterling. Machinist's Mate Second Class. Platoon Chief.
WEAPON: H&K MP-5SD sub-machine gun.

Ron Holt. Radioman First Class. Platoon radio operator.
WEAPON: H&K MP-5SD sub-machine gun.

Martin "Magic" Brown. Quartermaster's Mate First Class. Squad sniper.
WEAPON: McMillan M-89 7.62 NATO sniper rifle/
            McMillan M-88 .50-caliber sniper rifle.

Eric "Red" Nicholson. Torpedoman's Mate Second Class. Scout for the platoon.
WEAPON: Colt M-4A1 with grenade launcher.

Kenneth Ching. Quartermaster's Mate First Class. Platoon translator/ Chinese, Japanese, Russian, Spanish.
WEAPON: Colt M-4A1 with grenade launcher.

Harry "Horse" Ronson. Electrician's Mate Second Class.
WEAPON: H&K-21A1 7.62 NATO round machine gun.

James "Doc" Ellsworth. Hospital Corpsman Second Class. Platoon Corpsman.
WEAPON: H&K MP-5SD/
            Mossburg no stock 5-round pump shotgun.

*(Third Platoon assigned exclusively to the Central Intelligence Agency to perform any needed tasks on a covert basis anywhere in the world. A Top Secret classified assignment.)

Lieutenant (j.g.) Ed DeWitt. Leader Second Squad. Second in Command of the platoon.
WEAPON: H&K MP-5SD sub-machine gun.

Al Adams. Gunner's Mate Third Class.
WEAPON: Colt M-4A1 with rocket launcher.

Miguel Fernandez. Gunner's Mate First Class. Speaks Spanish, Portuguese, Squad Sniper.
WEAPON: McMillan M-89 7.62 NATO round sniper rifle.

Scotty Frazier. Gunner's Mate Second Class.
WEAPON: Colt M-4A1 with grenade launcher.

Greg Johnson. Gunner's Mate Second Class.
WEAPON: Colt M-4A1 with grenade launcher.

Willy Bishop. Electrician's Mate Second Class. Explosives expert.
WEAPON: Colt M-4A1 with grenade launcher, Mossburg no stock 5-round pump shotgun.

Ross Lincoln. Aviation Technician Second Class.
WEAPON: H&K MP-5SD sub-machine gun.

Joe "Ricochet" Lampedusa. Operations Specialist Third Class.
WEAPON: H&K 21A1 7.62 NATO round machine gun.

1

Thursday, May 14

0130 hours
Fuching, People's Republic of China
Zhonghua Renmin Gonghe Guo

Lieutenant Blake Murdock, a ring-knocker and commander of the Third Platoon of SEAL Team Seven, stroked evenly through the chilly water of the Taiwan Strait between Mainland China and Taiwan. He and his platoon swam the chilly waters a mile off the coastal Chinese town of Fuching.

"That's Mainland China, you shit-bird," Murdock had crowed when he first looked at his orders. "Those fucking Chinese don't like anybody messing in their rice bowl over there."

Murdock was now more determined than ever to get in and out, to scoot and shoot, and not even let the Chinese Mainlanders know he and his men had been there. If he and his team could pull it off. That was the best possible scenario, but like most covert operations by the Navy SEALs, the best possible seldom happened. There were too many loopholes, too many factors that he and his men didn't control, and too many cluster-fuck problems that could leap up courtesy of Dr. Murphy and his law of potential disasters.

Murdock felt the gentle tug of the six-foot-long buddy line that connected him to his shadow, Radioman First Class Ron Holt. He handled the commo work for the platoon, and stuck next to Murdock whenever possible.

1

Murdock sensed that he was moving on schedule. He knew exactly how many strokes he needed to swim a hundred meters even when confronted with a two-knot current. Now and again he checked the attack board to make sure he was on the right line to the target.

They had been dropped a mile offshore by a submarine and told to be back before dawn. It wasn't healthy for a U.S. boat to be caught on the surface in daylight this close to the Chinese mainland.

The CIA had called on Third Platoon again to pull their spy stuff out of the fire. It was a simple mission to meet a half-blown CIA Chinese agent on the coast and receive some high-level military plans the agent had obtained.

There was a chance he had been fully compromised, so a SEAL platoon was assigned to go in and be ready for any type of reception. It might be a walk in the park, a picnic on the beach, or it could be slaughterhouse row with ranks of the People's Republic of China soldiers waiting for them. One way or the other.

The sixteen men of the Third Platoon of SEAL Team Seven had stepped into the sea with full attack swimming gear. They were paired into eight teams, two-man units.

There was a slight chop on the surface of the chilly Taiwan Strait, but Murdock and his men swam fifteen feet under the surface. He checked the attack board again. It was a chunk of plastic with two handgrips. In the middle was a bubble compass along with a digital depth gauge and clock. The dials were luminous, but at night the dark seas quickly blotted out their meager light.

The attack board compensated for this problem with a Cyalume chemical light stick with a knob to increase or decrease the amount of light so the operator could read the instructions fifteen feet underwater at midnight.

Murdock checked the compass and saw that he was a fraction of a degree off course. He corrected and kept kicking. They had been swimming long enough for the chill of the water to reach through their wet suits. Murdock shook his head. He'd been a lot colder than this in his mother's living room. This was nothing compared to the training all SEALs go through at the Budweiser in Coronado, California—BUD/S for short, the Basic Underwater Demolition/SEAL course.

Murdock and all of his men wore the Enhanced Draeger LAR-V underwater breathing devices. They were rebreathers using pure oxygen that recycled the exhaled air so there was no telltale trail of bubbles for an enemy to spot and follow directly to the swimmer.

The new models were worn in front and had 30% larger oxygen bottles for longer underwater swims. The weapons usually on the SEAL swimmers' chest were now tied down on their backs.

Murdock looked around, but couldn't see any of the other men. They were there, moving toward the target. Even with a good moon out, he could see no more than six or eight feet through the Far Eastern sea. All of his men would get to the target. He needed them there.

He settled down and kept up his rhythmic stroke through the salty sea.

Ten minutes later he felt a hand on his shoulder, and looked around at Ron Holt. The hefty young man pointed upward. Against the soft moonlight bathing the water above, Murdock saw two shadows. They were not seals or sharks— he could tell by the shape. Then he saw the shadows kicking, and he swore he could see swim fins.

What the hell? Swimmers out here? A human frogman defense line? China had enough bodies. A damn complication. None of his men would be that close to the surface. Murdock let the attack board drop on its short cord tied to his vest, and reached for his K-Bar in its sheath on his leg. Holt had already drawn his combat knife. Murdock gave a thumb-upward motion, and they moved slowly toward the shadows above them. Murdock cut the buddy line to give them maneuvering room.

The forms above stopped, and Murdock saw wet-suited legs drop downward. The swimmers were on the surface. They weren't SEALs. The two men had been swimming parallel to the shoreline. Murdock and his men were moving directly toward the beach.

The pair above faced each other. Murdock decided they were resting or observing. They had to be Chinese frogmen patrolling out there. Who else could it be? This house onshore must be more important than the Navy stars and CIA back in Washington thought. Security out here on the water? A waste of manpower. He wondered if there were more of the frogmen along this beachfront.

Murdock was six feet under the surface treading water easily with his fins. He made up his mind to attack. He used hand signs to tell Holt which Chinese he would take. Then on signal, both surged upward, caught the frogmen by the waist, and tugged them downward.

Murdock grabbed the threshing swimmer by the chest and jerked off his face mask and breathing mouthpiece. The man flailed in panic. The Chinese frogman desperately struggled to get at his knife. Murdock pulled the weapon out of the scabbard and dropped it. He forced the Chinese downward again, and then Murdock wrapped his left arm around the enemy's throat. The SEAL leader saw crazed eyes through the dark water. Murdock's blade drove deeply into the enemy's side. The blade sliced through intestines and into one lung. Blood poured from the wounded man's mouth.

The man's body contorted in one frantic effort. Then his held-in air bubbled from his mouth and his body went limp. The Chinese frogman struggled again for a moment with one last dying effort, but it was too late. He had been caught by surprise. Another long burst of air bubbles streamed from the dead man's mouth.

Murdock held his man until he was sure he was dead. His body remained limp and his eyes stared sightless through the dark water. The platoon leader pushed him downward and looked for Ron Holt. Holt and his adversary faced each other, both with knives out. They were only ten feet away through the moonlit water near the surface. Murdock put on a burst of swimming speed, holding his K-Bar straight in front of him with his arm stiff. He came from the side and slightly behind the enemy frogman.

The victim must have sensed someone nearby, and turned

toward Murdock spoiling a quick kill. The Chinese swimmer surged to the side away from Murdock, and slashed at him with a long knife as he passed. The blade grazed Murdock's shoulder. He wondered if it had sliced through his wet suit and into his flesh.

Holt powered forward with a hard kick, forcing the Chinese swimmer to turn toward him again. Murdock swam fast at the target. The Chinese frogman faced Holt, his knife high. Fighting underwater to Murdock was like wallowing in molasses. Every move an effort, each attack slow and easy to counter.

Now the Chinese thrust at Holt, then backed away. Murdock held his blade at arm's length and drove forward again, coming at the man at the side. The Chinese man turned his head toward Murdock just in time to see the long blade jolt through fabric and stab deeply into his side. The heavy knife point slanted upward past ribs and through a part of his lung, and sliced through the Chinese sailor's heart.

He looked at Murdock in surprise, his silent cry of terror shown in his tortured expression through his face mask.

He dropped his fighting knife, his arms floating uselessly, his body collapsing. Murdock jerked his K-Bar free of the man and let him drift down and away from them with the slight current.

Murdock pointed to Holt, who caught the trailing buddy line and retied it to his skipper.

The lieutenant took out his MUGR (Miniature Underwater GPS Receiver). It was no larger than two packs of cigarettes and totally waterproof. Murdock pulled free a small floating antenna that drifted to the surface only a few feet above, with a wire attached to the MUGR. There it went into action picking up signals from the nearest three Global Positioning Satellites. The triangulation from the satellites pinpointed his location. A readout on the MUGR reported his position within plus or minus ten feet.

He hit the button marked POS, and looked hard at the line of alphanumerics displayed on the instrument's small,

lighted screen. The coordinates showed that the team was
less than seventy meters off target course. Great.

Murdock bobbed his head. He and Holt were off line due
to their small unpleasantness with the two Chinese swimmers. He pointed, and he and Holt shifted their direction and
swam again.

Twenty minutes later they could hear the roar of surf
ahead of them. Murdock pulled on the buddy line and when
Holt looked at him, the Platoon Leader motioned upward
with his thumb. They broke the surface just enough for a
sneak and peek. They were still fifty meters off the beach,
and in thirty meters the swells turned into breakers rolling
up on a dark-looking shore. It didn't show white or even
gray in the moonlight. He remembered the briefing. The
beach here was about twenty meters wide at high tide when
they arrived, and was covered with medium-sized stones
and pebbles. No sand.

Rendezvous time. Murdock treaded water and watched
the sea around him. Two men popped up twenty meters
away, then two more on the other side. He needed ten more
men. Three teams came up almost at the same time, then
the fourth. All were within thirty meters of him. He was still
one team short. Concern shadowed his face. There was
always the possibility of a team getting lost or taken out by
some enemy on a mission like this. He scanned the water
around him again.

On any operation, when a SEAL or a team became lost or
wasn't able to reach the rendezvous or continue the mission,
standing orders were to return to the drop-off point and call
for or wait for pickup. It had only happened to Murdock
once, and he didn't want to do it again. As he thought about
the chances, the last team surfaced. The men moved into
their proper order, in the First and Second Squads, and
removed the buddy lines. Murdock checked his watch. It
was 0218. Good. He hated to start any attack on the hour.
It was a giveaway.

Their briefing and planning had been detailed and specific. The house onshore in front of them had once been
owned by a local strongman who had worked closely with

the Communists, but had also maintained his own local power base. Two years ago he had lost favor with the central government in Beijing and had been arrested. A year ago he suddenly become ill and died in prison. His house was immediately taken over by the local party officials. Later it had been given to a wealthy manufacturer of the new Hoy-25 machine gun.

Tonight this house was the contact point for the SEALs and a Chinese "Christians in Action" CIA agent who had information so valuable that this SEAL operation was set up. Murdock hesitated. Why had there been Chinese frogmen patrolling this insignificant stretch of beach? Had their Chinese agent been broken and had the SEALs been lured into a well-armed killing field? Was there a welcoming committee of Chinese regulars with plenty of firepower to overwhelm sixteen SEALs? Murdock worried for a moment. There was only one way now to find out.

He went over his selection of weaponry. Half of the assault force carried the old standby, the Heckler and Koch German-made MP-5, a submachine gun spewing out 9mm messengers. The SEALs used the MP-5SD4 with its integral sound suppresser. That's a fancy word for a silencer, which doesn't really silence but cuts the sound down to a minimum.

The model had been especially crafted for the SEALs with a unique handgrip, safety, and stock. The tritium dots on the sights were for night shooting. There had been some problems with the sound-suppressed models because when you dampen the sound, you also cut down on the range and power of the weapon. The effective range of the muffled MP-5 was only fifty meters.

That was fine for house-to-house work and clearing rooms. Murdock liked them for that because the rounds wouldn't jolt all the way through a body and kill a civilian or a hostage. One of his four-man fire teams held the H&K MP-5SD4's.

The other four-man team used the M-4A1, once called the CAR-15. It had a short, sliding stock. These also had attached sound suppressers that were only eight inches long

and screwed onto the flash hider. These shooters spouted
.223 stingers at high velocity. Each of the M-4A1's had a
M-203 40mm grenade launcher mounted beneath the barrel
the way the M-16 did. To top off the weapon it had a laser
aiming light, an AN/PAQ-4 that shot out a small beam of
laser light that you could see with night-vision goggles.
Even though muffled, these weapons had a much longer
range than the MP-5.

Magic Brown in the First Squad carried his sniper rifle, a
bolt-action McMillan M-89 shooting the 7.62 NATO round.
The weapon had a shortened barrel and a fixed sound
suppresser. It had attached a Litton M921 3-power Starlight
Scope.

Harry "Horse" Ronson, one of the new men in the First
Squad, gave them firepower with his Heckler and Koch
21A1 machine gun spouting 7.62 NATO rounds.

Every one of the sixteen men had a backup weapon, a
standard-issue Sig-Sauer P-226 9mm pistol in a tied-down
thigh holster.

The troops had spread out ten yards apart in their
preplanned attack positions. Each man knew exactly what
his job was on this mission and what he had to do. They
waited.

Murdock could see the target house. There were other
houses around it, but this one stood on a small point of land
that lifted it half a story above the others. Status. They could
see two lights still burning in the house.

Murdock signaled the men to move forward. They swam
another twenty yards, then moved in with the breakers until
they were prone on the black rocks with an occasional wave
washing over them.

Now they saw the house clearly. It had a two-foot-high
wooden fence between it and the sea. Three slender and
wind-whipped trees grew near the fence. The house looked
as if it were plastered on the outside, and had some metal
sheets on the roof and some wooden panels. A brick
chimney extended from the far side of the roof.

One three-foot-wide window showed toward the sea. It
was dark. A line at the side of the house held flapping

laundry. The structure was one story high and had a door on the front and one on the side, just as they had been briefed. They would ignore the front door and use the side one. It wasn't a palace, Murdock decided, but maybe by Chinese standards it was upper-class. Due to the tight security in China, the SEALs did not have a floor plan of the house. Once inside, they would play it by ear using their much-rehearsed Kill House techniques.

The Kill House was their name for a mock-up house in the California Desert where they practiced attacking a room with dummy bad guys and hostages placed inside. They had to identify the bad guys from the hostages and use live rounds to shoot them. The SEALs trained in the facility dozens of times a year.

Now the platoon lay on a dark beach of smooth black rocks. The color blended in well with their all-black wet suits and gear. Their faces were blackened and they wore dark Nomex flight gloves to protect and hide their hands.

Murdock took the M-89 from Magic Brown and checked the layout with the Starlight Scope. He saw three men who were trying to hide themselves near the side and front of the house. None was looking at the sea. They seemed concerned with a street on the far side of the house.

He gave the weapon back to Magic and hand-signaled that there were three guards. Magic found them quickly. The M-89 coughed. Murdock watched through his one-lens night-vision goggles and saw the man in front of the house slam backwards and lay still.

Down the line the other M-89, in the Second Squad, coughed and the guard on the far right of the house tried to rise, then collapsed into a heap.

Magic drilled the third guard with a silenced shot. The man had seen the second lookout wounded and tried to go to him. Then all was quiet.

Murdock gave a hand signal that was passed down the line. The men took off their swim fins and tied them to their equipment vests. They kept on their Draeger breathing units. If anything went wrong they might have to leave in a rush and there wouldn't be time to put on the breathing apparatus. They could live without fins, but it would be a dangerous swim without the underwater rebreathers.

After that, Murdock didn't have to give any orders. The assault team with the MP-5's rushed up the beach to the house. They cleared the yard and knelt near the side door. Six more men raced silently to the front of the house. Four men spread out at the sides of the lot for security.

Murdock came up to the side door. He brought down his NVG (night-vision goggles), checked the troops, then lifted his MP-5 and kicked in the door. Holt pitched a flashbang grenade inside and then flattened against the outside wall.

The flashbang grenade is designed to render both blind and deaf anyone in the same room with the non-lethal device. The explosion is a series of ear-shattering blasts accompanied by a string of strobing light pulses so brilliant that anyone not covering his eyes is temporarily blinded.

When the last strobe of light from the grenade stabbed into the night through the opening, Murdock charged past the kicked-in door cutting to the right, watching for any movement or sound inside the room. From many hours of practice in the Kill House, he and his men knew exactly what to do. Murdock's sector was the right half of the room and he swept his MP-5 that direction looking for tangos. No, they weren't terrorists this time, just Chinese soldiers.

Murdock saw movement through his green-field NVG on his side and spewed a three-round burst of 9mm greeters at a man who raised a pistol. Holt fired two three-round bursts on his side of the room, the suppressed sub-machine gun coughing quietly. In a small window of silence, Murdock heard a long death rattle.

Enough light came through a door to the next room that Murdock could now see the three men down and dead, two with chest shots and one a pair of head hits. He flipped up his NVG. "Clear," Murdock said into his mike.

"Clear," Holt echoed.

Two more of the assault squad charged through that room to the next and more firing erupted. Murdock rushed to the door behind them. A lightbulb burned in the middle of the room on a cord from the ceiling. A blood-smeared

Chinese man sat in a chair bound by his chest, legs, and ankles. He mouth and face had been beaten bloody and raw. His chest and arms showed dozens of knife slices that bled continuously. One eye was closed, and the lid had been smashed or cut off the other eye.

Two Chinese men in civilian clothes, warned by the flashbang, had put up a fight. Both had handguns out, but they were no match for the MP-5's. A third man tried for the back door, but died before he got to it with six slugs in his side and back. The same two assaulters rushed into the next room and Murdock jolted forward to the doorway. He heard more firing from the suppressed sub-machine guns, then silence.

Machinist's Mate Second Class David "Jaybird" Sterling crashed into his Platoon Leader at the doorway.

"Some dip-shit tore out the backdoor," Sterling said. "Red is on his tail. He'll have him down and dirty within a block."

Torpedoman's Mate Second Class Eric "Red" Nicholson was lean and fast. If any of the squad could catch a running man, Red could. Murdock heard the "clear" calls from the other men, then went back to the prisoner bound to the chair.

There was no way this could be a setup, a plant. The Chinese might have known that this man was a CIA operative, but they must not have known what was happening tonight. Murdock seriously doubted they knew there would be foreign visitors who would hold a beach party.

Murdock looked at the tied-up man. His hands were behind his back. He was naked to the waist. His head hung down. Now he struggled to bring it up to look at these new men. When he opened his mouth, Murdock saw the jagged, smashed-out remains of his front teeth.

"Please, water?" the Chinese man whispered in English, his words slurred. His chest and arms had been sliced many times. It was the old Chinese torture of a thousand cuts. No one slice will kill you, but after a few hundred you will bleed to death.

"Untie him," Murdock said to Holt. The radioman cut the heavy cords that bound the man to the chair, and the tortured

Chinese agent almost fell off. Murdock caught him, then knelt beside him and steadied him. Murdock lifted a canteen to the CIA man's mouth and he drank.

"You are Americans," the Chinese man said. "I have what you came for." Then he tried to smile. A moment later he passed out.

2

Thursday, May 14

0222 hours
Beach house, Fuching
People's Republic of China
Lieutenant Blake Murdock held the Chinese agent in the chair after the tortured man slumped back unconscious. "Doc, get over here," Murdock barked. "We've got a problem."

James "Doc" Ellsworth, Hospital Corpsman Second Class, appeared quickly at Murdock's elbow.

"Let's hope he just passed out," Doc said. The corpsman broke open smelling salts and waved them under the agent's nose half a dozen times, then gave him a longer whiff. The Chinese man coughed, snorted, and then roused. At first he was wary. Then he relaxed, softened, and nodded.

"Yes, the Americans are here. I am grateful. Sorry about the bad reception by my misguided countrymen."

"The papers?" Murdock asked, his voice soft and low. "Do you have some papers to deliver to us?"

"Yes. I didn't tell them where I hid them. They asked me with much persuasion. You must take a look. . . ." He stopped. His face glazed with pain and his eyes closed as he shivered and his whole body spasmed twice, then again. He sagged against Doc, and for a moment he didn't breathe. Then the wave of agonizing pain passed and he looked up at the medic. He growled low in his throat and shook his head.

13

"Not yet. I'm not ready to die. No. The papers you want. They are outside in the roof, under a loose tile near the front door. Easy to find."

Murdock nodded at "Magic" Brown and Ron Holt, and they hurried out the front door.

"Let me lay you down and tend to these slashes," Doc said to the man.

The CIA agent shook his head and held out his hand.

"I am Hang Lee Chang, lately with the Company. I bring you the secret papers. They contain all that your people want to know. Now I must go back with you to your boat."

Doc looked at Murdock and slowly shook his head.

"You're too severely wounded to be moved, Mr. Hang," Murdock said. "We'll talk about that later. Why don't you lie down and let our medic help you."

"No. I must sit up. If I lie down, I'll die. If I stay in this house after you leave, I will be helpless and the first government man who sees me will capture me and the torture will start again. They know that I stole the plans. They didn't know about you coming." He gasped for breath and his face contorted with another spasm of pain. His eyes closed and he trembled twice. Then he gasped and his eyes opened again. "Now all is well, the Americans are here. You will take me back to your ship and then to Taiwan."

Brown and Holt came in with a roll of papers wrapped in heavy plastic. Hang looked at them and nodded.

"All there," he said. "Now we leave. You must take me with you. No other option. They will kill me the moment they find me. They will send troops here quickly if even one of them escaped your people."

Murdock looked over at Doc. The medic shook his head again. "Mr. Hang, you've lost far too much blood to risk a move. Your system is in deep shock. I don't have the equipment to help you recover. There isn't a chance that you could swim a mile through the ocean. It's simply impossible for you to come with us."

"My family is all on Taiwan. I taught English there to students. I must get back home. They will kill me if I stay here." His face contorted again. "I can't stand any more torture. I'm tired. I want to go home to my family in Taipei City."

Doc listened and reached into his kit. "I can give you a shot of morphine to ease the pain, Mr. Hang."

The Chinese CIA agent shook his head. "Must stay alert for the swim."

Murdock knelt down beside the Company man. "Mr. Hang, what our medic tells you is true. There's no chance we can take you with us. It's impossible. We're spending too much time here as it is. We're due to leave in thirty seconds."

Hang lifted his brows and nodded at them. "Understand. What is, must be. Old Chinese proverb. What must be, must be." He looked at the fighting knife on Doc's harness. "What a beautiful blade. I used to have one like it. Could I look at it?"

Murdock nodded at Doc. The medic took out the eight-inch blade with two sides and the point honed to perfection, and handed it to the agent.

Hang examined it a moment, touched the sharpness of it. Suddenly he turned the point toward his chest, gripped the heavy handle with both hands, and before either of the SEALs could prevent it, Hang drove the killing knife into his heart.

His head nodded once as the blade went in. Then his eyes rolled back showing only the whites and his hands fell away from the blade. The Chinese agent toppled lifeless to the floor.

"Damn," Murdock said. He looked at his men. "Time for E and E out of his dump. Let's move. Half out the front, rest out the side. Go, go, go!" Doc paused to pull his knife from the corpse, wiped it off, and pushed it back in its scabbard. Then he ran.

Murdock was the first one out the side door. He had flattened the roll of papers, stuffed it inside his wet suit next to his skin, and closed the suit up again. He went through the door at an angle and hit the dirt outside.

Holt went to ground on his right and Magic Brown on his left.

"Hear something?" Murdock asked.

"Trucks," Brown said. "Two, maybe three coming fast and they probably got us in their sights."

"Nicholson didn't nail that slant who got away," Holt said.

Murdock tapped his lip mike. "Got company this side 2IC. Your situation?"

"Yeah," Murdock heard in his earphones from Lieutenant Ed DeWitt, his second in command. "Company here too, coming down the side street."

"Join up here. Get those forties ready."

Rifle fire barked into the quiet of the Chinese night. Rounds slammed over the heads of the SEALs, who hugged the ground looking for targets.

The trucks stopped forty yards away, and the SEALs could see shadows melting from one house to another and moving closer.

Ed DeWitt, leader of the Second Squad, slid into the dust beside Murdock.

"Looks like a shit-pot full of them, L-T."

"Let's cut down the odds." Murdock brought up his MP-5 with a fresh clip and fired at the winking lights fifty yards in front of him.

The men with the M-4A1 carbines with the M-203 40mm grenade launchers opened up with deadly HE rounds. One round hit in front of one of the Chinese trucks, blowing the engine apart and rupturing the fuel line, which resulted in an explosion that tore the two-ton truck in half.

A Willy Peter round landed just behind the burning truck showering a Fourth of July spray of hotly burning white phosphorus into half-a-dozen Chinese troopers, who screamed as the globs of WP stuck to their uniforms and quickly burned through cloth, skin, tissue, and bone. The rifle fire slackened.

Murdock had been evaluating. He had one corridor, only four rifles firing along it, to the right front. He motioned, and Magic Brown laid down a deadly stream of 7.62 rounds into the area. Three high-explosive rounds from the launchers silenced the shooters. The SEALs heard screams, and one man rose firing a rifle, but was cut down by three rounds of NATO that tore into his chest and jolted him backwards.

Murdock came to his feet and waved his arm forward. The fifteen men behind him caught the sign and raced out of the yard, over the low fence, and down a short lane to safety behind a second house.

Four Chinese charged around the side of the house in the moonlight surprised to find an enemy waiting for them. Murdock took out the first man with a three-round burst that stitched up his throat and face. He spun and lost his AK-47 rifle crashing to the ground in front of the other three men.

The other Communist grunts never got a round off as the SEALs blasted them into instant communication with their ancestors with three-round bursts from the MP-5's.

Murdock made his plan in a heartbeat. They were now thirty yards from the beach. He heard Chinese troops approaching along the street just behind the house.

With hand signals he put Magic Brown on one side of the house and Gunner's Mate Second Class Miguel Fernandez on the other side. Both men had the McMillan M-89 sniper rifles.

"Hold them off two minutes, then regroup on the beach directly in front of us here," Murdock whispered to Magic.

Murdock signaled the others, and they lifted off the dirt and ran low and fast toward the beach and past two houses. They heard the coughing of the silenced M-89s behind them; then two M-40 grenades exploded courtesy of Gunner's Mate Third Class Al Adams, who had paused a moment with Fernandez and fired the rounds before he caught up with the group.

Red Nicholson beat them all to the beach. He paused to wait for the rest, and Murdock motioned them to go prone on the beach. He checked his men. All present except the two rear guards.

He waved at Harry "Horse" Ronson, Electrician's Mate Second Class, to bring up his machine gun. He spotted it just at the edge of some tall grass where a street ended and the beach began.

"Cover for the two rear guards," Murdock whispered.

Horse nodded, set up his bipod, and angled the weapon toward the houses in front of him.

Murdock waited. He heard firing from in front that covered up what must have been the silenced rounds from the two M-89's. Then two black shadows surged from beside the last house and charged the beach. As soon as they cleared the line of fire, Horse drilled a series of bursts from the MG alongside the house. The chatter of the machine gun shattered the sudden silence.

Murdock sent the two rear guards racing to the beach with the others and told them to tell the rest to put on their fins.

After the MG had chattered a half-dozen times more, Murdock touched Horse Ronson's shoulder. "Let's haul ass out of here."

By the time they got to the others, all were ready to swim. They all backed silently into the sea. None of the Chinese soldiers had come near the water to challenge them. They were sixteen dark shadows merging with the equally dark water.

Just before they slipped underwater, Murdock saw two Chinese fighters silhouetted against a searchlight they had driven up that was far too late. He slapped on his mask, ducked into a wave, cleared the mask, and swam into the dark water.

Murdock had tied his buddy line on to Holt just before they submerged, and now pulled up his attack board and angled directly away from shore and into the Taiwan Strait. They had a mile swim and plenty of time. Their radios had been stashed in waterproof pouches on their webbing, face masks and Draeger rebreathers positioned. Murdock sank fifteen feet below the surface and began the clockwork swim along his compass bearing.

He had the plans. Now if they were everything that the CIA thought they would be, it would be a good night's work.

Keeping his platoon together in the opaque darkness underwater was a problem for every SEAL commander. Not all of them could have attack boards. The buddy lines helped, but all sixteen couldn't be tied together.

There had been no chance to use their IBSs on this mission. They were too easy to spot, even at night. The Inflatable Boat, Small would hold eight SEALs, and with silenced motors helped the team move quickly and quietly. But not on this mission.

There could be no radio contact underwater. They had gone over the exfiltrate plans a dozen times in the submarine. Each SEAL had a waterproof wrist compass. Each man knew the correct azimuth to swim to, and with two men in each team reading the lighted devices, they should be able to rendezvous somewhere near the right spot.

Murdock checked his attack board again, made a slight change in direction, and swam forward at an even fifteen feet below the increased chop of the Taiwan Strait. He knew exactly how many minutes it would take him to swim a mile.

It was a little over a half hour later that Murdock and Holt surfaced in the rough waters. They looked around and saw no one else in the three-foot seas.

Holt let out and activated a tethered sonar signal ball that the submarine could home in on.

Murdock found the right flap in his gear and took out a heavy folded plastic package the size of a cell phone. He unfolded it, pressed a small trigger, and watched the plastic inflate with helium into a ball a foot in diameter. The inflation broke two chemicals inside the tough plastic and when they interacted, produced a fluorescent glow in the ball. A ten-foot-long monofilament line held the ball in tow. Murdock tied the mono to his webbing, and it rose to the end of the ten-foot line.

It was an SLVB, a Self Lighting Vue Ball, to serve as a guide at night on land or water with a visible signal locator device. It could be used in various ways, but always when there was no danger of enemy activity. This particular model could be seen for about half a mile when Murdock rode to the top of the swells.

He and Holt settled down to wait for their chicks to come home.

It gave Murdock time to think about Mr. Hang, the CIA operative in Fuching. He had made his choice. Murdock could tell the man was terrified of falling back into Chinese Communist hands. They would continue the "death of a thousand slices" and find more ingenious ways to torture him until he at last could feel the release of death.

He had chosen not to face that kind of an ending. The heart thrust had been deliberate, skilled, and fatal. Mr. Hang knew exactly what he was doing.

So far, it had been a productive mission. They had the plans. Whether they were useless or earth-shaking was yet to be determined.

A pair of swimmers stroked in from the north. David, "Jaybird" Sterling, Platoon Chief and machinist mate second class, waved and pushed his rebreather out of his mouth.

"This is a fucking mile? Somebody's stroke count has gone haywire. I wouldn't want to say whose it is, but there ain't many of us kicking shit here."

Murdock snorted. "Good to have you among the living, Chief. Where's the rest of your asshole crew?"

They heard splashing to the left and two more came in. Ten minutes later all but one team had joined the platoon leader.

"Missing?" Murdock asked the platoon chief. Jaybird had been keeping track.

"Lampedusa and Johnson."

"Mr. DeWitt, any intel on that?" Murdock asked.

"Lampedusa said he caught a ricochet back on the beach but it was nothing but a scratch."

"I should have looked at it," Doc said. "Why didn't I know?"

"Lampedusa and Johnson were the last ones off the beach," DeWitt said. "He assured me that he was fit for duty and would have no problem with a mile."

A hundred meters to the north, the sea foamed and a huge black hull rose out of the depths like some prehistoric sea monster. The nuclear submarine *Dorchester* flattened out and reversed engines, and came to a stop fifty meters away.

"Move out and board," Murdock said. He gave the vue ball to Holt and untied him from the buddy line. "Fasten this to the tower somewhere up high."

Murdock followed his men to the side of the sub, where they were helped on board. He stood on the deck watching the dark water around him. Where were they? He'd only lost one man on a mission and he didn't want to double that score now.

He scanned the waters on both sides a dozen times. A two-striper came out and paced with him.

"Two men short?" he asked.

"Right."

"We can give them a half hour. Then we move out."

"They'll be here," Murdock said. He spun on his heel and walked the other way down the sub's deck.

Five minutes later, Murdock heard a splash and looked starboard. Two figures moved slowly toward the big black fish. He soon saw that one man swam and one was being towed.

A half-dozen sailors jumped to the spot and helped get the SEALs on board.

Ten minutes later in the sick bay, Joe Lampedusa, Operations Specialist Third Class looked up at his skipper and shook his head.

"Damn it, L-T, I knew I could make it. Wasn't bleeding much at all. Just a nick on my upper arm."

Doc Ellsworth scowled. "You dumb-assed shit-for-brains stupid dry-humping moron. An arm wound always gets worse when you swim. I would have put you on a tow float from the git-go. Now pay attention while these Navy medics get some piss-blood back in you and take about twenty stitches in that little 'scratch' you got. Some damn scratch. I'm not losing anybody because of a fucking, some-bitching, whore-chasing scratch."

3

Thursday, May 14

0415 hours
USS *Dorchester*
Taiwan Strait

It had taken fifteen minutes to get Joe "Ricochet" Lampedusa into sick bay on the submarine and start treatment. Murdock had been met as soon as he came inside the submarine by the boat's skipper, Captain Johnson, and Don Stroh, the CIA spook who had been chaperoning and passing orders to the SEALs lately.

Murdock had been respectful but firm. "First I see that my man gets the medical attention he needs. Then we talk. Fifteen minutes isn't going to kill anyone." The captain's brows went up in surprise at the abruptness, nearly insubordination, of the junior officer, but Don Stroh took the man aside and explained it to him.

Stroh told him about the SEALs' unity, their cohesion, the way they were closer than most families and how they depended on each other for their very lives. It was a bonding that was equaled nowhere else in the armed services.

When Murdock met the other two in the officers' mess nearly twenty minutes after their first talk, the captain looked uneasy. Don Stroh waved Murdock to a chair with a pair of cold Cokes on the table in front of it.

"Now," Stroh said. "Murdock, let's see what you fished out of Mainland China for us."

Also on hand was Kenneth Ching, Quartermaster's Mate First Class, the Third Platoon's language expert, newly signed on. He'd been a SEAL for four years, had seen his share of the action, and was fluent in reading and writing Chinese and speaking various dialects. A civilian Chinese man who came with Stroh was also present.

Murdock took out the documents from inside his shirt and gave them to Stroh. He opened the plastic and scanned the papers a moment, laughed, and gave them to the Chinese civilian. "It's all Chinese to me," he said. Nobody laughed.

Stroh motioned to Ching, and he and the Chinese civilian looked at the papers critically.

"I am Hubert Wong," the Chinese civilian said to Murdock. "These characters are in the simplified Mainland style, perhaps Mr. Ching will do better on these papers than I can."

"What does it say?" Stroh asked. "What's the title page say?"

Ching looked up at Murdock, who nodded.

" 'Classified Secret' is all over the first page. A stamp of some sort. The lead title is: 'Final Plans for Invasion of Chinese Island of Taiwan.' "

Stroh shouted in delight. "Good. Now we've got our work cut out for us. Let's get to it."

Murdock signaled Stroh and stood. "Let me know what they are doing. Then maybe we can work out some way to help stop them. I need to check on the rest of my men."

He left the room, and again the captain lifted his brows.

Murdock made sure his platoon had quarters, a place to shower, and fresh uniforms. The EM mess would be open to them as soon as they were ready. He went to his assigned quarters, a closet-sized room, and showered, then put on dungarees to match the ones worn by his men. Next he called the steward and had him bring a large steak with all the trimmings and two cups of coffee to wash it down. By then he felt ready to face the committee and the Chinese plans for an invasion.

By the time he got back to the conference room two hours after he had left, sleeves were rolled up, papers littered the table, and Ching kept translating the documents, with occasional help from Hubert Wong. Much of it consisted of orders for various units and troops. These were stacked to one side.

Soon it was evident that there would be four main parts to the invasion of Taiwan by the Mainland Chinese forces.

Captain Johnson frowned at the CIA man. "Mr. Stroh, sensitive information like this must be on a need-to-know basis. This is top-secret material. What's an enlisted man doing here? And what's the clearance level of Lieutenant Murdock?"

Stroh smiled. "Captain Johnson, let me put you at ease. Your security clearance is the lowest of any man in this room. This is on a need-to-know basis, and if at some point I have to ask you to leave, I'm sure you'll understand."

The captain scowled for a moment, then nodded. "Aye, aye, sir. I'll be getting back to running my boat. Let me know of any special orders you have for me." The captain saluted Stroh, lifted off his chair, and marched out of the small room in a bad mood.

Stroh waited for the door to close, then looked at Ching and Murdock.

"So what the fuck do we have here? Looks like they have hard plans for invasion. Is there a date on their attack?"

Ching looked up and nodded. "Today's the fourteenth of May. Their target date is May eighteenth. We have four days."

"Not long enough," Stroh said. "What were those four main attacks they planned?"

Ching looked at his notes. "First, they will detonate a small nuclear weapon fifty miles south of Taiwan over the South China Sea to demonstrate the power of the blast. Second, they will launch poison-gas-filled missiles from two ships in the strait, striking each of the fourteen major Taiwan military bases to kill everyone on them and for two miles around.

"Third, they will send transport aircraft aloft with three thousand paratroopers to drop into key strategic points on the island and capture those areas. They will fly from a mainland air field.

"Then, when port facilities are secured, China will send three transports loaded with fifteen thousand troops for three separate dockside landings in Taiwan to facilitate the capture and total occupation of the island."

Stroh stood with a sheaf of notes. "I'm going to get on the radio and run this past my people as well as State, Defense, and the President. Some high-level decisions have to be made quickly if we're going to stop this without a full-scale war on our hands."

He looked at Murdock. "Does this sound like an interesting exercise for your men? I want you to start planning now how you could take down one or all of these operations and stop the invasion cold. Preplanning to be sure. Even if we don't move on this, you've lost nothing and it will be a good practice exercise. I understand the bulk of your equipment is on the carrier. We'll move toward the flattop at max speed as soon as I notify the captain.

"Mr. Ching, you should go over the plans again to see if we missed anything or if any other interpretation could be put on those documents. Wong, you help him out. Let's all get to work."

Murdock found his men in a small dayroom the submariners had turned over to the SEALs for temporary use. Most were cleaning and oiling their primary weapons. They had on clean dungarees and had been fed.

Platoon Chief Jaybird Sterling got to him first. "What's up, Skipper? That paper we brought back tell them anything?"

"We could be busy for the next few days." He gathered them around and briefed them on what the secret Chinese plans spelled out.

"They're finally gonna try it," Gunner's Mate Second Class Scotty Frazier said. "After threatening to do it for fifty years, they're gonna give it a try. Damn me."

"We don't know if it's a go for us or not," Murdock said. "Stroh is on the horn right now with the brass and the President figuring it out. What we need to do is get down to the dirty-dirty here and do some planning. How can we be four places at once, and how can we shoot down this planned invasion before it gets started? Any ideas?"

Most military commanders are shocked to their core by the SEAL methods. Every SEAL operation is a joint process. Planning and tactics and operations are all worked out by the men who will be doing the mission. Officer and enlisted rank means less here than in any part of the military. Every man does his job or he's booted out of the SEALs and back into the "real" Navy where he can chip paint, swab decks, and clean latrines.

Combat veterans of the SEALs know what it is to put their lives in the hands of their team members. They all have been through the most rigorous training in the world, have experienced pain and fatigue and cold and months of harassment and more pain. Few men can stay the course and graduate from BUD/S at Coronado, California. Those who do come out scarred, cocky, self-assured, profane, talented, and with an undying devotion to every other SEAL who has passed the test and weathered the system for six months or more to get his Budweiser pin. That's an eagle, a trident, and a flintlock pistol—the emblem of the SEALs.

The SEALs are a breed apart, and not at all loved by the rest of the Navy, and certainly not by many of the penny-pinchers in Washington when they find out that it costs $80,000 in cash to turn a sailor into a SEAL.

"Let's take them from the top," Platoon Chief Jaybird Sterling said. "That's the big bang. How do you stop somebody from dropping a bomb?"

"Easy," Magic Brown said. "Don't let them get the boom-boom on the delivery vehicle, whether it's a boat or plane."

Murdock nodded. "Bottle up the heavy stuff wherever they hold it. Our people should know where the Chinese have their atomic weapons manufacturing and storage facilities. The word is that there aren't a lot of finished nukes in China's arsenal yet. They must have at least one or two. If this mission is a go, we'll get info from Stroh and his satellite friends about the China nuke workshop and storage. What's next?"

"The poison gas," Seaman Ross Lincoln of the Second Squad said. "What kind is it and where do they store it? They plan to deliver it by ship, you said, so that means naval cannon rounds or missiles."

Doc Ellsworth had just broken down his MP-5 and was in the middle of oiling and reassembly. "I've heard about some of the gas warfare stuff the Chinese have. One great one is the HDL-7. A nerve gas that is as potent as anything our chemical boys own. It's said that a teaspoonful in a big city water supply can kill a hundred thousand people in an hour."

"So we go after the supply and the delivery," Chief Sterling said. "Twice the fun. Can we find out where they store the goodies?"

Lieutenant DeWitt chimed in. "Washington has a complete rundown on the Chinese chemical warfare capabilities, and I think that includes where they make the stuff and store it. We'd need to know what class of ship will be used for the delivery, probably one of their missile-cruiser class. That would cut down on the number of ships needed."

Murdock sat back and listened to his men. None of them were dummies. Most of them read a lot—between brawling, whoring, and drinking, that is. After all, they were SEALs. He wondered how the work was going in the conference room with the interpreters. He also was more than a little interested in how Stroh's talk with the President was going. He'd be surprised if they got any kind of a go-no-go for a covert action within twenty-four hours.

4

Wednesday, May 13

1815 hours
White House Conference Room
Washington, D.C.
"Yes, sir, that's thirteen hours, precisely, that Mainland China's west coast is ahead of us timewise," Secretary of State Matthew Burdick told his President. "It's now 6:15 P.M. here, so it's 7:15 A.M. tomorrow morning in Taipei and China."

"That's because of the International Date Line, correct?" The President asked.

"Yes, sir."

There were only five of them in the Oval Office clustered around the big desk. Burdick had loosened his tie. He puffed on a big cigar, to the annoyance of the others, who nevertheless didn't comment. "Damned difficult situation," he said. "We've halfway committed to telling the Mainland Chinese that they can have Taiwan back eventually. Yet we throw up a fleet of carriers and hundreds of warplanes when they hold live missile-firing exercises in the Taiwan Strait."

Across from him sat Lambert J. Waldpole, the current director of the CIA. He was a tall man, with gray hair, a full salt-and-pepper beard kept trimmed to half an inch, and gray, watery eyes that never let you know what he was thinking.

"We've got to give the Navy SEALs the go-ahead and try

29

to stop this invasion," the head spook said. "If we don't, we could get sucked into a full-blown war with one and three tenths billion Chinese. We don't need that. I've seen the results of these commando SEALs. They are ten times as good as any of the commandos who operated during World War II, ours or the British."

"A damn bunch of cowboys," the next man in line growled. He was Secretary of Defense Franklin Inge. He sat slumped over, small and wiry, with a cherub face and a big smile, behind which was a deftly concealed sharp knife looking for an opening.

"What can half-a-dozen men do against Mainland China, for gawd's sakes?" Inge asked. "A division of Marines, maybe. We're playing with fire. Sure, keep it as covert as hell, but what if something blows, or we leave some dead SEALs or U.S. equipment behind? What the hell happens then, win or lose in our strike?"

"Then the international shit hits the big fan," the President said. He looked at the last man in the room, Chief of Naval Operations Admiral Lucian Quenton. He was the first black four-star admiral in the U.S. Navy.

"Lucian?"

"As everyone has said, a tough call that only you, Mr. President, can make. I know these SEALs. I've seen them train. I've walked through what they call a Kill House and seen the precision, the skill, the speed with which these men function. If it can be done in three days, this platoon of SEALs can do it. I'd vote for a go."

They talked over every aspect of the situation for another half hour. The group was split on which way to go.

The President stood, picked a quartet of multi-colored M&M's off a dish on his desk, and popped them in his mouth. He walked to the end of the room and came back. His hands had been clasped behind him. He nodded at them all.

"Gentlemen, thank you for your time. I'll let you know what I decide within a half hour." They all stood and started for the door.

"Oh, Lucian, would you remain, please," the President asked.

The admiral sat back in his chair, his hands on the upholstered arms. When everyone else had left and the door closed discreetly, the President turned to Quenton with a slight frown.

"Lucian, what do you know of this SEAL unit that went in and brought back the Chinese invasion plans?"

"Best platoon of SEALs we have, Mr. President. Best leader, too. He led the SEALs on that nuclear threat by the Arab militant fringe in the North Sea on that oil-drilling and refining platform a few months back. Saved our hides on that one. He's had several SEAL missions before that. The nuclear matcrial coming into the Near East on that Japanese freighter that was hijacked.

"If there's a man and a platoon in the SEALs who can do the job, it's Lieutenant Blake Murdock and his fifteen men."

The President winced. "Sixteen men to take care of four major invasion threats like these? How is that possible, Admiral?"

"The SEALs believe that anything is possible, Mr. President. I've seen them in action close up. Their planning is intensive. This isn't admirals and secretaries of defense setting around a table in the Pentagon spelling our strategies and assaults. These are the men who will go in and do the work. Two officers and fourteen enlisted men, and every SEAL in the unit can have his say about how to do an operation.

"All of Murdock's men are bloodied. All have been on recent combat operations. It's your call, Mr. President. But I'd say a covert action right now is our best bet. Even if we don't pull it off, we'll hamper their invasion to some degree. On the other hand, if we don't act, they will swarm all over Taiwan and we lose another battle."

The President stood. "Thanks, Lucian. I can always count on you for the facts. I'll let you know which way we'll go."

"Thank you, Mr. President."

5

Thursday, May 14

After five hours of work laying out preliminary plans for attacking the four phases of the Chinese invasion of Taiwan, the men of Third Platoon turned in for some long-overdue sack time. Murdock had made a quick rundown on the plans with Stroh, who made a couple of suggestions and said he hadn't heard from the Commander in Chief yet.

Murdock decided a few hours' sleep would be beneficial to him as well, and he hit the bunk in his closet-sized room. He had made sure that his men had proper quarters before he turned on the snooze alarm.

David "Jaybird" Sterling, platoon chief of Third Platoon, lay on his bunk with his eyes wide open. He hadn't slept for well over twenty-four hours, but he still couldn't get to sleep. His mind charged from one of the four actions they had outlined to the next. Evaluating, working up possible improvements, different tactics. Then it all came crashing down. This speculation was worthless until they got the word. They couldn't do a damn thing until the President decided if they would try to stop the invasion.

He laced his fingers behind his head and stared at the bunk above him. A year ago he would never have thought he'd be where he was now. He had thirteen men to watch, to bitch at, to coddle, to persuade, to order if he had to into whatever project or job they had at hand. He had thirteen men depending on him. He was responsible for their lives.

When in hell was the brass in D.C. going to decide what they would do?

He pushed the thought aside and concentrated on Coronado. Coronado, California, and that long spit of land that connects the Jewel City to the mainland at Imperial Beach. On that strip of sand and earth perches the Naval Amphibious Base. Part of that facility is the headquarters of Naval Special Warfare. It's on the San Diego Bay side of the strand just off State Highway 75.

On the Pacific Ocean side is the BUD/S training center with the headquarters built around a courtyard. There are many slogans carved in wood and printed in that area. One says, "The more you sweat in peace, the less you bleed in war." Another one says, "The only easy day was yesterday."

SEAL training. Damn. Jaybird would never forget it. He had arrived nervous and scared. He'd heard all sorts of harsh and devastating stories about the rigorous training the SEALs underwent, but he knew it couldn't be as tough as they all portrayed. He was wrong. It was harder.

The stories didn't come halfway to the truth of the pain, the sweat, the pressure, the agony of SEAL training. Nor of the ecstasy when he completed it and knew he had won the biggest fight of his life, the fight with himself.

One of the purposes of the SEAL training is to stretch each man's capability to his limit, to let him relax a moment and then stretch him again beyond where he had been before, and eventually far, far beyond anything he had thought he was capable of.

A lot of SEAL candidates quit. The dropout rate reaches 90% in some classes. One class closed because every man in the group quit. The usual dropout rate is about 50% for each group.

At one corner of the courtyard at the headquarters is a large brass "quitting bell." It used to be a man could ring the bell three times, put down the helmet, and quit the training.

Now they had stopped using the bell. The Navy decided that using it created a serious psychological problem for those leaving training. Bullshit!

Even now, Jaybird found it hard to believe that the training lasted for twenty-six weeks. That's six months of Hell for the men who try it. Jaybird had heard that SEAL training was 90% mental and only 10% physical. He had never believed that. But the mental strain was tremendous.

Those with a weak commitment or a flagging will almost certainly don't make it through the training. Those who survive the twenty-six weeks of fatigue, pain, and grueling exercises beyond anything they had ever known are the strong ones. They can be counted on in combat when the lives of the SEALs are on the line and they must perform their jobs flawlessly, quickly, and with decisiveness. Then you are a SEAL.

Jaybird remembered the obstacle course at Coronado. Damn, it was the toughest in the world. He'd learned to hate the diving tower, a fifty-foot-deep tank filled with water. He'd almost drowned there once. One phase of their training was "waterproofing." The trainees were tied hand and foot and dropped into the tank. They sank to the bottom, then paddled slowly to the surface, took big breaths, and then sank to the bottom again. They don't use that tank anymore. Now they have a new twelve-foot-deep pool instead.

The idea is to train the men not to fear the water, and not to panic. Most people drown because they panic in the water.

The long strand of clean sand beach and the Pacific Ocean just outside the fence from headquarters were also part of the exclusive SEAL training areas. He quickly became acquainted with the IBSs, the Inflatable Boat, Small. Jaybird became devilishly familiar with them while learning teamwork. One of the exercises was for the seven men to lug an IBS around on their heads.

Climbing ropes tore up arms and shoulders regularly, but also served in the long run to build those muscles for top upper body strength. Then there were the telephone poles that teams of SEALs lifted and held and carried until their bodies ached beyond belief.

It had taken Jaybird only a week to learn that while individual training was important, the emphasis in BUD/S was on teamwork. That teamwork became so ingrained in the candidates that they would later function as a team without thinking, reacting to a situation as they had been trained.

The SEAL trainee starts with a Fourth Phase program, a four-to-seven-week time slot in which he gets his equipment, learns how to use it, and is given an outline of the training requirements.

Jaybird had looked in awe at the posted tests:

Swim a half mile in the pool without fins in thirty minutes.

Swim a mile in the pool without fins in sixty minutes.

Take a one-mile swim in the San Diego Bay with fins in fifty minutes.

Run a two-mile course in sixteen minutes.

Swim a mile and a half in the Pacific Ocean with fins in seventy-five minutes.

Run a four-mile course in thirty-two minutes.

Officers who take the BUD/S training have no rank during training. They are treated the same way the lowest seaman is—with vigor and toughness and with an eye toward washing out anyone who can't measure up. The officers are treated differently in one aspect. In certain written tests the officers must score ten points higher than the enlisted candidates to pass.

Jaybird remembered the log.

Not just any log. His boat team's log. The boat team is a training unit that helps teach team effort. Jaybird would never forget the first day they met their log.

Seven men made up a boat team, and they would be together for the rest of the training. They marched out to a stack of telephone poles, each twenty feet long and weighing three hundred pounds. The seven of them picked up one pole and carried it where instructed.

Then they were told to lie down and bring the log onto

their chests. The next order puzzled them at first. They were commanded to do sit-ups with the pole held to their chests. The whole point was that all seven men working together and at the same time could do the sit-ups lifting the telephone pole at the same time. But if one of the seven didn't lift his weight, the other six bodies couldn't do it by themselves.

They were starting to learn the teamwork that is the hallmark of every SEAL who ever graduated from BUD/S training.

For weeks their pole was never far from their sweating bodies. They did push-ups with their toes resting on top of the log. They raised it over their heads while lying flat on their backs, held it all the way up, halfway up, then did push-ups with it.

Once they ran a race along the beach for fourteen miles with the seven of them carrying the log. Sometimes they ran over sand dunes to the surf. There they had to drop the log, flop into the surf, then pick up their very own log again, and run back to the starting point.

Platoon Chief Jaybird Sterling turned over on the bunk trying to find a comfortable position. When the hell were the brass in D.C. going to make up their minds? It was a simple answer, yes or no. He checked his watch. It'd been an hour since the SEALs had finished their preliminary planning. What in hell was going on?

The next thing Jaybird knew the L-T was shaking his shoulder.

"Up time. Let's move. We catch a chopper in fifteen minutes. We're taking a damn quick ride to the big floating football field on the ocean. Move."

"What's the word, go or no go?" Jaybird asked.

"Wish I knew. Let's get out of here. We'll find out for sure on the carrier."

6

Thursday, May 14

The big Sea Stallion CH-53-D had come in from the south and hovered two feet off the deck of the sub, and the sixteen SEALs crawled on board with all of their equipment used in the shoreline attack.

Joe "Ricochet" Lampedusa had to be helped into the chopper because he was well doped up on painkillers and antibiotics. By then he wasn't feeling the pain in his arm. Neither bone had been broken, and he bellowed that he'd be ready for duty in four hours. Murdock knew he wouldn't be.

Don Stroh jumped in behind them along with one other civilian Murdock didn't know and Hubert Wong, the CIA Chinese interpreter.

An hour later they walked off the chopper on the deck of the supercarrier *Intrepid*, and were led by a white shirt to their quarters. A white shirt on a carrier deck is the safety officer who helps route pedestrians in and around the flight deck so they don't get killed. Murdock checked out the living space for his men, approved it, then went to the cabin assigned him and L-T DeWitt. The room was large compared to the submarine's offering. Before they got their gear stowed, a knock sounded on the door.

Don Stroh stood there with a phony grin. "Hey, guys, I

think it's time you both had some background on this China-Taiwan tussle. Family feud is what it is. Herb Wong, who met you before, can give you a briefing in about an hour. It's worthwhile."

Murdock scowled. "Why just the two of us? If it's worthwhile for us, it's just as important for the rest of our men. SEALs don't have 'officer country' secrets. You should know that by now, Stroh."

The CIA op grinned. "'Deed I do, Lieutenant. Just thought I'd give you the option. We can do this in the crew's quarters if they'd be happier there."

Murdock dropped his Draeger rebreather on his bunk. "Fine, let's do it right now. Any go from the White House yet?"

"Not a whisper. You'll probably know which way before I do. I'll let you lead the way to your men."

Ten minutes later, Murdock was glad they were getting the briefing. In addition to several dialects of Chinese, Hubert Wong spoke perfect English. He should. He was from Boise, Idaho. He had been a practicing attorney before he went with the CIA.

Murdock settled down and listened.

"What we're dealing with here is the oldest organized nation on earth, and a second outfit that is an upstart of a mere fifty years. The People's Republic of China is not a republic or a democracy and is ruled by an elitist clique with dictatorial powers. One estimated population of China is one point three billion people. That's a B as in billion.

"This tiny neighbor, just ninety miles off the mid-China coast, was originally called Formosa by the Portuguese rulers, and has been called Taiwan or Nationalist China or the Republic of China, and now calls itself the Republic of Taiwan. Taiwan has about twenty-two million people. That means China has sixty times as many citizens as Taiwan does.

"The only thing certain about Taiwan's future is the uncertainty of the island's future. Will it become a full-fledged nation in its own right, or a province of China, or remain in limbo as it has for the past fifty years?

"Physically, Taiwan is dwarfed by China. Taiwan is about two hundred and fifty miles long and eighty miles at its widest point. Some twenty smaller islands are close by and considered a part of Taiwan. It is about the same size as the state of Massachusetts. It includes two islands near the China coast, Matsu and Quemoy, that have caused problems in the past.

"There is proof of human life on Taiwan dating back ten thousand years. These were aborigines and not Chinese. Many think they came from Malaysia. In the early history of the Chinese dynasties, there is little mention of Taiwan other than to say it was not a part of China.

"In 1517, the Portuguese found Taiwan and named it Formosa, or beautiful island. Spanish invaders took over the island in 1626, but were booted out by the Dutch in 1628.

"I bet all these dates are boring to you men. Enough to say that Dutch ruled for thirty-three years.

"A Chinese rebel defeated the Dutch in 1661 and brought thousands of Chinese to the island. He fought the dynasties on the mainland, but at last his island was captured by Manchu troops from China in 1683.

"After a quick war with Japan that China lost in 1895, China ceded Taiwan and the Pescadores to Japan. Japan's ability to organize and develop served Taiwan well, and it was soon on its way to becoming a modern society. All developments in business and industry were channeled to Japan, and more than ninety percent of its exports went back to Japan.

"In World War II, Taiwan was described by Japan as an unsinkable aircraft carrier. It was used as the base of operations for the Japanese invasion of the Philippines and other lands, including Indonesia.

"At the end of World War II, Taiwan was stripped from Japan and Generalissimo Chiang Kai-shek was assured that control of the island would be returned to China. Chiang was then in control of Mainland China. Chiang's Nationalist China sent military forces to Taiwan and his officials handled the administration of the island.

"In October 1945, Nationalist Chinese authorities for-

mally took over political control of Taiwan. It was known as
Retrocession Day, and Taiwan became a part of the Republic of China.

"That's the Nationalist China bunch we're talking about
here under Chiang Kai-shek. Soon he was fighting the
Chinese Communists, who were trying to take over China.
The situation on Taiwan went from good to extremely bad.
The Chinese sent to Taiwan didn't know how to handle the
advanced technological developments the Japanese had left.
The civil rule and law and health all went into a serious
tailspin, and soon the local Taiwanese thought the Mainland
Chinese were worse than their long-time occupying forces
from Japan.

"Then in 1949, Chiang's forces were defeated by the
Communists and he and most of his government fled by
boat to Taiwan where they would be safe from the Communists. More than a million and a half people surged into
Taiwan when the economy was already in serious trouble.

"In the spring of 1950, Mao Tse-tung planned to invade
Taiwan and return it to China's rule. Bad planning, few
boats, and a terrible health crisis brought on by liver flukes
in China delayed the planned invasion. In mid-1950 the
Korean War started, and the U.S. sent the Seventh Fleet to
the Taiwan Strait to shield Taiwan from invasion by China.

"With peace and protection by the U.S., Taiwan could
look to reform. They began with land reform, returning the
land to the people, and with U.S. help did an outstanding
job. That was the start of reforms that soon transformed
Taiwan into a place with the fastest-growing economy in the
world.

"As Taiwan's economy, her standard of living, and more
and more freedom for her people soared, China was
stagnated with too many people, not enough industry, and a
sluggish economy that had no firm foundation. This aggra-
vated the Mainland Chinese even more and some say this is
the main reason why the Communists want to capture
Taiwan and bring the island into line as a China province."

Wong took a pull from a soft drink and looked at the men.

"So, are there any questions?"

Magic Brown turned his big brown eyes and his black face upward and stared at the speaker. Then he grinned. "Mr. Wong, just why the hell do we need to know all this?"

There was an immediate hurrahing and lots of laughter in the quarters. Wong looked surprised. Then he grinned.

"You need to know it because your commanding officer said you did. Best damn reason I can think of."

"Yeah, me too," Brown said, and they all laughed again. Murdock stood and shook Wong's hand.

"If China ever gets her act together, those one point three billion Chinese are going to be a real pain in the butt."

Stroh laughed at that and he and Wong started out. Stroh made it to the outside door, where a sailor handed him a piece of paper. He read it and headed back to Murdock.

"Hey, Lieutenant, you've got a phone call. The Chief of Naval Operations himself back in D.C. wants to talk with you. He's on the horn right now and we're due up in the communications room."

Murdock stared at him. "The CNO? You sure? Admiral Lucian Quenton himself? I've never met the man. He doesn't know that I exist."

"He does now, sailor. Let's get up there before he hangs up on you."

7

Thursday, May 14

On the way from the men's quarters to the communications room, Murdock asked Stroh if he knew what this was about.

"Not a clue, frogman. We better get hopping."

Murdock took a swing at Stroh, who chuckled at his own joke and led the way. They got lost twice in the big ship, and had to ask for a guide to take them to the communications complex. When they finally got there, a chief, two radio operators, the captain, and two commanders stood around waiting, their nervous twitches obvious.

"Glad you found time to come, Lieutenant," the captain said. "Right over here. It's the satellite link and just like talking on a telephone. There will be a slight delay, but you'll get used to it. We've got it on the speaker so we all can hear."

Murdock took the handset. "Yes, sir, Admiral Quenton. Lieutenant Murdock reporting, sir."

A light chuckle came over the handset. "Murdock. I've been hearing good things about you. We just got word from the President. It's a go for your mission to try to stop that damned invasion. We can't make it overt. Don't leave any of your dead behind, use all the sterile equipment that you can. We don't have a chance to talk about tactics, but all of us here wish you well."

"We'll try for containment and prevention, get them before they can get into action on any of the four phases. It should work. If we're lucky, sir, and the creeks don't rise."

The admiral laughed. "Understand. I've already talked with Captain Victor there on the *Intrepid*. You have his cooperation for any materials, transport, weapons, rehearsal areas. Just tell your contact what you need and you'll have it."

"Thank you, Admiral. We'll also need the satellite guys there in D.C. to give us all the data they have on the Chinese nuclear site where they build and store their bombs. The same for anything they have on Chinese poison gas facilities and storage. These two elements are vital for our operation."

"Our boys have been checking out those two elements for the past few hours. I'll get printouts and photos sent to you by satellite just as soon as they're ready. Anything else from the home office?"

"Anything about the Chinese defenses along the coastline opposite Taiwan would be helpful. Airfields, barracks, naval stations, that sort of thing."

"No problem. You'll have that material within an hour."

"Thanks, sir. Now we better get to doing our detailed planning."

"Good luck, Murdock. We're counting on you and your men."

"Yes, sir. We'll do it."

Murdock hung up the phone and looked at Stroh. "You heard it."

"So, what's next?"

Murdock looked at Captain Victor. "Who will be our contact with your people, Captain?"

One of the commanders spoke up. "I am, Lieutenant Murdock. Jason P. Wandemere. The captain told me you get anything we have on board or that we can fly in here in a rush."

Murdock took the man's hand. "Thanks, we'll be needing lots. First, how about a good-sized conference room, lots of big blank charts, and all of the intelligence you have on the Chinese mainland across from Taiwan. We'll especially need to know where their airfields are and all of their close-by navy facilities, and anything you know about where they store their nuclear material and weapons."

The commander brought out a notebook and took notes quickly.

"We have a medium-sized classroom one deck up from your quarters that should work well for you," he said. "It has overhead projectors and lots of old NCR blank charts. Room for twenty men.

"Let me make some phone calls and I'll get this other information you need brought right down there. We can talk later about what transport you'll need. Do you have any time schedule planned yet?"

"We've only got four days. We'll want to hit them as fast as we can, probably tomorrow as soon as it gets dark. We'll see how our data comes in. Let's see that training room. Could you have a runner go bring my men to that same training room? They've had enough sleep for this week."

The commander grinned, motioned to one of the sailors in the room, and then left himself to do his phoning.

"Sir, I'll take you to that training room," another sailor said. Murdock nodded. Don Stroh doubled up his fist and punched the air once.

"We're on our way, Murdock. Watch out, you Chinese bastards, the SEALs are coming after your ass."

An hour later Third Platoon wallowed in data, locations, estimated troop strength, position of airfields and barracks, and a hundred other bits and pieces of data about the Chinese position on the mainland.

Murdock had them separating and classifying the information.

"We put everything we know about their airfields in one stack on this table," he said. "The same for their nuclear ability and possible locations goes over here." He looked at the scatter of maps and satellite printouts and reports and grinned. "At least we have enough intel on this project. Down here goes the poison-gas and germ-warfare ability and locations. Then the next table is for the naval facilities and where their troop transports probably will be stationed and load out."

It was another hour before they had the material sorted. More kept coming in every ten minutes or so from the satellite, and from the map room of the carrier.

Murdock assigned them to each of the four phases of their attack for a more detailed study. He, Lieutenant DeWitt, Chief Jaybird Sterling and Magic Brown worked on the nuke problem.

"Figured they might have a facility way back in the interior somewhere," Murdock said. "From the intel we get from the satellite guys, they say the major Chinese nuclear center is in a huge solid granite cave on an island near the mainland just south of Fuching."

"That's where we went ashore to bring back the invasion plans," Magic said.

"True. This is a small island south of that somewhere. According to the satellite guy, it's named Tayu. Tightly guarded, accessible only by ship, and about three miles off the mainland. As far as the spy guys know, this is the only facility in China where they store ready-to-use nuclear weapons. Logic tells us that the Chinese nuke bomb should come out of that hole. Our job is to stop it from emerging."

"This our first attack?" Lieutenant DeWitt asked.

"Should be," Jaybird said. "They'll need some lead time to get the bomb to the surface, then loaded on a secure boat and taken to a port were it will be loaded on a secure truck and taken to the airfield where the delivery plane is waiting. At least a twenty-four-hour lead time to be safe."

"So we hit this first," Murdock said. "Just how, we'll work out soon. What's the next-priority target?"

"The gas missiles, looks like to me," Magic Brown said. "Doubtful if they would keep anything that potent in place on one of their ships. It would be on an 'on need' basis. So they would have to use transportation again. Where is their gas-warfare center?"

Murdock went to the gas-warfare table. He left the other three at the nuke table to start working out a plan of attack and destruction without setting off one of the nuclear weapons.

Doc Ellsworth looked up at his L-T and shook his head. "These bastards have some rugged shit in their inventory. Where did they get all of this potent nerve gas? Amazing. If the spy guys are right, they could wipe out everyone on Taiwan and send over a couple of million new inhabitants and have it all their own way."

"Where do they make the stuff?" Murdock asked.

Doc pointed to a map of China. "Way to hell and gone up in here at a little place called Chitai. That's almost all the way across China, about twenty-five hundred miles from Fuching."

"They keep the shit there?"

"Nope, make it there. The ready-for-delivery gas is kept in rockets ready to use at the Amoy Naval Base, maybe two hundred miles south of Fuching. Big fucking navy base there with all the goodies."

"Do they know where on the base?" Murdock asked.

"All the spy people can tell us is that the missiles loaded with poison gas are in building twenty-eight," Doc said. "We don't have the slightest where that shack is situated."

"At least the two hundred miles is within our transport capability. That all-the-way-across-China shit didn't sound good at all. Work at it. Figure out some ingress into the navy base. How secure is it? Where can we get in, under, around, or through?"

Murdock went to the next target in line, the airfields that would launch the three-thousand-paratroop drop to seal off any opposition and capture the port facilities needed to land the invasion troops.

Gunner's Mate First Class Miguel Fernandez led the SEALs working over the airfield data. "Could be one of two fields, L-T. Not the fuck sure which one. We'll have to wait for the satellite to show us a buildup of some kind. Latest photos were eighteen hours ago. They're repositioning the satellite to get a better sweep on this coastal area. Figures to be close to the coast, which narrows it down to two fields.

There's a new one just south of Amoy, big with long runways.

"The other one is inland about five miles from Foochow. That's about thirty miles north of Fuching. So far the spy boys can't give us any positive on either one. They lean toward the Amoy field since it's newest and has the best facilities. Oh, they said there were new barracks there that could house the three thousand troops for a limited number of days. They'll watch for the troop buildup and the gathering of transport planes around either field."

Murdock nodded, and told them to work out some attack plans on each of the fields—infiltration, weapons use, and how to haul ass without losing any men.

At the last table he saw better intel. Ron Holt, his radioman, had taken charge of the troop transport table. He grinned and showed Murdock satellite photos. They detailed three huge troop transport ships at the harbor in Amoy.

"Looks like they are loaded and waiting," Holt said. "Look at the waterline. Must mean that each one has its complement of five thousand troops, equipment, ammo, and supplies. Ready and waiting to hear that the docks are captured in Taiwan."

Murdock grinned. "So that makes your job easier. We have two targets in Amoy harbor. Once we penetrate, we can send one squad at each target, get the job done, and E and E."

"We thinking some limpet mines to blow off the screws or to sink the turkeys right there in the mud dockside?" Holt asked.

"Either one. We'll be ready for either chance and see how our time is working out. This will be the second night. About twenty-four hours before their attack time. We've got to make each phase work."

Holt nodded. "Right now we're trying to figure out the distance from the harbor mouth to the transports. Just a nice swim. We shouldn't even break a sweat."

Murdock told them to keep planning. "Work out the

equipment, arms, transport, IBS, timing, coordination with the carrier. I'll be back."

He went to the nuke table and huddled with DeWitt and Jaybird.

"We've got three targets tied down and a question for the fourth," Murdock said. "Two of them are in Amoy harbor. That would be the second night. One is near Fuching here, and the other one either up thirty miles north at Foochow or down at Amoy airfield. This is looking more doable all the time."

"Get a submarine next door to Fuching and go in with IBSs, do the job, and then back to the sub?" DeWitt asked.

"Could," Murdock said. "Then if it's Foochow, we can go by sub up that way and use the IBSs again to go ashore and blast that field wing tip to wing tip with transport planes. Then back to the sub and lay over during the day.

"The next night we meet a chopper and get airlifted two hundred miles south to Amoy and do our work there. By the time we're done, the sub should be off Amoy to pick us up, or we can beacon in a chopper for an airlift home."

DeWitt held up his hand for a high five and the three grinned.

"Now, let's get down to the dirty-dirty details," Murdock said. "Everything on paper now."

8

Thursday, May 14

**2014 hours
USS *Intrepid*
Taiwan Strait**

Somewhere in the afternoon or evening they had eaten. Food had been brought to them in the classroom as they worked over plans and equipment and details for each of the four missions.

An officer came in from the commo room.

"Lieutenant Murdock, we have confirmation from the satellite photos. There is a definite buildup of aircraft and personnel around the airfield near Foochow. It's a definite."

Murdock thanked the ensign and hurried over to the table detailing the strike on the airfield. He told them the news and they adjusted their plans, mostly for transport, infiltration, and egress.

At the Amoy table he checked the plans. They looked solid. He talked to Lieutenant DeWitt.

"So we go first on the nuke. That's up at Fuching. Fine. If all goes well we get in and out in an hour. Then we need to move our asses all the way up to Foochow. That's over thirty klicks, and how the hell we gonna get there?"

"Use our IBSs in and out of the island and the nuke, right?" DeWitt asked.

"Probably the best, give us a base of operation."

"We bug off the nuke island after our hit, then call in our

handy-dandy little submarine for a joyride thirty miles north. At twenty knots, that's going to take an hour and a half. Lots of night still left."

"Then we move into this airfield. The only trouble, it's about five miles inland." Murdock figured it could be done. Two missions the same night was nothing new to them.

"Yeah, a long walk but not a tough one," DeWitt said. "All we have to do is not make any noise or rouse any Chinese farmers or villagers."

"So we get in, no problem," Murdock said. "Getting out might be a little hairier. They'll have choppers to throw at us if they can find us. And those damn jets of theirs, the SU-27s, are no slouches. They can carry a shit-pot of missiles and bombs."

"So we get in, do our job, and get out before the sun comes up," DeWitt said. "Sounds interesting. We taking both squads on each mission?"

"So far that's the plan," Murdock said. He heard someone come in the door and looked up. He couldn't believe it. His father, the U.S. Congressman, who should be back in his office in Washington D.C., taking care of business. Murdock pushed away from the table and went to meet his father. He grabbed his hand and pulled him toward the door. In the companionway he frowned at the politician.

"What are you *doing here*?"

"Checking up on you. I'd been in Taipei on a fact-finding trip and I heard that some of our SEALs were out here. I took a chance one of them was you. Oh, it just happens that Captain Slash Victor who runs this floating island is a longtime friend of mine. Called him from Taipei and he said, yes, indeed you were on board."

Congressman Murdock chuckled. "Hey, swabbie, a congressman has more clout than an admiral, especially when he's on the House Military Affairs Committee."

Lieutenant Murdock nodded. "To say the least, you are one hell of a surprise. We're right in the middle of planning one of the biggest operations I've ever been on. I should get back."

"Take ten and let me talk to you. If those men of yours are

as good as everyone says, they can get along without you for ten damned minutes."

The SEAL nodded, led his father into the classroom, and tapped the coffeepot the mess steward had set up at the far end of the room. They found a small table and two chairs and sat down to sip their brew.

"I've got something in my pocket I can't help telling you about," the older man said. "It's an absolute plum, a situation that only comes along once every ten years or so. It's all mine."

"Dad, I told you before."

The congressman held up his hand, cutting off his son. His voice was low, yet intense. No one could hear him except Blake Murdock.

"A man high up in the Administration owes me. It's time to collect and I want to make it count. You can do ten times the good for our country in this spot as you can out here getting all wet and getting shrapnel in your ass."

The congressman chuckled. "You bet I heard about your last little job over there in Lebanon. This spot is one that would bring you an immediate promotion to full commander and one of the top spots in the Navy."

"Dad, I know you mean well, but I'm happy doing what I'm doing. This is important work."

"Probably, but so is being the top aide to the Chief of Naval Operations. Admiral Lucian Quenton."

Blake looked at his father as his own jaw dropped. He was rarely surprised, but this time he couldn't find a thing to say. He stared at his father and shook his head. At last his vocal cords came under his control.

"You said top aid to the CNO?"

"Right. I've talked with Lucian about you. He says he couldn't be happier with anyone else. He'll be delighted to have you on board."

Blake Murdock could grin now. He knew his father. The old politician wasn't telling the whole story.

"Dad, didn't Admiral Quenton say something else after you tossed my name in the hat?"

The congressman moved around in the hard Navy chair.

Then he sipped his coffee and looked away. He took a deep breath and then nodded.

"Yeah, he said you would turn me down."

"Dad, he was right. I talked to him this morning by radio. He gave me this new mission. It's important. So important I can't even tell you what it is. This is a job that must be done, and right now my men and I have been tabbed to take on the load. We do the job or we go down the hard way trying, and if we go down, the whole damn United States and the West is in heavy shit right up our eyeballs."

Blake stood and held out his hand. "Dad, thanks for stopping by. I'm sure you can get transport back to Taipei and then finish your junket."

"Oh, damn. I didn't think it would be this hard. I should have known. I had hopes that after this stint of maybe five years with the CNO I'd set you up to run for my seat in Congress, then six years later you'd get elected to the Senate, then in about ten years we'd make a big boost and run you for President."

Blake laughed. "You're a dreamer, Dad."

"Oh, somebody else said to give you a big hello. Jeannie Reilly."

Blake grinned. "Little Jeannie. Haven't thought of her for years. What's she doing now?"

"She's a lawyer, working for State. Damned good, from what I hear. Graduated second in her class at Harvard Law few years back."

"Little Jeannie. We were quite a pair in high school."

"Always figured you two would get married." The congressman darted a quick look at his son. "Wonder if it's too late for anything to develop there."

"Way too late, Dad. Now I really do need to get back. We have four separate missions two hundred miles apart and the coordination is vital. Thanks for coming."

Lieutenant Blake Murdock shook his father's hand again, walked him to the door and waved, then closed it behind the congressman.

Murdock headed for the nuke table. It was well past time that they settled on the type and numbers of weapons for each man and what kind of explosives they would carry. Then there was the timing they would need. When would they insert into the Taiwan Strait from the submarine? When would they get picked up again by the undersea craft?

The serious business of getting the detailed planning for each of the four missions moved along.

9

Friday, May 15

Ten minutes past midnight, the Third Platoon had finished its work. The details down to the smallest item had been planned, checked, critiqued, worried, and at last approved for each of the four attacks. Murdock had alerted the galley an hour before, and on command they brought in a midnight dinner of steak, spaghetti, three vegetables, bread and coffee, and big dishes of ice cream.

A well-fed SEAL is a well-fed SEAL, the saying goes. They headed for their bunks shortly after they ate with an 0900 chow call.

Murdock hit his sack and watched DeWitt drop off to sleep almost on command. The man could sleep anywhere, anytime. Murdock wished he could.

His mind kept churning over the preparations they had made. They had the right weapons. Mostly H&K. No U.S. made guns to leave a telltale trace.

His men were ready. With them helping on the planning, it made for a more cohesive unit when they hit combat. Besides, he had a lot of combat experience in those men. He was pleased with the makeup of his new platoon.

The two old hands in new positions had done well in their first taste of combat in their new slots. Jaybird Sterling had

59

been good. The three new men in the platoon had also performed well. It had turned out to be a small warm-up for the real mission. Nobody had intended it that way. It was just the way it had worked out.

Murdock turned over in his bunk. Tomorrow morning they would do what little rehearsal they could on the nuke attack. They would have plenty of explosives along to do whatever job needed to be done. It would be a play-it-by-ear since they had no intel at all on the inside of the facility. They would fight their way in—that was a given. Some rocket-propelled grenades might come in handy for that job.

They would carry the potent TNAZ explosive as well. It was Trinittroaze Tidine which had replaced plastique C-4. It had 15% more bang and 20% less volume and weight than the C-4.

He turned over again.

Before he knew it, his mental alarm went off and it was morning.

He had a quick breakfast at the officers' mess and beat everyone but Jaybird to the training room. The rest of the troops poured in quickly. Among them was Joe Ricochet Lampedusa with a large bandage on his arm. It was the first time they had seen him out of sick bay.

Murdock called him and DeWitt over to one side.

"Lampedusa, you won't be going on this mission. That slug dug in deeper than we thought."

The seaman scowled and nodded. "About what I figured. Damn, I'd like to be along."

"Not a chance, Richochet," DeWitt said. "We'd lose you on the first swim and we could have three or four more depending on how it goes."

"Understood. I just don't like it."

"You want to get flown back to Balboa Hospital or stay here? We could use you here for our contact. We'll need new supplies and gear for our second night's work."

"Yes, sir. I'd like that. Whatever I can do here. I want to stay with the program."

"Fine. See me after this rehearsal."

They had a full commander who was the resident expert on nuclear warheads. He told them what the Chinese might have.

"We know it isn't highly sophisticated. We also know that it works. What we don't want is to set off one or all of their nukes in that cave. It could blast the whole island apart and spread radiation across half of China.

"We figure that their triggers are put in place just before arming. That would be done in the plane. Yes, we also have about decided the best bet is that they have an airdrop device. So we treat it with care. If they are plutonium-powered, the problem is greater. The big program here is not to subject any of the devices to what we consider a triggering force.

"True, we don't know just how much that force is, but we have a ballpark figure of five thousand pounds of TNT."

"Sir, how much of this is speculation and guesswork and how much is fact?" Murdock asked.

"Damn few facts here, Lieutenant. We go with what we know and build on that. Best we can do. Best anyone can do. I don't know your plans, but they could change once you get on-site.

"Any more questions?" the commander asked. There were none. Murdock thanked the three-striper and he left. It was evident that the ragtag bunch of SEALs made him nervous.

Murdock took over the meeting again.

"Schedule: We chow down at 1200 hours. We make final assembly of our gear for both hits and chopper out of here at 1800 hours. Gets dark in this latitude about 1900 hours. This carrier is steaming on its regular circuit around Taiwan as it's been doing for months. The mainland won't even notice. The chopper will get us to our meet point with the same sub we were on before. She'll be our base ops for both missions.

"We leave the gear on her for the second hit, then get out our IBSs and head for that little nuke island. The sub will get us within five miles, then kick us off. We motor into the nuke island and take it down. Any questions?"

"Yeah." It was Jaybird. "How close can the sub come to the nuke island in case we run into trouble? A couple of rounds into those IBSs and we're fucking swimming."

"Covered. The sub can come in submerged within a mile of the island if they get a signal from us from a homing sonar."

1900 hours
USS *Dorchester*
Taiwan Strait

The big Sea Stallion CH-53D put them down within two feet of the submarine's aft deck, and the fifteen SEALs tugged out their equipment and hustled it into a hatch. The last bits out were the IBS bundles. The SEALs at once began inflating the boats and stowing their gear inside.

"Time?" Murdock asked DeWitt.

"It's 1905. We're about five minutes ahead of sched. The boat commander said as soon as the chopper leaves he'll start moving toward the island. We're about ten miles off it now. He can come into five miles on the surface without wetting his drawers."

"Good, let's check the boats."

The big chopper edged away from the submarine, then churned gently away from the mainland heading back to the carrier.

The submarine got under way nosing toward land.

"We should be on station in twenty minutes," Murdock said. "Let's double-check everything again." They carried four rocket-propelled grenades. They had two sets of cutting charges that would use their shaped form to cut through six inches of steel.

Half the men carried the H&K MP-5SD4 for close-in work. One man in each squad used the H&K HK-21A1 machine gun with 7.62 NATO rounds. Magic Brown and Red Nicholson had the McMillan M-89 silenced sniper rifles, as did two men in the Second Squad. Doc Ellsworth carried his favorite toy, a fully automatic shotgun with a five-round magazine.

Fifteen minutes after the chopper left, the men boarded

the two IBSs and checked equipment. Fins and rebreathers
were stowed. They would motor straight into the beach a
hundred yards from the front gate of the facility.

"Time," an officer on the conning tower called. The
SEALs unlashed their IBSs and the big boat began to slide
under the water. In a matter of seconds they were floating,
the nearly silent IBS motors powering them away from the
rear of the submarine and the turbulence caused by sub-
merging.

The SEALs wore black Nomex flight suits under their
combat webbing, which was loaded with tools of their trade.
They also wore American Body Armor operations vests.
They had pouches on the front for loaded magazines. A
waterproof pouch was in back for each man's encrypted
Motorola MX walkie-talkie. There were grenade pouches
with room for more goodies.

Each man wore a headset and earpiece inside his left ear.
A wire went down his neck and plugged into the Motorola
unit in his harness. A filament mike perched just under his
lower lip. A touch on the transmit button brought a *tsk-tsk*
through the headset.

Murdock listened for the series of signals. All of his men
were hooked up and tuned in. They wouldn't use the radio
until they had to. He checked the azimuth and corrected the
boat slightly as it powered gently through the swells toward
Mainland China.

They were doing something no U.S. military unit had
ever done, invading modern Mainland China. They'd better
do it right or there would be hell to pay, and a chance at
starting World War III.

Murdock pulled down his night-vision goggles from his
forehead. He had a Litton single-lens version. You could use
it with one eye and keep the other eye available for normal
night vision. He studied the lime-green view and found the
other IBS ten yards to port. He powered closer to it until he
could see it through the China night without the NVG.

It would take them the best part of an hour to travel the
five klicks at five knots. There was no other choice. The
submarine couldn't risk moving in any closer. Radar might

pick it up. There was little chance that even the best radar could pick up the IBS. They lay low in the water and the movement wasn't fast enough to cause a blip on the radar screen.

Later, Murdock heard the surf before he saw anything. It sounded like a moderate set of breakers. It was a sand beach, and they would leave the IBSs inflated and ready for a quick exit.

Murdock moved his IBS closer to the other one and with hand signals indicated that he would go in first, followed by the second boat.

A minute later he could see the outside of the swells. They were larger than he had guessed and they broke rather sharply. He watched them through the NVG a minute, and decided he had to charge straight over the top of the breaker and try to keep the boat right side up. All of their equipment was tied down if the inflatable did flip.

Then they were riding the top of the swell. It rose and rose, and then he saw the white curl, and a moment later they came crashing down a four-foot breaker of foaming seawater. The bow of the IBS nudged under the sandy water, then righted, and the breaker slapped it forward like a roller coaster taking that first high plunge.

He turned off the motor and the swell drove them up the beach. When the wave receded, the men jumped out, carried the boat high into dry sand, and pushed it behind a small mound covered with sea grass.

They untied the equipment they needed, checked and cleared their weapons and charged them with a live round, then watched the other boat come in.

It came over a swell, got turned sideways, and barely managed not to be flipped. It came in backwards, and the men picked it up and dashed up the beach. They were all thankful for the many hours of IBS training they had done through the breakers on the Silver Strand beach near Coronado.

Not a word was said. They had to move to the right. Hand signals grouped the men into the two squads. Murdock led his men out first. They would bypass the main gate by fifty yards and set up their firing positions. The Second Squad would set up on the near side to put the gate in a cross-fire.

When he was in position with his men ready, Murdock tapped his mike three times. *Tsk, tsk, tsk.*

It was over a nervous minute later when Murdock and the rest of First Squad heard the answering *tsks* in their earpieces. Magic Brown and Red Nicholson had leveled in on the front gate through their Litton M-92 Starlight 3-power scopes. Both had selected targets and sighted in on them.

Murdock had checked the gate through Magic's scope moments before. Four guards walked in front of a steel-bar gate near a small gatehouse. Twenty yards behind it was another gate manned by two soldiers.

Murdock tapped Brown and Red on the shoulders and their weapons chugged out a greeting to the Chinese. Murdock saw one of the guards at the gate go down as he watched through his NVG. Then the other one crumpled. The third guard started forward to help his buddy, but he slammed backwards from another round. The fourth guard was caught with another silenced round from the Second Squad shooter before he could move.

The snipers turned to the second gate. Only Magic had a shot. He jolted one round into the guard just outside the small guard building. That brought out his partner, who took two rounds from Second Squad gunners.

At once the squad came to its feet and moved cautiously toward the gate. Two men guarded the rear. Murdock ran ahead, checked the four guards, then ran on to the second gate. It was a simple lift bar. He raised it and his fourteen men darted through, past a double barbed-wire fence and another that looked electrified. They were inside.

They had studied the enclosure from the satellite photos for hours. Their best guess was that the concrete building to the left of the main gate would be the one covering the entrance to the massive underground nuclear production facility and storehouse.

The men ran that way, their soft-soled boots making no sound on the concrete paving.

Just then a small jeeplike truck came rolling around the far corner of the complex, the twin beams of its headlights stabbing ever closer to the fifteen SEALs.

10

Friday, May 15

2028 hours
Tayu Island
Just off Mainland China

The four SEALs with silenced sniper rifles needed no orders. They opened fire as soon as the headlights flashed their way. The first four shots took out the headlights. Six more shots through the windshield killed the driver in his seat. The utility vehicle went out of control and jolted into the concrete wall of the building and stalled.

Jaybird Sterling raced the thirty meters to the jeep and checked inside. There was only the driver, and he was greeting his ancestors.

Jaybird darted back to the unit and the men moved ahead cautiously. The compound door to the windowless, concrete slab of a building showed directly in front of them. It was not guarded.

The SEALs in their black flight suits and with blackened faces blended in with the shadows around the big building. The large truck door was designed to lift and roll back into the structure. There would be no chance there. At the lower right-hand corner of this door was a man-sized opening with an electronic control panel next to it filled with Chinese characters.

Murdock eyed the door again, then spoke into his mike with a whisper. "Cutting charge," he said.

Gunner's Mate Second Class Greg Johnson ran up beside Murdock and knelt.

"Small door, three sides, go," Murdock said.

Johnson and Fernandez ran to the door unrolling the lead-sheathed triangles of high-velocity explosives. The point of each triangle focused the shaped charges' powerful force into a thin line. It could blow a pencil-wide slice through four inches of steel. It took thirty seconds to position the charges around the door and set the electronic detonator.

Johnson came back with the trigger in his hand and nodded at Murdock.

"Fire in the hole," Murdock whispered, and Johnson pushed the button.

The strips of shaped charges around the door exploded with a cracking sound like a stick of dynamite does when it's hung on a string from a tree and set off. In one moment the door was solid. Then a fraction of a second later the steel door had been cut out and blasted inside the building.

Four SEALs surged through the opening, Murdock in the lead and angling to the right. His MP-5 covered his section of the room ahead. It was a lobby, a reception area with a bench along one side, a desk in the middle, and ten meters behind it a pair of polished wooden doors. Only one man was on duty. He had been blasted off his chair behind his desk.

He came to his knees and fumbled at his belt for a handgun. Murdock sent a trio of 9mm slugs into him blasting him backwards into a quick death.

Two armed men surged through one of the wooden doors and were cut down by Jaybird and Ron Holt with their silenced MP-5's. Jaybird's three-round burst caught the first Chinese soldier in the throat and worked upward into his head, spraying brains and blood against the polished wooden door.

Holt's rounds took his victim in the chest and drove him back against the door, where he dropped his rifle and slid down to the floor.

Murdock stared at the two doors. Which one? A crap-

shoot. He charged the door on the right. The First Squad
followed him and according to the plan, the Second Squad
dispersed around the room behind what cover they could
find to secure the area against any opposition.

Murdock led his seven men into a corridor that slanted
downward. It was a death-trap box if anyone challenged
them with machine guns from the other end.

They sprinted downward for thirty meters, then came to
a branch. Chinese signs designated directions. Kenneth
Ching was a step behind his L-T.

"Supplies, maintenance to the left," Ching called. "Production and storage to the right."

Murdock waved them to the right. The eight men charged
along the corridor for another thirty meters, then came to an
open area with a guard station. They faded back in the
poorly lighted tunnel and looked out. There were six
soldiers visible. A machine gun had been mounted above a
sandbagged position. The wooden barricade looked temporary. Behind the sandbags they saw a vehicle also with a
mounted weapon on it.

Ron Holt carried one of the RPGs. Murdock motioned
him forward. Holt put the shoulder-mounted launcher in
place and flipped the arming switch, then zeroed in on the
machine gun emplacement and the truck behind it. He gave
Murdock a thumbs-up sign. Murdock held up his finger and
motioned sharply to Holt.

He fired.

The blast of the rocket in the tunnel was like a swarm of
angry bees. If left a fiery trail for twenty meters, then
exploded on the sandbags and the truck. The vehicle's gas
tank blew up in a gushing ball of fire that sent two guards
still alive running. Magic Brown and Red Nicholson brought
the two down with their silenced sniper M-89's.

A siren wailed somewhere ahead.

The fire effectively blocked the tunnel. The could feel the
heat, but they were far enough away to avoid any problems.

Murdock gathered his troops.

"Now we're alive and with sound. They know someone's
here. When that fire simmers down, we charge past it. There

will be a reception committee somewhere on the other side. First two men through are Ronson with his machine gun and Magic. Charge past the heat, hit the deck, and give us some protective fire down whatever is ahead. This damn tunnel has to end soon."

They heard sporadic gunfire from beyond the flames, but no rounds came near them.

Murdock looked at Ching and Horse Ronson. "You both still have the juice?"

They nodded. The carried the new explosive, the TNAZ that had more punch than C-4.

The fire burned lower. Murdock hadn't heard any shooting from beyond the flames for five minutes. "Let's go," he said.

They charged the flames. Brown and Horse Ronson roared to the front, shielding their faces as they burst through the open area past the still-flaming truck and into the smoky darkness as the tunnel continued beyond.

The air-conditioning sucked the smoke away from Murdock and his men as they continued down the passage. It was larger here and they could see bright lights ahead. Brown and Ronson flopped to the sides of the tunnel and looked for targets. They saw none. They didn't fire.

Murdock and the others caught up with them and nodded. He put Ronson on point and they moved down the corridor silently, black-on-black heavily armed figures coming out of the smoke.

Sixty meters ahead the downsloping tunnel ended in a huge natural cavern. It was set up as a manufacturing layout, with assembly tables, overhead wires and beams, and what looked like a "clean" room at the far end.

The SEALs saw no one. Either a shift had finished work or there was no work in progress.

Four Chinese guards with automatic rifles surged from behind the clean room and opened fire.

The SEALs dove behind whatever cover they could find. Magic Brown caught one of the Chinese with a round to the chest and he quit the fight. The other three advanced behind the workstations on the floor of the big cavern.

The flat crack of the AK-47s on full auto-fire sang
through the cave. The gunners were forty meters away and
advancing. Murdock checked his men. He used his mike.
Radio silence was no longer required. Who had the best
arm? They hadn't brought any grenade launchers.

"Horse, you have any fraggers?"

"A shit-pot full."

"Toss a pair down that way to discourage the bastards."

Horse sent the first four-second-fuse hand grenade over
the top of the assembly tables heading for the three Chinese.
It landed short, bounced once on the concrete floor, and
air-blasted fifteen feet from two of the shooters. Both went
down with multiple shrapnel wounds in the face and neck.
The last Chinese tried to run for it the way he had come in.

Magic Brown tracked him and fired. He missed. His
second round connected and the runner tumbled into eternity.

Murdock listened to the silence for a few seconds, then
looked at Ching. The Chinese SEAL shook his head.

"Hell, I don't know. No more signs. We want the bomb
storage, right?"

Murdock nodded. He scanned the area ahead. Two
tunnels led out of the assembly area. Both had heavy doors
on them. He chose the one on the right.

Doc Ellsworth carried their other RPG. Murdock brought
him to the front of the unit.

"Blow that door into fucking hell, Doc. Then we'll see
where it leads."

Doc grinned. Although he was a medic, he carried all the
arms and had the killer instinct of every other SEAL. He'd
been through BUD/S like the rest of them. At times he was
too gung ho and Murdock had to hold him back.

He sighted in, checked his back-blast area to make sure it
was clear, and fired. The round went downhill to the heavy
wooden door. It bounced off the concrete and slanted up ten
feet to hit the door to the left of center.

The explosion was magnified in the cavern. For a few
seconds Murdock couldn't hear. Then the sensation came
back. Already he had the troops moving. They charged the

door, kicked aside some splinters, and surged through into another tunnel. This one was not finished with concrete. It looked more like a miners' tunnel, but was high enough and wide enough to be used by small trucks.

They worked along the tube for fifty meters and came to a guard station. It was not manned. Another thirty meters ahead they came into another huge natural cavern. It was more than fifty meters high and three times that wide. It had formed in the shape of a large oval, and there was no way out of the large cave besides the way they had come in.

In the center of the big cavern there was a small structure that looked like the top of an elevator shaft. Around it were what seemed to be worktables of some sort. There were a dozen small electric forklifts that could be used to move a nuclear bomb.

The rest of the cavern was empty. The floor had been paved only along two strips, one leading to the elevator-type house, and another leading away from it, circling around and coming back to the access tunnel.

Murdock could find no armed protection. His men stayed in the mouth of the tunnel for cover. Murdock used his sectioning method of examining the area. He sectioned it off and checked every possible place that could hide troops or offer cover. He found none. He had returned to the mouth of the tunnel, and was just about to order his men forward, when a section of the floor just behind the elevator shaft opened and two machine guns with gunner on them lifted to the surface. Two more sections came out, and twenty armed soldiers stood with their weapons pointed at the cave entrance.

A voice came over a loudspeaker in Chinese. Ching had moved up beside Murdock, and translated the words quietly as the voice sounded.

"Idiots. Don't you know that your presence here and any powerful explosion could activate one or more of our nuclear devices? How stupid can you be. You must be from Taiwan. Yes, they are this stupid. Lay down your arms and surrender. If you try to resist, you will be crushed immediately."

Murdock used his radio mike. "Snipers get in position. When you're ready give me a signal."

The four men moved forward to the very front of the tunnel and got into places from which they could fire.

"Take out those machine guns first. The gunners, the ammo men, then the troops. We've got a thirty-meter range. Our MP-5's will help. As soon as the MGs are down, bring up our H&K 21A1's and settle the matter."

Murdock got four single *tsks* on his radio.

"Go" he said. Four silent rounds jolted through the cavern and knocked both the gunners and loaders away from their machine guns. The snipers each fired four more times, cutting down anyone who tried to man the machine guns.

The MP-5's opened up on the rifle troops. They fired back, but had no real targets. The 9mm whizzers from the MP-5's kept the Chinese troops prone until the H&K SEAL machine guns got in position. The rifle fire from the Chinese slackened, then stopped. No one moved in the defensive position.

When all firing stopped, there was a pause as some air-purification device sucked the smoke and cordite smell out of the air. The Chinese voice spoke again.

"You are not easily discouraged, but we have ways of handling that," Ching translated.

"You have five minutes to clear this facility. At that time doors will close sealing in this complex. It will then be flooded with enough poison gas to kill everyone inside within sixty seconds after inhaling it. There will be no escape. If you don't leave, you all will die. You have five minutes starting now."

"The voice is bluffing us about flooding this area with poison gas," Murdock said. "Unless it's contact gas, it would take hours to get enough gas in here to kill anyone. Forget it. We move on the shaft in the middle. Fire only at a definite target. Now. Go, Go, Go."

The eight men of Third Platoon lifted off the deck and stormed the small shaft in the middle of the cavern. It was only thirty-five meters away. There was no opposition. Not a shot was fired.

Murdock came around the side of the shaft, which was made of heavy steel plates, and looked at the front. It was an elevator, and evidently fully operational. The door stood open.

"Sign says safe occupancy by no more than ten people," Ching said.

"Ching, Brown, Doc, we're going for a ride down. The rest of you spread out and keep this thing operational. It it's clear down there, we'll send it back up for reinforcements. Bring down two more men and leave Holt and Nicholson up here for security. We want to be sure we can get back up this shaft."

Murdock waved the men on board. Ching studied the control panel.

"Only two operational buttons, L-T. One is down, the other up."

"Let's go down, Ching, and see where the hell this goes to and what the cluster-fuck in July is down there."

Ching pushed the button. The door closed and the elevator started down.

Murdock nodded. Now they would see what the Chinese had developed in their nuclear weapons program.

11

Friday, May 15

The enclosed elevator car felt like a tomb for a moment. Then Murdock looked at Ching.

"Any indication how far we're going down?"

"None, L-T. It's quite a drop even though we aren't going fast like the ones do in the Empire State Building."

"This will do. When we stop I want us lined up in back of the car. Have your weapons aimed at that door when it opens. We don't know what the fuck we're going to find down here. That guy on the loudspeaker has to be somewhere. He could alert them that we're coming down."

The car slowed and ground to a stop. Doc stood in the center of the rear of the car, his shotgun pointing at the door. It slid open with a slight whine and two Chinese soldiers gaped in surprise at the weapons aimed at them. Their own rifles were slung over their shoulders with muzzles down.

As the doors opened, Doc got off one round from his shotgun. The thirteen .32-sized slugs tore into both men. Half the torso of one billowed with blood and internal organs spewed out. The man beside him had his arm torn off and enough of the slugs drilled into his heart to kill him instantly.

Murdock looked around the door of the car. They were in

a much smaller cave, one that looked to be blasted out of granite. Three steel huts were at the near end of the room. It was no more than twenty meters long and about that wide. The overhead was only four meters above them.

Murdock saw no other guards. The four SEALs darted from the elevator to the closest of the steel buildings. They had no obvious doors, no windows.

Ching read the sign on the front.

"This sealed container holds two nuclear devices, ready to be given the final charge and the arming detonator."

"Maybe six bombs," Murdock said. "Check the other two huts."

Ching ran to them and came back nodding. "Six must be their total. What now?"

"We mess up everything down here that we can. Those electric forklifts, put small charges on them with two-hour timers. Nothing that will break down the steel doors to the hutches. Get on it now. You have five minutes."

He grabbed Ching. "Let Brown juice the forklifts. Suggestions on how we wreck this place?"

"We don't know how solid those steel buildings are, so we better not blast the ceiling down. I'd say we blow everything down here, then go up the elevator, set a moderate charge with a timer, and send the box down here. Then we blast the top of the elevator."

Murdock nodded. "About what I'd been thinking. Then we blast every tunnel shut as we leave it. Take them a damn long time to haul out all of the rubble. Good, start laying your charges with that TNAZ. Remember, it's more potent that the old C-4 we usually use."

Magic Brown came back in four minutes. "I put one-eighth of a stick on four of the forklifts and latched them together. They all have delay timers set for an hour."

"We're ready. Let's move up the ladder."

Murdock led the four into the elevator and they pushed the up button.

At the top of the ride, the four SEALs stayed at the sides of the car as the doors opened. Rifle fire tore into the back wall of the elevator. The fire let up and Murdock yelled,

"Cover us!" He heard MP-5's chattering to the left, and the rifle fire held off. The four SEALs came charging out firing with all the power they had.

Murdock saw the rest of his men crouched behind some upturned tables to the left and sprinted that way.

The four men dove behind the tables just as the Chinese rifles opened up again, the flat crack of the venerable AK-47 on automatic fire.

Murdock skidded to a stop half on top of Jaybird.

"What's happening, Chief?"

"Six of the dry-humpers came out a hidden door down to the left. They fired on us before we knew they were there. We nailed two of them, but four have us pinned down."

"Fraggers," Murdock said. "The range can't be more than thirty meters. How many fraggers we have?"

The found six among the men. The best throwers took the small bombs. "Two at a time, then wait for a reaction," Murdock said.

Brown and Horse lifted up and threw the grenades with the 4.2-second fuses. They didn't let them cook at all. The distance would mean almost instant detonation on contact. Both bombs went off with a sharp roar and they heard shrapnel zinging all over the place. One Chinese soldier screamed.

The firing from behind the tables across the way stopped.

Murdock nodded, and the men threw two more. These dropped over the edges of the tables and went off at once. More screaming came, and then the survivors began to retreat. Brown shifted to his sniper M-89 and picked one soldier off before he could get through the hidden door in the wall. The second one made it.

"Checkout time," Murdock said. "Go, go, go!" He stood with the MP-5 on his hip and charged forward firing three-round bursts at the tables where the Chinese riflemen had been. The other men of First Squad were beside him as they rushed the strongpoint where the Chinese had hidden.

They kicked over the tables and sprayed the bodies there with more rounds.

"As you were!" Murdock bellowed, and the firing stopped. "Let's get those charges set so we can get out of here."

Ching and Brown ran back to the elevator. They set two charges, one on each side of the car, and wired them together. Then they wired them to a thirty-minute timer-detonator and punched the down button on the elevator. It still worked. The doors closed and the car headed for the cavern below and the six Chinese nuclear weapons.

As soon as the car cleared, Ching had the second charge ready to demolish the top of the elevator. Nobody would be bringing out any nukes from that cave below for a long time.

"Set that one for half an hour," Murdock said. "Now, let's move out of here. Jaybird, you take the point and keep Brown close behind. Doc, you bring up the rear. Let's move."

When they hit the mouth of the tunnel leading away from the large cavern, Magic Brown had a charge of TNAZ ready. He plastered it against the tunnel ten feet inside from the mouth and set a fifteen-minute timer-detonator, and they moved away. At the end of that tunnel they set another charge with the same-timed detonator. This was where they had blasted in a door with the RPG. Ching set a charge there and dialed the timer for ten minutes.

They hurried across the assembly area. There was nothing there worth blasting. They found the up-slanting tunnel on the far side of the huge natural cavern. There was still the smell of smoke in the tunnel. They set another charge in the tunnel twenty feet in from the cavern and positioned the detonator for ten minutes. By now the charges were placed and the timers set almost without missing a step.

Halfway up the long tunnel they came to the burned-out truck and the Chinese bodies. They continued past to the spot where the tunnel branched. Ching put a charge that would block both tunnels, and they continued upward.

A minute later they came to the reception area. Before they got there they heard firing. Murdock recognized the chatter of the MP-5's. His boys from Second Squad were mixing it up with someone.

They got to the mouth of the tunnel and checked outside

carefully. The reception area had changed. Murdock found three of his other seven men pinned down behind some upturned tables and the receptionist's desk on the far side. The other four were on the near side behind metal file cabinets and tables.

Rifle fire came from the blasted-open man-sized door. Magic Brown flattened out near the mouth of the tunnel, kicked down the bipod on his sniper rifle, and sighted in on the metal door leading outside. He waited, watching through his scope. Then he fired. A scream sounded outside.

Murdock used his radio. "Troubles, DeWitt?"

"Too damn many. About twenty of them charged through the door. We beat them back, but can't join our forces. Three on the left, and four on the right. We're out of fraggers."

"RPG?"

"Used up."

Horse Ronson had set up his H&K machine gun. He signaled to Murdock that he was ready. Murdock put the rest of his squad on the left of the chatter gun. When Ronson opened fire, he slammed nine-round bursts through the metal door. That was when the rest of First Squad charged out the tunnel and around to the left of the room and got as close to the outside door as they could. Brown, Murdock, and Jaybird all threw grenades at the blasted-in doorway. Two of the three went outside and exploded. The third one bounced off the metal truck door and rolled far enough to the right so the shrapnel missed the First Squad.

Ronson cut off his firing. All was quiet outside. Magic Brown threw two more grenades. Both went through the opening and blasted outside. Murdock and his men charged the door, firing their submachine guns through the opening as they ran. Murdock went through the blasted door first and slanted to the right, his Kill House territory.

Two Chinese solders limped away. He put them both in the dirt with three-round bursts. He heard firing from his left. Another Mainlander had risen from his position close to Mother Earth, and was greeted with two hip-fired rounds from Magic Brown's rifle.

Then all was quiet.

Murdock touched his mike. "Come," he said. Second squad came out of the metal door and dispersed in the darkness.

"Casualties?" Murdock radioed.

"I've got one man nicked in the leg," DeWitt said through the earphone. "He says not serious. I'll watch him. What's next?"

"We've attracted too much attention. Let's haul ass for the beach and our IBSs."

They moved away toward the beach at ten meter intervals. No lucky grenade or shell would get more than one SEAL. They heard sirens wailing from inside the facility. The best part about this island strike, Murdock decided, was that the Chinese couldn't truck in a thousand men to hunt them down. The garrison on the island was all they had. He wished he knew how many fighting men that involved.

The SEALs could see headlights to the left, inland on the island, which they heard was about two miles across. The beach was only a hundred meters away. They picked up the pace to double time.

Lieutenant Murdock came to the beach and turned right to find the IBSs. He found the spot. Both boats had been slashed, ruined, and looted. Nothing left of value.

"Hit the dirt!" Murdock bellowed. A moment later machine-gun fire erupted along the grass dune that separated the dry sand from the land.

"Waiting for us," Murdock said in his radio. "Take cover and let me find this bastard."

Murdock saw where the fire came from. The gun was on the dune thirty meters down from the boats. His rounds were high, but he'd get them down. Murdock checked his pouches and found two more fraggers. He wished he had another RPG or some M-40's. He began to crawl forward on his elbows and his knees, digging into the sand, moving more slowly than he wanted to.

Thirty meters. Too damn far to throw. He checked behind him and found Holt tailing him. He must have some hand grenades left too. They moved into the grass. The rounds were still high. The gunner was kicking out five-round bursts. He knew what he was doing. He didn't have NVG, that was for sure, or half the platoon would be dead by now.

They crept closer. At fifteen meters Murdock stopped and let Holt come up beside him.

"How many?" Murdock asked.

"Three."

"We'll alternate. I'll throw one. Five counts later you throw one. We do that twice."

Holt nodded. Murdock remembered that Holt had been second in accuracy with live grenades on the range. The kid could throw. Murdock pulled the pin on his grenade, waited for Holt to pull his, then with a stiff-elbow throw arched the bomb toward the machine gun.

A second after the fragger ripped the China night apart, Holt lifted up and threw his hand bomb. In 4.2 seconds the second grenade went off with a chopping roar. The machine gun stopped firing.

Murdock motioned Holt up, and they both took their MP-5's and charged the machine gun firing as they ran. Three Chinese lay dead around their weapon. Murdock shot two rounds into the receiver so the MG wouldn't fire again, and ran back to his troops.

"Swim time," he said on the radio. "Our IBSs are both slashed and dead. Let's swim." He pulled off the mike and headset, stowed them in the waterproof pocket in his vest, and charged his men into the water.

The water is home to the SEAL. When all goes bad he can always take to the water for protection and comfort. It also can hide him and save his Navy hide to fight again another day.

They had no breathing apparatus. Their emergency fins and face masks had been in the IBSs on the beach. Now they would be part of the "evidence" the Chinese might use when the story came out. If it came out. He hoped it would embarrass the Chinese so badly they wouldn't mention the intrusion.

The SEALs waded into the water, ducked under the first three breakers, and assembled just beyond the white water.

"Buddy lines," Murdock said. "I want groups of four. DeWitt, how's your man?"

DeWitt swam over. "He's better off out here than on land. He tells me he can breaststroke ten miles. We'll see." They tied themselves together. Three sets of four and one of three. Ron Holt was with Murdock.

"Holt, you have that sonar signaler?"

"Always."

"Activate it. We want that sub to come in until his nose scrapes Chinese sand. We'll move out a mile and wait for him."

"Damn dark tonight, L-T."

"True. Another hundred yards off shore and I'll put up the SLVB. Give the men and the sub something to watch for. Free swimming this way, we've got to stay together."

They took two rounds of rifle fire from the beach, and then no more.

The SEALs kept up their steady stroke away from the shore. Murdock tried to set a course, but soon realized that it didn't really matter. The sub would be homing in on the sonar signal sent out by the handy-dandy little rig that Holt had slipped into the sea on a cord tied to his webbing.

Murphy's law had hit them hard. The Chinese finding the IBSs was the worst of it. Now they had a tough swim. He hoped that the sub skipper would come in to the one-mile mark. If anything else went wrong they would still be swimming when daylight broke over the eastern horizon.

Now it was all up to that sonar device. Work, damnit, Murdock demanded. Work!

12

Friday, May 15

Murdock figured the SEALs were a half mile offshore from
Tayu Island when he heard the engine. It was too high-
pitched to be a submarine. Submarines made hardly any
noise at all, even when traveling on the surface.

He listened closer.

Holt turned toward the sound. "Company," he said.

"A patrol boat of some kind," Murdock said. "Fast and
heavily armed. Sounds like he's coming right at us."

"They must have figured we'd go directly away from the
island," Holt said.

Murdock could see the four groups of swimmers. "Company coming," he called loud enough for all of them to hear
him. "Probably our Chinese friends with a patrol boat.
They'll have a searchlight. When they get close with the
light, we play duck-dive just like in training. Everybody
copy?"

A chorus of ayes came back at him.

"We convince these sailors we aren't here, they'll go
home. You know the hide-and-peek drill."

They swam forward silently then, the sound of the patrol
boat fading and then coming closer as it worked some
search pattern behind them. Gradually it came toward them.

Murdock saw the light first. It swept in long arcs across the two-foot swells in the strait. The Chinese sailors had a tough mission. In these nighttime seas it would be tough to find somebody who wanted to be located. Not wanting to be found would be harder yet.

"Coming at us," Murdock said.

The craft powered straight at them, then turned on its search leg. The light in the bow swung toward them, but was too far away to touch them. Then it turned away and it was gone.

"Next time they cover our area, so be ready," Murdock said. "We still have four units?"

Jaybird sounded off. "I'm in group two and I can see three more so that makes damn near four. Watch it, here comes that Chinese cocksucker with the long dick-light."

The patrol craft growled toward them at five knots and the beam of light, four feet across, swung closer to their position. Murdock had pulled in the string holding the vue ball and let out the helium. It collapsed. As the light edged toward them, the SEALs duck-dived, sliding under the water at the last moment.

Murdock took four downward strokes, then leveled out and watched the beam of bright light sweep over the waves where he and his men had been moments before. It came back over the same spot again and then faded as the boat moved away. He stroked to the surface slowly, pushed his nose out of the water for a big drag of air, then broke his face out.

Blessed darkness.

The patrol craft had worked beyond them in what looked like a routine search pattern. It was if the crew didn't expect to find anything and was simply going through the motions.

Good.

Murdock called softly, and heard replies as the groups surfaced around him.

"Everyone accounted for, L-T," Jaybird called. "Looks like the dry-humper is gone."

"He'll be back," Murdock said. "Let's keep moving due east. That pig boat has got to be out there somewhere."

Murdock motioned to Holt, who swam over closer. "You have a backup on that sonar sending device?"

"Yep."

"Let's get it in the water and turned on. I really don't want to have to swim the ninety miles over to Taiwan."

"Roger that, sir. Have it out and activated in just a minute. I always keep two of them with me."

They swam forward, eastward, away from Mainland China.

Twice more the patrol boat swung its big beam of light across the sea where the SEALs swam. Twice more they had to dive and hold their breath until the wave of light passed over them.

Finally the patrol craft switched off its light and the motor sound picked up as the boat headed back to its mooring.

A light wind kicked up the swells into a froth on top, sending the water into the swimmers' faces. Murdock figured they had been in the water about an hour. Not long by SEAL standards, but the Nomex flight suits were leaving the men colder and colder.

Murdock felt the cold start to sap his strength. They could last another hour at the most. Where the hell was that submarine? With two sonar beacons out, it should be able to home in on one of them.

They heard the engines before they saw the craft. Then their anticipation turned to despair. A huge hull rose out of the ocean not a hundred yards away. It was a supertanker heading up the strait into the East China Sea.

The SEALs cursed silently to save their breath and kept swimming to the east.

Ten minutes later they saw another huge black shadow moving toward them. The craft had no running lights and hunkered low in the water. Murdock bellowed out a call, and the craft turned slightly toward them and slowed.

The USS *Dorchester* came to a stop ten meters away from the swimmers. A dozen sailors helped pull the SEALs on board and they hurried down a hatch into the big boat. Murdock made sure all fifteen bodies were accounted for.

Murdock checked his watch: 2212. They had almost eight

hours of darkness left for the second half of their mission. As soon as all the SEALs were on board, the submarine had turned north and picked up speed. She was on the surface at fifteen knots. They were scheduled for a two-hour trip north to Foochow. Their landing zone was a deserted, marshy area next to the Min River and along a good-sized bay.

Murdock made sure the men were fed and got dry uniforms. Since most of the next mission would be on land, they would be wearing the three-color desert camouflage suits, tan and pale green with splashes of pink. For gloves they had the fire-resistant sage-green Nomex. Swim fins would go over regular-issue jungle boots if they had to hit the water moving in to their objective.

They would use two new IBSs stashed on the sub for the last mile in from the cold waters of the East China Sea. Then they had about five clicks overland to get to the Chinese air base where the planes were parked that the paratroopers would use for their drop on Taiwan.

Murdock, DeWitt, and Jaybird went over the latest satellite photos of the air base near Foochow that had come in less than an hour before. They could see the concentration of aircraft on the field. They were parked wing tip to tail feathers. The satellite guys in D.C. said they had spotted forty of the transports ready for action. They were the Chinese SAC-YD four-turboprop transports. Each one could haul eighty-two fully equipped paratroopers. Forty of them would mean over three thousand men in the air. If they got off the field.

After the SEALs had been fed and clothed, they came to the room where the weapons had been stashed. This would be a different kind of attack for SEALs. They hoped they wouldn't have to get within five hundred yards of their enemies.

"What we have here is a job a little different than most we do," Murdock told his men. "We're after those planes on the tarmac. There are forty of them, packed so close together it looks like a carrier deck loaded with planes.

"We hope they are fully fueled and ready to roll. We'll be going in with twelve rounds of RPGs and ten McMillan

M-88 bolt-action sniper rifles that blast out a .50-caliber round. These are not small or light weapons. They are fifty-three inches long and have a bulbous muzzle brake on the end of the barrel. They have a bipod out front and a fixed five-round magazine. We'll have fifty rounds for each weapon.

"You've all fired this piece in training. You'll be doing a lot of shooting tonight. Ten of you will have the eighty-eight, and your fifty rounds of fifty-caliber. Some of those ten will have an RPG as well. It's a heavy load. The other four men will carry the M-4A1, the CAR-15 with the forty-millimeter grenade launcher attached.

"We're now a long-range, high-firepower unit. We shoot and scoot hoping we cause so much hell on the base that they won't think about trying to run us down."

"L-T, we go in five klicks over land. That means we got to go five klicks back to get to our IBSs?" Al Adams asked.

"It should be less than five, maybe a mile depending on the bay and how far we can motor up it. We go as far as we can in the IBSs, then hit the land. If they find our IBSs we'll have to swim home. But this time we'll take the minutes needed to deflate and hide the rubber ducks."

"When do we push off?" Jaybird asked.

"I've got an appointment with the captain to deboat us at ten minutes after midnight and we should be a mile from shore."

"Any changes from the way we planned it?" Doc asked.

"Our only change is one less man to do the job. I'm moving Red Nicholson to Second Squad to even us up at seven men each. Any other questions?"

"Will those fifty rounds be explosive or tracer?" Ronson asked.

"Both. We want to blow up those fuel tanks and get a chain reaction down a whole fucking line of those SAC-YDs."

Murdock looked around. No more questions. "Okay, here's the roster. Holt, Ellsworth, Murdock, and DeWitt will carry the CAR-15s. Each of those men will also have two RPGs to haul into the fire zone.

"All the rest of you will tote the M-eighty-eight. Four of you with the eighty-eight will also have one RPG. Those men are: Brown, Ronson, Fernandez, and Johnson. Everyone with an eighty-eight will also carry his own fifty rounds.

"Any questions now?"

"Will we have the cloth bibs to carry the RPGs?" Doc Ellsworth asked.

"Yes, some of us call them yokes. A hole for your head with one round in the cloth pouch in front and one in back. Leaves your hands free."

"Those yokes and our web vests?" Johnson asked.

"You want to leave any of your goodies at home?" DeWitt asked. Johnson grinned and shook his head.

"Okay, time. It's now 2312. We'll push away in just an hour. Chief Sterling, check the two IBSs and make sure all the gear is attached including the second inflation canisters.

"The rest of you gather around and draw your weapons and ammo. Don't overstock yourself. Those RPGs are not lightweights. Let's move."

A half hour later the men were ready. All had on their gear, with their faces blackened and their various headgear in place from black stocking caps to balaclavas. They jogged up and down and adjusted their loads of weapons, ammo, and gear. Then they sat down in a row and waited for the call to disembark.

13

Saturday, May 16

East China Sea
Off Foochow, China

The pair of IBSs rode off the aft deck of the submarine and slid into the China Sea a little over a mile off Foochow. The silent-running motors powered the little boats away from the wash of the sub and toward land to the west. Murdock checked his watch. Two minutes behind schedule. Close enough.

Murdock went over the plans again. He could find no flaw. They would motor into the Min River Bay, which they estimated to be three miles long. If they could work the IBSs in that far, they would leave them in a brushy marsh on the left-hand shore almost near the end. They would deflate the boats and hide them for use later.

If all went according to plan.

The airfield was about three miles from the bay to the north. They would infiltrate to the border fence and determine if they had a good field of fire. There was no telling how far the fence was from the parked planes, or if the planes would be in the same position as four hours ago.

The men in the two inflatables stayed in visual contact with each other. They would use up most of an hour moving against a slight current and the start of an outgoing tide, but there was no way around that.

Later Murdock checked his watch. He had just heard the first sound of the surf. It was 0116. Still pretty much on schedule. They prepared to go through the surf. Murdock had checked his compass twice in the past five minutes and was sure they were on the right line. But the surf shouldn't be this high if they were at the bay.

They were still fifty meters off the breaker line when he saw the bay opening to the left. He got the attention of the second boat and powered parallel to the beach until they were in the quieter waters of the bay mouth.

He checked the shore a quarter of a mile on each side. He found no guards, no military. He drove the small boat into the center of the bay mouth through swells that didn't break, and then they were inside.

The left shore held trees and grassy areas. The right had houses and shacks and buildings. They hugged the left shore.

Lights blossomed on the left shore, and they heard a truck start up and gear down as it rolled away from them.

"Troops?" Jaybird asked in a whisper.

Murdock shook his head. No way to tell. They moved through the bay expecting at any moment to meet a patrol boat or to be targeted with a searchlight and a stuttering machine gun. Nothing happened.

They could see the dim outline of the end of the bay ahead, and Murdock checked the shore, then steered the boat into the edge of the water and grounded it. Six men jumped out and pulled the boat up the grassy bank. One man hit the valve that held in the air, and the boat deflated quickly.

Five minutes later both IBSs were buried under a scattering of dirt and leaves and tree branches.

"Now, let's remember where they are," Jaybird said. He found three flat rocks and piled them on top of each other near the shoreline. It would do.

As they worked on the IBSs, Red Nicholson had taken a quick scout beyond the woods and to the north. He came back with his report before they were ready to leave.

"Nothing between us and the boundary fence of the

airfield, L-T. But you ain't gonna be happy with the view."

"Why, Red?"

"Can't see the planes at all. This is in a little low point and there's a rise on the runway and no fucking way can we hit them planes from down here."

Murdock noted the report and spread out his men in the usual formation. He put Nicholson on point, followed by himself and then his radioman, Holt. Besides their short-range Motorola MX-300 belt radios, they had a backpack radio. It was the new AN/PRC-117D. It weighed only fifteen pounds, was fifteen inches high, eight wide, and three deep. Holt carried it on his back, sometimes under protest.

The tactical radio operated on several modes and multiple frequency bands and replaced three different radios the SEALs had used before.

It picked up and sent UHF satellite communications called SATCOM. It could reach anywhere in the world through that linkup. It had a UHF line-of-sight ability to talk to aircraft and direct air strikes. It handled VHF or FM, used for tactical contact by most armies in the world, which was the same band their Motorola MX-300 walkie-talkies used.

Holt could change bands by flipping a switch and setting up an antenna. Power went anywhere from ten watts down to one-tenth of a watt. A special encryption system for coding transmissions was built into the radio. The crypto system could be changed at any time by entering a new set of numbers. They could also transmit with compressed data bursts that lasted only a millisecond.

With this radio Murdock could talk directly with the President, the CNO, or Coronado's Third Platoon dayroom.

If they needed some help in a rush they could ask for it. Here in the wilds of China the odds of them getting any close air support, say, was not good. But they could ask.

Red led them through the woods and parallel to the fence. All growth had been cut back ten meters on both sides of the fence, which was chain-link with razor wire on the top. They could cut through it if they had to.

A half mile along the fence, the land rose and they could

see the aircraft parked on the hard runway. They were at
least seven hundred meters away.

"Too damn far," Murdock said. He sent a guard both ways
thirty meters along the fence, then called on Gunner's Mate
Second Class Greg Johnson, who had a pair of wire cutters
with fold-out handles for lots of pressure on the blades.

"Right here, Johnson. We want a three-foot-high hole and
we need it last week."

Johnson ran for the fence, touched it briefly with his
fingers, then began slicing the chain-link fence wire. It took
him four minutes to cut a line three feet high and three feet
across the top. Then he folded back the far side and slid
through the opening.

The rest of the platoon followed him and they established
the point man again with Second Squad fanned out behind
the First in a proper diamond. DeWitt served as rear guard.

The land had been bulldozed, some of it recently, and
they found the remains of houses, stock pens, and water
holes. It wasn't a neat job, but it had knocked down
everything that would interfere with a jet plane landing or
taking off.

Two hundred meters from the fence, Red Nicholson hit
the dirt and the rest of the SEALs ate dust like dominoes.
Murdock ran up to Nicholson bent over, and flattened out
beside him.

"What?"

"Mounted patrol. Looks like an old jeep. Coming along a
dirt track about a hundred meters ahead of us."

Murdock could see the rig then and the lights. It did not
have a searchlight that was turned on and probing.

"Let him pass," Murdock said.

Red nodded. He pointed to the left where a low building
of some sort stood. It looked to be made of concrete block
or stone. It had no electronics on it and was over two
hundred meters ahead. If they could reach the building, it
would put them in range of the middle of the parked
transport planes.

Murdock watched the transports through his night-vision
one-lens glass. He spotted figures moving around the

planes. Service personnel or guards, he couldn't tell which.

The jeep rolled past, shifting gears to get out of what looked like a spot of soft dirt or sand. When the rig cleared, the SEALs waited two minutes, then moved again to the left at a slow jog to eat up the distance.

Thirty meters from the concrete block building, Red stopped and waited for Murdock.

"Nothing shows from this side. Thought I saw a shaft of light a minute ago, like a door in front had opened and let out some yellow rays."

"Let's check." Murdock and Red eased up to a crouched position and ran to the rear of the building. Now they could tell it was twenty by forty feet and had no windows in the back or the side they could see. They edged around to check the far side. There was no alarm. Evidently no sentry or guard was outside.

They checked the front. It had three windows, all wide and low. The structure was no more than eight feet high. One door on this side opened inward. As they watched, the door swung in and a khaki-clad man came out, walked ten meters away from the building, and urinated.

Red gave a throat-slash move, but Murdock shook his head. They held still as the man went back in the door. He didn't have to unlock it to get inside.

Murdock took out a fragger and a flashbang grenade. He motioned to Red who took out one fragger. They both pulled the pins on the grenades but held down the arming spoons. Then they edged up to the door. Murdock went past it to the far side. He looked at Red and nodded. Murdock rammed open the door and threw both his grenades inside. Red pitched in his fragger and they let the door swing shut.

The five ear-shattering blasts of high explosives from the flashbang was followed by a string of bright strobing light pulses. The flashbang went off just before the two fraggers. The three windows in front blew out and the strobe lights winked through them.

When the last grenade exploded, Murdock charged through the door and covered the right half of the room spotting with his NVG. He saw two bodies on the floor writhing. He sent two silent rounds into both with his CAR-15 and swept the rest of the room with the night-vision goggles.

Red had fired three times, and Murdock saw the bodies spasming on the two bunks to the rear.

"Clear," Red said.

"Clear here," Murdock said. Then the Platoon Leader continued. "Make sure," he said. The SEALs went to the bodies and put a round in the head of each. Now they were sure.

Murdock examined the place. It was one large room. The fraggers had blown out any electric lights that had been on inside. Below the windows were panels that at one time must have been useful. Now they were scraped and torn and twisted from the shrapnel. The windows looked out directly down the first runway. The SAC-YD transports were parked cheek to tail fin on a taxiway fifty meters to the left of the runway. Murdock figured they were within two hundred meters of the near end of the line and four hundred meters from the far end of the parked transport planes. Fish in a fucking barrel.

"Bring up the squads," Murdock said into his lip mike. "We've found our firing positions."

As the men came up to the blockhouse, Murdock placed them. He put the four RPG men with two rounds each, including himself, on top of the building, which he found had a solid tarpaper and rock roof. The other men with RPGs would fire them from the sides of the blockhouse. These men also had their M-88 .50-caliber rifles locked and loaded and ready to go.

Murdock made a radio check. All thirteen gave him a quick "ready" on the Motorola. He had told them which areas of the line to fire in. Those on the roof took the far half of the line. The men on the ground drew the closer targets.

"Check your range and hit those motherfuckers," Murdock had told each man.

Now he sighted in on the center of the line of planes. As soon as he fired the rest would blast away. He concentrated on the sights, armed the rockets, and pulled the trigger.

The whoosh from behind him was always a surprise on an

RPG. He could follow the trail of fire as it arched into the sky, then came down. Before it hit, six more RPGs were in the air. Murdock watched his round hit. It blew up directly under one Chinese transport on the near side of the parking lot. A moment later the fuel tank exploded showering burning jet fuel over a dozen of the big SAC-YDs. He knew they had thirty-eight-meter wingspan. A lot of fuel in there.

Then the other RPGs began hitting. Three flew farther than Murdock's did. One fell short; two more landed among the parked planes and went off with a roar. Then RPGs began to fall on the planes closer to them. Three hit their targets, and one exploded beyond the planes in a hangar.

A moment later the heavy .50-caliber rifles began to speak. The rounds were aimed at the wing tanks and cockpits. Murdock caught himself watching the show, then remembered his last round. He fired his last RPG at maximum range, and figured they would not destroy the planes all the way to the far end with the RPGs. He watched four more hits in the row of planes. Sirens wailed and red lights from fire trucks blazed through the night. He could hear loudspeakers blaring in Chinese.

Then he saw the domino effect taker over. One plane exploded, and that set off two more, which roared into a firestorm exploding their fuel tanks, which set off half a dozen more planes as the whole row soon began burning.

He rolled off the roof, went below, and told the riflemen to concentrate on the far end of the row. One plane began taxiing away from the fireballs. Magic Brown put four slugs into the ship before it got far, and it burst into flames from the exploding rounds and kept on rolling as a blazing inferno.

Two planes closest to them had escaped the destruction. Murdock pointed them out and Ronson and Johnson drilled them with a half-dozen rounds, resulting in one of the planes blowing sky-high and taking the undamaged one with it in a flaming toast to Sino-American relations.

An armored car of some kind faded from the firelight and rolled toward the blockhouse. The troops inside the building began taking machine-gun fire. The sniper fifties returned fire and knocked out the rig with ten rounds. The armored half-track surged to one side, rolled, and wound up on its roof.

Murdock watched his handiwork. Not a single transport had escaped. He touched his lip mike.

"Let's get the hell out of Dodge," Murdock said.

They grouped up behind the blockhouse. A mortar round exploded fifty meters to the right.

"Any casualties?"

He heard no response. "Let's move it then, double time. You know where we're going, to that hole in the fence. We'll have company before we get there. Let's keep our rough diamond formation. Go, go, go."

They trotted back toward the fence. All were considerably less loaded down than on the march in. They were still a hundred meters from the fence when a mortar round went off thirty meters in front of them. Another one bracketed them twenty meters behind.

"Right flank!" Murdock shouted. "Run like hell, we're bracketed!"

They charged to the right and before they had moved thirty meters, they heard the whispers of mortar rounds, then the flash of six fire-for-effect HE rounds as they exploded tearing up the airfield landscape where the SEALs had been moments before.

They hit the fence and moved to the left. They found the hole and were through it when two mortar rounds hit in the trees beyond the fence.

"Stay with the fence and run downstream!" Murdock bellowed. "Keep away from any airbursts in those trees!"

They ran again keeping a suggestion of a formation. More mortar rounds hit behind them walking through the trees to the bay.

Murdock cut their pace to a fast walk. "They think we're in the trees. The problem is they know someone is down here. Before we can get to our boats and inflate them, there will be some Chinese navy boats swarming all over this bay."

"We've still got our fifties," Magic Brown said.

"Sure, but they'll have mounted fifty-caliber machine guns and maybe some forty-millimeter stuff."

They cut to the shore of the bay and Red Nicholson swore. He had just stumbled over the pile of three rocks they had left as their marker.

Murdock had never seen his men work faster or with more skill. They unearthed the IBSs, inflated them, and had them in the water in platoon-record time. He put three men with the fifties in the front of each boat, and they began moving downstream on the bay toward the ocean.

Murdock looked at Jaybird. He had an amazing knack for tactics. "Shoreline or center of the bay?" Murdock asked.

Jaybird shook his head. "No contest. We stick with the shoreline. We can vanish in these trees a lot easier than getting sunk in midstream. We don't have the equipment we need to play frogmen this time."

"You're right."

That was when they heard the growl of the high-speed patrol boat heading their way from the mouth of the bay.

14

Saturday, May 16

0217 hours
Min River Bay
China Mainland Coast

"A Chinese patrol boat?" Jaybird asked.

"You guessed it, and coming fast," Murdock said. "Head for the tree side," Murdock ordered. "Up ahead there are some trees that overhang the water. If we're lucky we can get in there and be hard to spot."

Both IBSs headed for shore at what seemed to Murdock an agonizingly slow speed. The patrol boat growled closer. Now they could see the headlight. It wasn't a searchlight, but aimed the right way it could be dangerous to the black boats and cammie-outfitted SEALs.

It would be close.

The IBSs edged into the overhanging branches of the trees, and were almost completely covered by the time the Chinese patrol boat roared into the area. It had been making S-curve searches, scanning the bay and both shores. Here the bay was nearly half a mile wide and the boat had a lot of water to cover.

The craft paused as it sighted the overhanging branches. The headlight played on them for a moment as the forty-foot craft turned past them from fifty meters. Evidently the searchers saw no movement and nothing else suspicious through the thick growth. The patrol boat turned in another large S and moved on up the bay.

Murdock put the silent-moving craft back into gear. "We've got over two more miles to get to the ocean," Murdock whispered to DeWitt in the other boat. "If we make it, we charge straight east and hope for a pickup. If we get separated, same plan. You have a sonar signaler. We'll stick together if at all possible."

They hummed along the far shore, watching for more patrol boats. Surely the Chinese had more than one in the bay or available for use here.

The second, then the third patrol boat appeared quickly. Each seemed to be working one of the shorelines from the ocean inward. The near shoreline here had trees, but none that grew close enough to the water to hide under.

"If we get spotted, we use the fifties and blast the cockpit of that sucker," Murdock said. "Maybe we can kill any radio transmissions. Then we go for any mounted machine guns we see and then try to shoot out the waterline and sink her."

The word was passed to the second boat. Each had five of the .50-caliber sniper rifles.

Six minutes passed. Murdock checked his watch. It was 0232. Less than six hours of darkness left. If they got caught in the bay or on the land come sunup, they were as good as dead. They would have to take their chances swimming their way out the bay and into the ocean. They had fins and masks on the IBSs, but no rebreathers. They would have to dump all their weapons and ammo and hope. A damn lot of hope, Murdock knew.

The near-shore patrol boat had an active searchlight. It sent out a three-foot beam with a lot of power behind it.

"Get ready to shoot and scoot, you guys," Murdock whispered to the five men in his boat with the big fifties. "We gonna have uninvited company in about two minutes. We shoot first. Brown, take out the searchlight."

Usually the squad leader or platoon leader opens fire first. This time Murdock didn't have a fifty, so he brought up his CAR-15 with the selector on full auto.

The Chinese patrol boat moved closer. It had slowed and the searchlight swept the shore continuously. The beam was twenty meters from the lead IBS when Murdock aimed at

the lighted pilothouse of the forty-foot craft and fired a
five-round burst.

The heavy fifties barked in immediate response. Bolts
were thrown quickly, new rounds were inserted, and another
blast of ten of the heavy .50-caliber explosive rounds jolted
into the small Chinese craft. The first volley blew out the
searchlight and most of the running lights and crippled the
steering. The patrol boat slewed sideways. The fifties kept
pounding, now aiming lower at the waterline hoping to hit
an engine or fuel tank.

Just as the first five-round magazines were running dry
on the McMillan M-88's, an explosive projectile hit the fuel
tank on the patrol craft and it blew up. A huge fireball
blossomed and slowly lifted upwards as the boat disinte-
grated. Parts of the patrol craft fell into the water fifty
meters away. When the sound of the explosion faded,
Murdock could hear a siren from upstream and then the
angry growl of the other two patrol craft heading his way.

"A mile and a half," Murdock said so his men could hear.
"We charge ahead, but these IBSs aren't exactly outboard
racers." He turned his .50-caliber sharpshooters around the
other way. "As soon as you can see any running lights back
there, start shooting at them. We might discourage them
enough to keep them back at long range."

"Yeah, and we might not," Magic Brown said. "We
staying near the shore in case we catch a lucky round that
deflates this little gem we're riding in?"

"Damn close to shore. We might be able to ground one of
those beasties back there. Let's hear some sound out of
those fifties."

The other IBS saw the reverse targeting and did likewise.
Murdock hoped it would be enough. Now, with a definite
target, he was sure the Chinese would have radioed to their
base and alerted some heavier craft and maybe some
airpower. He knew the Chinese had good attack choppers
and some sleek new fighters. Either one would be bad news.

Jaybird Sterling gave a shout of joy. "Put out one of the
damn running lights," he chortled. "Don't know what else I
hit. They must know by now that we have some firepower."

The two patrol boats behind them did seem to slack off their forward charge.

"They are regrouping," DeWitt said. The other rubber boat had come alongside. "Wish we could capture one of those patrol boats and use it to charge straight out the bay and into the night to the east."

"Dreaming, L-T," Ronson said. "I figure we'll be swimming before this fracas is over. These Mainlanders don't like to lose even a little skirmish, and we spanked their asses good back there at the airfield."

The sniper rifles continued to send messages to the patrol boats. Murdock had checked ammo totals and told the men to conserve. They didn't know what they might need the big fifties for down the road. The two patrol boats were definitely holding back. Murdock wished he knew why.

Then he found out.

Both the Chinese boats opened up with .50-caliber machine guns. They must have had to change mounts or bring them from the aft decks. The big rounds began slapping into the water short. Murdock and DeWitt turned their boats away from each other. DeWitt was closest to the shore and he hugged it. Murdock guided his IBS thirty meters away toward the center of the bay.

"Cease fire," Murdock said into his lip mike. "Hide, don't give them a target."

The fifties went silent. The attacking boats behind them closed to a shorter range and fired the heavy fifties in bursts now that tracked across the water where the SEALs still moved slowly toward the mouth of the bay.

Murdock cautioned his men to stay low in the boat. "They probably don't have radar on those buckets, but we don't want to give anything away."

They moved forward, the silent IBS engines propelling them closer to the mouth. Murdock figured they were still a mile short of the ocean.

The machine guns behind them fired again, picking up the series of five-round bursts. Most of them went toward the shore.

"Trouble!" Murdock heard in his earpiece. It was DeWitt.

"We've taken two rounds, our IBS is going limp, and we have a casualty. We can make shore. Will save all of the masks and fins. Mind joining us?"

Murdock turned his boat toward the shore. Before he motored into the hail of .50-caliber rounds, the Chinese slowed, then stopped the firing.

"They must be encouraged that they haven't had any return fire," Ronson said. Murdock agreed.

"DeWitt, some help here?" Murdock said into his mike.

Murdock's radio sounded. "I see you. Turn left about ten meters and then straight into the shore. We've found a little cover here. Some logs and an old foundation of a building. Our IBS is flat."

"Roger that."

Murdock had almost thirty seconds to decide what to do. One boat down meant both boats were down.

"We're going in. Grab your masks and fins and hope we can use them later. Right now we have some dogface ground-soldier work to do. That L in SEAL still stands for land. Let's hit the beach running. If we can hide the boat, fine."

There was no way to hide the boat. When they were all out with their equipment, Murdock slashed it twice with his combat knife and pushed it into the water to deflate and sink.

They found DeWitt and his men behind crumbling rock foundations ten meters from the shoreline.

It was the best protection Murdock had seen all night.

"We stay silent unless they spot us," Murdock said. "Don't even breathe heavy."

The fourteen men crouched in place. Only Doc Ellsworth was busy.

"We have one casualty," DeWitt whispered to Murdock. "Johnson took a hit through the chest up high, but it's one of those damn fifties. We patched him some. The round went out his back. Missed his lung, I'd say."

They heard the Chinese patrol craft working slowly toward them. The boats fired now and then. Once they put on a burst of speed and snapped on searchlights working both sides of the shoreline.

"Gonna fucking miss us," Jaybird whispered.

Doc crawled over and touched Murdock's shoulder. "He's hit bad. Lost a lot of blood. I patched him up some. Took two shots of morphine to keep him quiet. He won't travel good."

"Swim?"

"Float in a body bag."

"Thanks. Stay with him."

The boats worked closer. The one on the side of the bay snapped on its lights every ten seconds or so, let it burn for a quick look at the shore, then snapped it off.

Murdock had a hole in the foundation through which he watched the boat come closer. The searchlight jolted on and swept the beach directly in front of them. Murdock sucked in a breath. Half of one of the IBSs showed on the muddy bank. It was deflated flat, but looked out of place. It would be a bright beacon for the Chinese.

The light held on the raft. The patrol boat cut its engine. Machine-gun fire raked the beach and the tall grass behind it. When the firing stopped, the SEALs could hear the Chinese chattering.

The boat still had its running lights on. Murdock figured it was no more than forty meters off shore. The heavy machine gun spoke again, this time spraying the grass and the end of the foundations. Everyone was in the Chinese dirt two feet below the top of the native rocks and mortar.

Murdock checked his peephole.

The boat came forward slowly toward shore.

"We've got to take them out," Murdock whispered in his mike. "Let's get ready. On me. Here we go." He lifted up and put his CAR-15 over the top of the foundation. The searchlight on the boat was off. He sighted it on the bow where the machine gun had to be and fired a five-round burst.

Ten .50-caliber weapons and three CARs fired a half second after he did. The rounds ripped into the suspicious boat with the force of a 105 round exploding. The small

pilothouse windows crashed, the deck was swept with
.223-caliber rounds, and the exploding fifties broke up the
ship from stern to stern. For a moment it wallowed, then
went dead in the bay waters.

They heard splashes on the far side. No more sound came
from the patrol boat.

Murdock called a cease-fire. All was quiet. They could
see the running lights on the other patrol boat a half mile
away on the far side of the bay.

"Will it run?" Murdock asked his mike. "If it will it's an
even trade. Ronson and Sterling, get out there and see if we
left enough of that tub intact so we can use it to make a run
down the bay for glory."

15

Saturday, May 16

Lieutenant Blake Murdock watched his two men slide into the water and swim strongly toward the Chinese patrol boat. It drifted slowly toward the mouth of the bay. Outgoing tide. He had forgotten about that. It could be a help. The dead craft floated twenty meters offshore.

He heard the growl of the other Chinese patrol boats across the bay. It was less than half a mile away and coming toward them fast. Murdock could see the lights on the craft as it cut slightly downstream to counter the tidal current. It would be five minutes before the Chinese came close enough to evaluate their sister ship.

He watched through the dusky China night as Ronson and Sterling climbed on board and vanished inside the patrol boat. His other men had strung out along the shoreline at combat intervals. Two men faced back the way they had come as a rear guard.

It seemed like an hour before Murdock heard the Chinese patrol boat's engine turn over, then catch and the heavy pounding of the diesel engine steadied down. The craft edged slowly toward shore. Ronson showed at the rail and waved. His fist pumped up and down. The Platoon Leader pointed at the two men nearest him and then at the boat.

They carried their gear, waded out, then swam the last twenty feet to the side of the craft, where they could push their weapons on board and crawl up. They waited to take Johnson on board until the boat was almost aground. Magic Brown and Ken Ching carried and floated the wounded SEAL to the craft, and four men lifted him on board. Doc was there, and put him on the deck and went to work on him again. Doc swore as he tended the bullet wound. Murdock scowled. That meant that Johnson was in bad shape.

The last two men off the shore were the two officers. The boat was so close to China that they tossed their weapons onboard and didn't have to swim.

"The control panel got shot up, L-T," Ronson said. "Twisted a few wires back together and she's good as new. Almost."

DeWitt checked the oncoming Chinese patrol boat. "She's about two hundred yards off and throttled down," he said. "I'd say her crew is looking us over. Hope they don't have night-vision goggles."

Murdock looked at the other boat, then at Ronson. "Ease her along the shore seaward. We'll see what our buddies over there do."

The craft turned and edged along the shore for twenty meters. Then the Chinese crew snapped on a searchlight and swept over Murdock's navy.

He had positioned four of the .50-caliber McMillans along the starboard side facing the other boat. The gunners had instructions to open fire if the enemy searchlight came on. The first booming shot from the heavy sniper rifles smashed the searchlight, and three more rounds slammed into the pilothouse. A small-caliber machine gun opened up aft on the other boat, but he didn't have the range.

Three CAR-15's splattered bursts of .223 lead into the aft section and the pilothouse, and the Chinese gunned their motor and pulled back another hundred yards. They returned some rifle fire, but evidently didn't have a bow .50-caliber weapon.

"Gun it," Murdock said, and Ronson shoved the throttles forward and the little boat jolted ahead toward the bay's mouth. Now the other Chinese boat turned and followed, with half-a-dozen guns slanting hot lead at the SEALs' ticket home.

The men with the McMillan fifties moved aft and kept up their fire. It was less effective now, but held the Chinese well off.

Gradually Murdock's crew pulled farther away from the trailer, and Murdock stared from inside the pilothouse at the bay mouth now less than two hundred yards ahead.

Jaybird was at Murdock's elbow. "So, say we make it out of the bay, what the hell then? They must have been alerted about us by now. They should have something in the air soon. I hear the Chinese have a good attack chopper."

"I don't know about their choppers, but they do have a good little jet fighter with rockets. I'm not sure it has night-attack capability. We just play it by ear out here. We're not into the open sea yet."

As if to punctuate the statement, a burst of machine-gun rounds from the chasing patrol boat slammed into the pilothouse and sent chips of wood and glass flying. Murdock felt a sting on his check, and found blood on his hand when he investigated. The three men in there ducked, but Ronson kept the boat on full throttle charging toward the bay mouth.

Murdock crawled from the pilothouse and moved two more fifties to the back.

"Get rid of some of your ammo," he told them. "See if you can cripple that hound dog on our trail."

The firing picked up from the heavy weapons, and fire from the other boat trailed off. Then they were at the swells of the East China Sea as the little craft slipped out the bay entrance.

"They must have some cutters or destroyers in Foochow," Jaybird said.

"Probably. Due east, Ronson. We need at least a mile offshore before we blow up this baby."

Murdock called for Doc Ellsworth, who came up shaking his head. "Ain't good, Skipper. Lost so damn much blood.

If we have to go into the water, he won't make it. Plasma won't do no good now."

Murdock nodded. Behind them the patrol boat had given up the chase. It sat just outside the bay for a couple of minutes, then sailed north toward Foochow.

That was when Murdock and the other men heard the heavy growl of a larger, high-speed ship. The sound came from the north.

"Called off the puppy and sent out a real fighting dog," Magic Brown said. "This mutt won't be scared off by our fifties."

"Frazier," Murdock called. "Rig two charges below with ten-minute timers, but don't set the timers yet. We're gonna get wet. Get your masks and flippers on, the SEALs are going back to mother."

Doc Ellsworth came over to Murdock. "You better come take a look at Johnson. He's getting worse. He can talk, but that's about all."

Murdock knelt on the aft deck where Johnson lay. Even in the faint night light he looked pale.

"Hang in there, buddy. We're out and away and should find that sub soon."

"Can't do it, Skipper. Been a good cruise with you. Take care of the guys."

A flash of pain jolted Johnson, and he lifted his head off the deck, then let it down. "Oh, damn, but that hurts. Why does it hurt so bad, Doc?"

"Don't know, Johnson. I'll give you another shot of morphine. That will make it stop hurting."

"Save it, Doc. You might need it. This is my last mission. Sorry I got in the wrong place."

"Johnson, we'll get you through," Murdock said. "Just hang in there."

Johnson closed his eyes, took a deep breath, and died.

"He's gone, sir."

"Yeah, good man. Goddamnit!"

"We taking him back with us, L-T?"

"Absolutely. Your job, Doc. Use a buddy line around his

chest. We're going in the water but we won't be moving fast." Doc nodded and left.

"Ronson, aim this thing southeast and tie down the wheel. When that motherfucker out there gets within three hundred yards, we all go over the side. Then you give her full throttle and get wet yourself."

"Roger that, Lieutenant."

The SEALs got ready to go back to the safety of the water. Whenever things get too hot or they need cover and protection, SEALs always go into the water. It's their second home. They're at ease there, comfortable, in familiar territory. This time all they had were their fins and masks. No scuba, no Draeger LAR-V rebreathing gear. Just them and the East China Sea.

Murdock checked on Doc. He had Johnson zipped up in a thin plastic sea-green body bag. Doc tied a buddy line around the bag at Johnson's chest.

"Never done this before, Skipper. Hope to hell I never have to do it again."

"We won't leave him behind, Doc. We'll pace ourselves to your speed. We'll be more than a mile off when we hit the water."

Doc nodded, and the platoon leader checked his other men. He found nobody else wounded except for some scrapes and tears and two of them dinged with scratches from flying glass.

The growl of the attack craft came closer now. They couldn't see it through the darkness, but it evidently had them on radar and had zeroed in on their course.

"Dump your weapons and extra ammo," Murdock told them. "Won't do us a damn bit of good against this mad dog coming. We're on swim-and-fin time. Evade and escape. Magic, I want you to stay with Doc and help out with Johnson.

"Holt, get aft and dangle one of those sonar beepers in the wet. Maybe our sub friend is nearby somewhere. He damn well better be."

Murdock could see a searchlight now from the cutter.

"Southwest, Ronson, tie her down."

Two minutes later they could see the hulk of the Chinese raider bearing down on them. She was bigger than Murdock had suspected.

"Let's go for a swim, men," Murdock said. "Doc and Johnson first. Set the timer on those charges. Let's get the hell out of Dodge."

The SEALs went over the side and grouped quickly. Ronson was next to last off and Frazier, who set the timers on the charge of C-4, was the last one out.

They watched the patrol boat steam away from them, and saw the dark shadow of the Chinese warship veer away from them as it followed the boat.

Five minutes after they went into the water they had joined up, established their buddy lines, and were set to move.

"We stay on the surface unless that ship comes back looking for us and gets too close," Murdock said. "We'll move east away from the mainland. That sub commander will thank us for every quarter of a mile we get away from Mother China back there."

Murdock put Doc in the lead with Magic Brown as they towed the body bag. So far it was floating thanks to the trapped air inside the plastic bag. Doc established a slow crawl stroke and they moved away from China.

Two minutes later a flash of light blossomed on the sea to the southeast.

"Right on sched," Frazier said. "Good-bye patrol boat."

They heard the large Chinese ship's engines again.

"They're coming back," Murdock said. "If he gets anywhere close or that damned searchlight is about to hit us, we duck-dive until it's dark and clear."

Five minutes later the Chinese cutter swept past them a quarter of a mile seaward. The big searchlight came nowhere near their position. They continued to swim away from shore.

Doc called to Murdock, who swam up beside him.

"Losing air out of the bag, L-T. The things weren't designed to be float bags. Air coming out around the end of the zipper. Another ten minutes and we'll be towing him underwater."

"You're on point, we'll follow at your speed."

They had been in the water for forty-five minutes by then. They hadn't planned on a swim and had decided back on the carrier not to wear wet suits under their land-action cammies. Now the cold was starting to get to all of them. Not as bad as a four-hour training session off Coronado in winter, but cold enough to numb fingers and toes.

"He's coming back," Magic called softly.

The hulk of the Chinese cutter was almost on them this time. They waited until the searchlight swung their way, then dove. It took both Magic and Doc to keep Johnson's body bag just below the surface of the choppy green water. They kicked downward and stroked down and managed to keep the green bag submerged until the yellow light above them swung past. Both surfaced with lungs burning.

They all came up and sounded off in a quick count, and Murdock knew he had all of his men. They watched the dark hulk of the cutter slowly move away from them heading for the coast.

"The cluster-fucking Chinese Navy has done it again," Jaybird said. They all laughed in a tension easing moment.

Doc and Magic moved out again to the east towing their dead friend behind them.

A half hour later they were still swimming. Murdock called a halt.

Doc said it for all of them. "Where the fuck is that damn sub? We've had that sonar beeper in the water for almost two hours. They chicken bastards and won't come in this close to shore?"

Murdock told them all to float and relax. He found DeWitt and they talked.

"Should have found us before now," Murdock's second said.

"Must have been that Chinese cutter that spooked them," Murdock said. "The screws might have sounded like a destroyer."

"That's been over half an hour ago."

"We could shoot up a red flare," Murdock said.

"Yeah, and have half the Chinese Navy on our backs in twenty minutes."

"I don't think so. They got their noses bloodied twice, they won't want to try for three in a row."

"You have a flare gun?" DeWitt asked.

"Always carry one." Murdock took the small flare gun from his fanny pack and broke open the waterproof plastic seal. "Loaded and ready to go."

"Let's do it," DeWitt said.

The muffled report of the flare gun and then the brilliant red flare on a parachute surprised the SEALs.

"This is crazy," Sterling said.

"Get ready to dive again," Chin agreed.

"Might work," Brown said. "Nothing else is fucking working."

The thirteen men watched the flare drifting to their right. The bright red flare burned for almost a minute, then sputtered out.

The SEALs waited.

Less than a minute later a bullhorn sounded to the east of them. "Got you, swimmers. Where are your two IBSs?"

The SEALs gave a cheer.

Ten minutes later they were all on board the USS *Dorchester* changing into dry clothes.

Murdock checked his watch: 0422. Plenty of dark time out there. They were scheduled to rendezvous with the carrier as quickly as they could get there. They would have a few hours of sleep and then get ready for the second half of their mission. Murdock grinned. This was beginning to feel a lot like Hell Week back at the Coronado BUD/S training command.

16

Monday, November 24

Lieutenant Blake Murdock sat at his desk in the home base headquarters of the Seal Team Seven. He stared at the list of names of the men in his two squads in the Third Platoon. He was still tired. He was grouchy as hell and he had a monster headache.

Third Platoon had been back from Lebanon for ten days. He'd given the men three-day leaves, and had tried to catch up on his sleep himself. His butt and both legs still hurt like they were on fire. The medics had told him to stay in bed for a week and let the shrapnel wounds heal.

Sure, a week in bed.

He stared at the list of men again, concentrating now on the three with red circles around them.

Chief Petty Officer "Koz" Kosciuszko was dead and buried on foreign soil. Murdock hated that as much as any part of the Lebanon mission. SEALs just didn't leave a KIA behind. This time there was no possible way they could have brought him out. Koz had been with the platoon a long time, longer than Murdock had, and he was the anchor of the operation. He had to be replaced.

Razor Roselli, his longtime Platoon Chief, was still in Balboa Naval Hospital in San Diego with a shattered ankle.

115

If it didn't heal right it would mean Roselli would be out of the SEALs. Roselli had more combat experience than any other man in the platoon. He'd be hard to replace.

His right hand on a mission, his radioman, Bill Higgins, was in critical condition with a badly shot-up side. If he lived he would probably never be fit for SEAL duty again.

Three good men. How did he replace them?

He stared at the roster again. Ron Holt. He'd seen a lot of good action from Ron. Ron was a cool head who obeyed commands in an instant. Yes, he'd move him up to be his radioman. That still left two big holes.

He had moved Jaybird Sterling up as Platoon Chief on the ship just after they got out of the Blackhawk chopper. So far Jaybird had done a fine job. He had persuaded, cajoled, threatened, and bullied the men to get their equipment squared away, their reports written and their lost weapons detailed. He'd be fine in that post.

So far he was measuring up. Several men in the platoon had more combat experience than Jaybird, but none had the guts, the bravado, and the cool decision-making and problem-solving in action that Jaybird had shown. Jaybird it was.

Murdock had his first cup of coffee, and then looked over the roster of unassigned SEALs there in Coronado.

Each man was listed with his name, rank, specialty, physical description, length of service and a picture.

Murdock picked out Electrician's Mate Second Class Henry "Horse" Ronson for his machine gunner to replace Kos. He was six-four and 230 pounds of muscle. If he passed an interview he'd be assigned to First Squad.

That left two slots to bring him up to TO&E. He needed a man who could handle explosives. All SEALs are trained to be sappers, but it was beneficial to have one man specially trained and outstanding at his work. He picked out Willy "The Priest" Bishop, an Electrician Mate Second Class, to fill that spot.

A linguist would help. He went over the available list of SEALs to see if any had been to language school. One man had. He could speak Spanish and French, Tagalog, Russian, and four dialects of Chinese. Yeah, that should cover most of the world. He looked at the man's picture. He was Chinese. Kenneth Ching, Quartermaster First Class.

Murdock made a phone call to personnel and told them to send the three men over that morning for interviews at 1100. The platoon should be back from PT by then.

Murdock moved cautiously on the pillow on his swivel chair. He'd have a sore butt for a month, maybe more. He was lucky at that. He'd made a hospital call that afternoon to Balboa and check on his two wounded men. Both had been detached from his command, but they were still his men. If they weren't being taken care of properly, there would be some serious shit flung around those clean hospital rooms, corridors, and offices.

DeWitt. The lieutenant and second in command of the platoon had come back from Lebanon with his left arm in a cast. A bad break. The medics had told him to take a two-week leave and rest up at home. DeWitt had said yes, sir, saluted the commander doctor, and reported back to duty the next day.

He was hurting. Doc Ellsworth checked on him twice a day with a shot of morphine ready. DeWitt was making it fine now with no training going on. Murdock didn't know how he'd fare during the tough training school he had worked out. It would be nasty and brutal. He had to integrate the new men and confirm Jaybird's leadership ability under tense and near-combat conditions.

"Oh, damn!" Murdock whispered as he shifted on the chair. Lacy pains darted up his thighs and buttocks, and he stared at the bottle of ibuporfen on his desk. He'd been gulping three at a time four times a day. The dope kept him civil most of the time.

Murdock looked down at the training schedule. It wasn't Hell Week exactly, but he did have a forty-eight-hour mission set up without sleep and with live firing out in the desert. Two canteens of water, no food, no rest, lots of double-timing, and a whole shit-pot full of beer cans to knock down at three hundred yards.

The two-day Hell would come after some intensive

day-long training exercises with definite objectives followed by evaluations and critiques. Jaybird would have a lot
to do with these. The troops were due to report back today
at nine. Jaybird would be in by eight. He hadn't taken any
leave, wanting to get to understand all of his duties. He was
a quick learner. He, in effect, would do a lot of the running
of the platoon while they were in garrison.

DeWitt came in, groaned, and drew a cup of coffee. He
sat down across from Murdock.

"Platoon back today?"

Murdock nodded.

"We going to hit the training sched?"

"Like we were a brand-new class of BUD trainees. I still
think you need that week's leave to see your parents up in
Seattle."

DeWitt looked at him from deep-set eyes under his just
renewed flattop haircut. "If the men do it, I do it, except
maybe the cargo net climb."

"You won't do that cast any good smashing it around."

"It's my cast, and my arm. What's on for this morning?"

"Start out slow," Murdock said. "Figured we'd do a little
log PT with cammies and life vests."

"Then a run with the logs?"

"An easy five-mile jaunt. You don't get to carry the log.
You can do the run."

"Thanks, Boss." DeWitt looked out the window. "I got
five more weeks on this cast. If anything pops in the world,
you take me along even if for nothing more than to hold
your goddamn fly open."

Murdock chuckled. "Nothing can pop. I've got a six-
week training schedule worked out. Not even the CNO
would mess up one of my schedules."

"I'll send him a fax so he's sure about your timetable."

The two grinned at each other. They had hit it off since
the first day when Murdock was named to replace Lieutenant Vincent Cotter, who had been KIA in the Shuba airport
raid in Iraq. Third Platoon had gone in to rescue a C-130 full
of UN weapons inspectors that the Iraqis had surrounded
and wouldn't let depart.

DeWitt hadn't been upset when a new man had been called in to take over the platoon that he could have inherited. They had both worked together like the well-oiled parts of an H&K MP-5 sub-machine gun ever since.

DeWitt was a stringbean, six-one, not over a hundred and eighty pounds, and tough as Southern fired shoe leather. He came from Seattle, and, served two years as an enlisted man before he got his appointment to Annapolis. A year after he graduated he applied for the SEALs and made the cut. That made him a Mustang, ring-knocker SEAL. He wasn't married and tended to like long-legged redheads, when he took the time. Being a SEAL didn't leave much time for social activities besides a few bars.

DeWitt rested his cast on the desk. "Yeah, I think Jaybird is going to make it as Platoon Chief. He's damn good with the men."

"He's coming along. Sure I can't write you a week's leave with an airline ticket for Seattle?"

"I wouldn't know what to do. Mom would love it, but I'd drive my dad nuts. He still carries mail for the Post Office."

"You can go fishing. Remember those big salmon you used to catch? When do the chinooks and kings run up there? About now? Even find some of those big flounders you were telling me about."

"Out here we call them halibut. Not as many of them as there were. I've lost my enthusiasm for fishing. Much rather help get this outfit ready to fight again."

David, "Jaybird" Sterling banked into the office, dropped two notebooks on his desk in the outer section, and filled a coffee cup before he came to Murdock's room and leaned against the door.

It was 0800.

"Sir, I have the latest intel from the men," he said to Murdock. "Seems you've picked up a new nickname. It has something to do with the recent unpleasantness in Lebanon which shall be nameless."

DeWitt turned grinning. "This I've got to hear. They've been calling me Broken Wing."

Jaybird laughed. "True, L-T. That's not such a bad

moniker. The guys are calling the commander Old Iron Ass in honor of all the shrapnel that wound up in his lower sections."

DeWitt laughed. Jaybird beamed. "It could be worse, sir. This way you could go down in history right next door to Old Ironsides."

"Not likely," Murdock growled.

"Good coffee," Jaybird said through his big smile.

"Don't change the subject," Murdock said. "We fall out at 0910 for training. You're in the mix, Jaybird. When the troops arrive get them into cammies, floppy hats, and issue each one a life vest. No weapons. Be a walk in the fucking park." He stared at them a minute, his growl showing on his face. "Now get out of here and let me finish my plans for a forty-eight-hour Hell Week."

They both left. Murdock popped three Motrins and washed them down with coffee.

Murdock had never wanted to be anything but Navy since he went on an Outward Bound trek the summer after his senior year in prep school. His family came from the wealthy enclave of Front Royal, Virginia in posh Royal County. His father was a longtime Congressman holding a key seat on the powerful House Military Affairs Committee. His dad wanted him to go to Harvard, then get into politics and some day run for the family seat in Congress.

Murdock wanted something more challenging, with more bite, and physically demanding. He wrangled an appointment to Annapolis, and four years later received his ring. A year later he applied for SEAL training, and worked his way through the six-month course right alongside the other SEAL candidates.

Officers get no preferred treatment in SEAL training. They do everything the other men do. It helps mold a strong bond between enlisted and officers, and has a way of breaking down the strict and traditional "officer country" psychology. When you're trusting your life to the SEAL behind you on an operation, it doesn't matter what insignia of rank he has on his collar. All that matters is that he can do his job.

Murdock had been in the SEALs for five years, including two years as a senior instructor at the BUD/S training base in Coronado. He was delighted when he took over Third Platoon about a year ago as platoon leader.

He was still single. He had met a girl, Susan, on the Outward Bound program in Colorado the summer before his last year at Exeter. Their relationship had grown and they had planned to be married. She was driving to his graduation at Annapolis when a teenager on cocaine hit her head-on three days before they were to be married. She died instantly.

He shuffled the papers again. Teamwork. That was the hallmark of the SEALs. In the field they had to operate as a team. Every man had to know what the SEAL beside him and behind could do and would do under any combat situation. There could be no guesswork, no lost time hoping somebody would do his job.

Those kind of glitches killed SEALs. He wanted no more dead men on his watch.

He dug into the paperwork again, working out specific exercises and problems to help the new men function smoothly with the experienced ones. He also had to see that the men in new positions, such as his radio operator, would know what to do and when to do it in every possible situation.

He worked over the papers again and when he looked up, Jaybird stood in the doorway with his red life vest on.

"The troops are ready for training, sir," Jaybird said.

Murdock hesitated. When he was here as a senior training officer he used to take out his training boat team wearing clean, perfectly pressed khakis in contrast to their sweat-, mud-, and sand-lathered cammies. No time for that today.

He stood, and couldn't suppress a groan. The damn shrapnel.

Jaybird frowned a moment. "L-T, Doc will be with us and he has his full kit with lots of Motrin and morphine."

"You didn't hear a thing, Jaybird. Let's get out there with the troops."

The platoon double-timed into the sand of the Pacific Ocean and directly to the pile of much-used telephone poles. The men were lined up in two squads, and Murdock halted them and grinned.

"Ladies, we'll have a meeting of the sewing society today. Each squad grab a pole and sit down and put it on your laps. It's review time."

The SEALs knew what was coming. They lined up, picked up a three-hundred-pound butt end of a former telephone pole, and sat down with it on their thighs.

"Move your friend the log up to your chests, ladies." The logs moved and Murdock nodded. "Ready? It's sit-up time. Hold the log in place and do sits-ups. Ten will be enough. Move!"

These seasoned veterans had been through the log PT dozens of times during and since their BUD/S training, but it still took the ultimate in teamwork and guts. If just one SEAL didn't lift his share, the log wouldn't come up and the whole squad would fail.

The logs came up, slowly at first, then quicker as the men counted off the ten sit-ups.

"Fair, fair," Murdock barked. "I've had raw recruits do it better. Some of you are getting old and sloppy. Okay, drop your friend the pole in the sand and on your feet."

He waited for them to stand beside their logs. "We'll play a little pickup, men. Lift that little toothpick to your knees." He waited as fourteen backs strained and lifted. "Now take it to your waist." They did.

"Up to your shoulders. Move it!"

Murdock waited until the logs were lifted quickly to shoulder height. Then he bent to the ground and worked on the laces on his boots.

The SEALs held the log in position.

Murdock stood and grinned at them. "Not bad, not bad. Now let's push it over your heads, arms straight. Move!"

The logs pressed upward, wavered, then were up clean for both squads.

Murdock nodded. "Yes, fair. Drop your toothpick to your

shoulders and we'll do that again, fifteen times. Count them off." He waited as the men pushed the heavy poles upward the fifteen times barking off the number with each completion.

Murdock shook his head. "Slow, you ladies are slow as my grandmother. Enough of that. Let's take a little hike. In case you've forgotten, we start out on the left foot. Works best if you all try to stay in step."

Lieutenant DeWitt marched along with his squad. With his broken left arm, there wasn't a thing he could do to help them.

"How far today, L-T?" a voice shouted from one of the men.

"Was going to be only five miles," Murdock said. "Now I think we'll do seven instead." He looked at the troops. "Any more questions?"

There were none.

"Let's move out," Murdock called, and the sixteen SEALs marched ahead in the soft sand along the Coronado Strand. They had done it before, but not for a long time. The log was unforgiving and a quick way to whip the SEALs back into fighting shape. Murdock knew it and the men knew it.

Somebody sang out with the ages-old cadence count chant. It was permitted.

"You had a good home and you left."

"Damn right!"

"You had a good home and you left."

"Damn right!"

"Sound off."

"One, two."

"Sound off."

"Three, four."

"Cadence count."

"One two three four . . . three four!"

A new verse came out.

"Love those girls all dressed in red."

"Love those girls all dressed in red."

"They don't mind giving us head."

"They don't mind giving us head."

DeWitt moved up beside Murdock, who led the march. "Seven miles?"

"Damn right. We don't have time to fuck around. We could get a mission anytime now that the saintly CIA is twisting our tails. Those Damn Christians In Action are always coming up with some world crisis. We might only have a week to get these puppies back in shape. Now that Don Stroh has pegged us as the CIA's pet tiger, they can unleash whenever they feel the need. We've got to be ready."

DeWitt didn't respond.

Murdock looked over at him. "Broken Wing, I like that. The downside is that if we get a call while that wing is still in the cast, we leave you high and dry here on the grinder."

DeWitt scowled and spat into the sand. "The thought had occurred to me. Not that I like it. I'm sticking pins in my CNO doll every night telling him not to call us for another six weeks."

"Yeah, hope it works. If we do leave you behind, I'll put Jaybird into your slot. Only thing I can do."

"Damn well better not come to that," DeWitt said. He looked behind and saw that his squad was functioning according to the book. Log on shoulders, held with both hands, feet in position lockstep, marching to the same drummer.

A little over forty-five minutes later they hit the three-and-a-half mile turnaround point and headed back. Murdock took them down to the wet sand, which was easier to march on.

"You get soft?" DeWitt asked Murdock as he pulled up beside him.

"Hell, no, the men are getting tired walking in that damn loose sand."

DeWitt nodded, then frowned and stumbled. He caught himself, looking sheepishly at Murdock.

"I'm fine, I'm fine. Just stubbed my toe."

A moment later he stumbled again and went down to his knees. Before Murdock could yell, Doc Ellsworth had pulled out of ranks and run up to where DeWitt had dropped forward to rest on his good right hand and his knees.

17

Monday, November 24

Doc Ellsworth dropped to both knees beside Lieutenant DeWitt. He looked at his face, then gently eased the SEAL sideways until he sat on the hard sand.

DeWitt shook his head and rubbed his face with his right hand.

"So damn dizzy. Can't figure it out. Where the hell am I?"

"Sir! Lieutenant DeWitt." Doc shook his shoulder gently. "You stumbled and went down. Complained of being dizzy. Sir, do you know where you are?"

"Damned grinder somewhere." He shook his head again, blinked, and stared at Doc. "Hi, Ellsworth, what's happening?"

"You stumbled, sir, and fell. How are you feeling?"

"Stumbled? Damn. Feeling? Oh, a little woozy, like a cheap drunk. What have I been drinking?"

"Only coffee, sir. It could be the pain pills they gave you at sick call. What meds are you taking?"

DeWitt blinked. "Pills?"

"Yes, sir, we'll figure that out later. Just sit still." Doc turned to Murdock. "A jeep would come in handy, sir."

Murdock looked over at his platoon, which had stopped on his curt command earlier. "Drop the logs on three. One, two, three. Nicholson. See how fast you can run up to the grinder and bring back some transport for the L-T. Anything that rolls and he can sit in. Go, go, go!" Nicholson had the best foot speed of anybody in the squad. He had run the 220 in high school.

"L-T, we've got some transport coming for you," Doc said. "Just take it easy."

DeWitt frowned and brushed the wet sand off his knees with his right hand.

"What the hell am I doing sitting in this fucking wet sand? Doc, answer me. Why am I sitting here?"

"You had a dizzy spell, sir. Almost passed out. I'd guess it's a reaction to some of the meds sick bay gave you. What are you taking?"

"Don't know. Said three a day so I'm taking three a day. Bottle is in my quarters."

Murdock had been listening. He straightened up and looked at his Platoon Chief. "Jaybird. Get those logs hoisted to shoulders and take the troops back to the toothpick pile. Then fall out around the tower climb. If nobody is on it, put each man up five times. We'll be along as soon as we can."

Twenty minutes later, Nicholson came racing down the wet sand in a white Shore Patrol Van with the red light on the top blinking. The rig eased up to them and stopped three feet from DeWitt.

"Let's try to stand up, L-T," Doc said.

"Hell, I can stand up." DeWitt tried, almost made it. Then Murdock caught one arm and Doc the other and they helped him take three steps to the van door and slide into the front seat.

Murdock fastened the seat belt around his 2IC. "Drive easy going back, sailor," Murdock told the Shore Patrol behind the wheel. Doc climbed in the back seat.

"Yeah, easy as it goes," Doc said. "I want the L-T in one piece when we get to the infirmary."

Red Nicholson and Murdock watched the van cut across the soft sand to the highway, turn left, and head toward

SEAL headquarters. Nicholson and Murdock began double-timing along the hard sand.

"Is the L-T bad off?" Nicholson asked.

"Not sure. Might just be a reaction to some of the pain medication. At least I hope that's it. That damn broken arm is giving him fits."

Murdock met his men at the tower climb. All the SEALs had done two climbs. He watched them do three more, then had the troops do twenty push-ups with him leading them.

That was when Murdock remembered the three men he had called over to interview at 1100 hours. It was almost 1130 hours. They would still be there. He turned the platoon over to Jaybird, and told him to get them to mess and have them ready at 1400 hours with cammies and floppy hats. Jaybird nodded.

Murdock took off at a ground-eating lope across the highway to his office. The three SEALs in garrison cammies sat on chairs just inside Jaybird's office. They jumped to attention when Murdock came through the door.

"Reporting to the lieutenant as ordered, sir!" one man said.

Murdock recognized him from his picture and the fact that he was at least six feet four.

"Ronson, into my office. I'll be with you other two in short order." He paused to get some breath back. "Bishop, Ching, glad you showed up. Relax."

Ronson followed Murdock into his office, and the other two SEALs sat down.

Murdock liked the looks of Ronson on first sight. He was big, he was rugged-looking, even with his shirt on. He could pack a McMillan .50 if he had to.

Ronson sat stiffly in the visitor's chair.

"Relax, sailor, you're among friends. You have your trident, I see. How long in SEALs?"

"Three years, sir. I was with SEAL Team Three, but caught a slug and took some Balboa time. They filled my slot, so I've been unassigned for a while."

"Ever handled a McMillan fifty?"

Ronson's eyes lit up and he grinned. He relaxed then and

nodded. "Yes, sir. Sweetheart of a weapon. My favorite. Course I like the M-60 too, along with a thousand rounds. I was the AW man with Three. I hear Seven has the new H&K 21A1 machine gun. It's a beauty. I fired it once in training. Damn things never break down."

"You married, Ronson?"

"No, sir."

"Your nickname is Horse?"

"Right. But I really can't carry that much." They both laughed.

"Ronson, how would you like to get into Platoon Three of SEAL Seven? We're on call by some heavy hitters and just lost three men wounded on our last social visit. You'll get all the action you want with us."

"Like to be with you, sir. Heard good things about Seven."

"I'll send the paperwork through this afternoon. Get your gear ready to move into the Platoon Three of Seven rest home."

"Aye, aye, sir!"

"On your way out, tell Ching to come in."

Ronson hurried out with a grin as wide as an IBS paddle.

Murdock talked to the other two men. They looked as good in person as they had on the personnel sheet. He signed them on and then put a call into the small infirmary they had on base. He went through two nurses, then got the doctor who had just seen Ed DeWitt.

"Nothing serious, Lieutenant. Looks like those pills he was taking dehydrated him. That walk in the sun didn't help matters. I've changed his medication and put him on light duty for a week. See if you can get him to take a leave for a week."

"Good idea, Doc, I'll do just that. Thanks for the good news."

He hung up and tried to figure how he could discourage DeWitt from taking part in as much training as he wanted to. He shuffled some papers on his desk, then had an idea.

The brass had not been pleased with the amount of equipment and weapons they'd lost and written off as combat casualties in Lebanon. Commander Dean Masciarelli, the CO of Team Seven, wanted some better explanations than the formal ones that Jaybird had sent through channels after their mission.

Just the small task for Lieutenant DeWitt to take care of this afternoon.

He looked at some of the paperwork on his desk and gave up. He called Navy Special Warfare Unit One, got through to personnel, and asked to have the three SEALs he'd interviewed transferred to Team Seven Third Platoon at once. Chief Murphy there knew Murdock, and said he'd cut the orders and send over a personnel request form for Murdock to fill out and get back to him yesterday.

While he was talking on the phone, DeWitt came in and slumped in the chair beside Murdock's desk. Murdock hung up.

"So, when's the funeral?" Murdock asked.

"No funeral, just some damn pills that dehydrated me to hell and gone. I'm fine now. Fit for duty."

Murdock nodded. "Good. I've got something here that has to be taken care of today. Masciarelli didn't like our 'loss during combat' report. I want you to go over there and explain it to him, item by item. We save the fucking treasury a few hundred thousand million in counterfeit hundred-dollar bills and Masciarelli is worried about a thousand-dollar weapon or two."

"Figured Jaybird sent that report in," DeWitt said.

"He did, but Masciarelli has forgotten his days on the grinder. He's getting officerfied. Go over there this afternoon and stroke him and placate him and explain any aspect of the mission he doesn't understand. You can do it. He'll believe it coming from you even if you say the same things that Jaybird wrote."

"Right after the swim?"

"Who said anything about a swim?"

"Figures. I know how you think. We did that seven miles with the log this morning. You'll want to really stretch these guys with a five-mile swim in the bay."

"Not a chance. It's a ten-miler in the ocean. We'll go from

here to Zuniga Point on the tip of North Island and back."

"That's only seven miles, Boss. I've made that swim too often."

"So I'm mellowing in my old age. It's a seven-mile swim. Enough for a warmup, especially with a four-knot tide working to the north."

"Just as glad I'm not going. You have a copy of Jaybird's report?"

Murdock handed him the three pages.

"Did you get me an appointment with the old man or do I just drop by?"

"I'd call him and set it up. He's getting very Navy all of a sudden."

"I'll win this one for the Gipper."

"You didn't even play football."

"Is that what the Gipper is all about? Damn me."

Jaybird slipped in the door with a cold Coke and a pair of hamburgers and put them in front of Murdock.

"Figured you didn't get any chow, Skipper. Don't want you to pass out on our swim this afternoon."

"Who said anything about a swim?"

"Nobody. Just figures. How far?"

"Point Zuniga round trip."

"Good, I was figuring ten miles. You still want the troops ready at 1400?"

"Yeah, right. That'll give my burgers time to digest."

Lieutenant Edward DeWitt brushed his flattop with his good right hand and stared hard at Murdock. Then he chuckled.

"You set me up, didn't you?"

Murdock laughed and flipped him a French fry he had found with his burgers. "Yeah. A habit. Comes with the stripe. That Seattle ticket is still open, on me."

DeWitt took a long breath. He crinkled his brow, then shook his head. "Fuck, no, I'm having too much fun here."

18

Monday, November 24

Murdock broke off the swim at two miles and before they reached the announced halfway goal of Zuniga Point on the far end of North Island. The SEALs had entered the water wearing their cammies, masks, and flippers. Murdock led them at an even stroke knowing precisely how fast to swim to cover a mile in thirty-five minutes.

After two miles he signaled for a halt and turned the men around.

"Jaybird, take the con, lead us back to the home beach in exactly an hour and ten minutes."

"That's a roger, sir." Jaybird was not the best swimmer in the platoon, but now it didn't matter. The men would move at the pace he set. A light breeze had picked up and the ocean showed an occasional whitecap. The water was not summer-warm yet—about sixty degrees, Murdock figured. It had often been much colder. Top summer sunshine might boom it to sixty-nine or seventy-four degrees, but that would be the top of the scale.

Open-ocean swimming is not easy with the swells and the current. Now the small chop and the whitecaps made it that much tougher.

"Remember that four-knot current we'll be going against,"

Murdock told Jaybird. The Platoon Chief waved and struck out for the distant shoreline just off the SEAL training base.

They had stayed on top of the water since they didn't have any breathing gear. Once they came to a small school of eight-inch jelly fish, their long arms trailing into the water.

Jaybird slanted them around the hundred or so creatures. They weren't the hard-stinging kind, but could bring a welt.

Once, looking seaward, Murdock saw a half-dozen Pacific porpoises jumping and playing around the hull of a two-masted sailing ship.

Nothing else distracted the SEALs from a relaxing afternoon swim in the bright blue Pacific Ocean.

Jaybird led them up the beach across from the grinder, and Murdock checked his watch.

"You're two minutes early, Jaybird. Guess it's better to be early rather than late. On a hot mission what would you have done?"

Jaybird took off his mask and picked up his flippers. "On a mission I would have checked my time of arrival. If I was early, I'd have kept the platoon at least five hundred meters offshore and waited for the exact time to hit the beach."

"Good. Now, the rest of the day is free. Tomorrow we really get down to the business of training. We should have the three new men we talked about. If all goes well, they should report in tonight. Get them set up with gear and equipment."

"Yes, sir. What's up for tomorrow?"

"A surprise, Platoon Chief, even for you. Arrange with the mess for a patrol-type full breakfast for the platoon at 0430. We'll be in transport by 0530."

The Third Platoon formed up in two squads and double-timed across the sand and into SEAL country. Murdock found Ed DeWitt waiting for him in his office.

"Those three replacements are here. I sent them over to supply. Master Chief MacKenzie said Jaybird would get them outfitted when he got back. Is that Chinese guy the linguist?"

"He is. He speaks a whole pot full of languages. I just

wish he knew Arabic. I figure we're going to have some more Near Eastern time before long. You like the looks of the three?"

"I do. Especially the big guy, Ronson. He going to be the HW man?"

"How did you guess? How are you feeling? Any more dizziness?"

"No. I just got the wrong meds. Fit for duty. What's on for tomorrow?"

Murdock took a sheet of paper from the top drawer of his desk and handed it to his second in command. DeWitt read the first few lines and then scanned it.

"We're back in Hell Week, only it's for just two days," DeWitt said.

"You want to come along? You do everything the rest of us do including the survival drill."

DeWitt read the paper again. Slowly he shook his head. "I can't make it through all those exercises and tests and drills with this damn broken arm."

"True. You want that week's leave or should I put through a light-duty form for you?"

"You cleared this training with the Commander?"

"No. The facility is not being used for the next three days. I reserved two of them. We leave at 0530 tomorrow."

"Masciarelli is not going to be thrilled, as you know."

"Keeping my platoon in top condition is my responsibility. I checked with the motor pool and we'll have a twenty-passenger bus ready and waiting."

DeWitt squirmed in his chair.

Murdock took three pills from the plastic bottle on his desk and downed them with some lukewarm coffee. He looked at his friend and combat buddy. "So, which way are you going?"

"Seattle for four days. About all I'll be able to stand. Then I'll be back here and working out with you whenever I can do the drill."

"Done. Master Chief MacKenzie will take care of your leave and your transport. Have a good visit with the family."

"I'll try. Provided you get the rest of that shrapnel out of

your ass so we don't have to call you Old Ironbutt
anymore."

Tuesday, November 25

0900 hours
Chocolate Mountain Gunnery Range
Niland, California

The twenty-seat bus had rolled out of SEAL country at 0528
the following morning with all fifteen SEALs of Third
Platoon on board. Murdock had had to go to the CO of the
motor pool to get permission for Red Nicholson to drive the
bus. He had a military driver's license, and said he used to
drive a school bus.

They had loaded up the rig with all of the ammo,
weapons, and gear they would need for their two-day stay.
There was plenty of field rations and supplies, but no
blankets or sleeping bags. The men had noticed that up
front.

"What the hell is this, fucking Hell Week all over again?"
Martin "Magic" Brown had asked, his black face more
curious than angry.

"How do you get a week jammed into two days?" Ron
Holt had asked.

"With a fucking SEAL shoehorn," Jaybird had screeched,
and they all had laughed.

The bus had rolled down the Silver Strand highway into
Coronado. Murdock got mad when anyone called it Coronado Island. Even some of the people who lived there called
it an island. They should have known better. Radio and TV
newscasters were always calling it Coronado Island. Actu-
ally, it is a large bulge on the end of a long narrow strip of
land that encloses San Diego Bay and is called the Silver
Strand. Technically Coronado is on the end of a peninsula.
A peninsula is described as a portion of land nearly
surrounded by water and connected to a larger land mass by
an isthmus. An isthmus is a narrow strip of land connecting
two larger land masses.

Murdock had long ago given up correcting people about

Coronado. It irritated him, and he made sure that his men knew the difference, but he'd given up on the rest of the English-speaking world.

The bus had gone across the graceful Coronado-San Deigo Bay Bridge, turned south on Interstate 5, and then slanted off on California Highway 15 north toward Interstate 8. Once on 8, the bus had nosed east heading for the desert.

"We going to the fucking desert?" Jaybird had asked.

"Now that you mention it, why don't we?" Murdock had rasped. "You guys haven't had a shot at the Chocolate Mountains in months now."

"I'm getting thirsty already," Ross Lincoln had said.

"Hold that thought," Murdock had said. "You're be a hell of a lot thirstier before the next forty-eight hours are over."

"Forty-eight?" Doc Ellsworth had asked. "Sheeeet. We can do that without even changing our wad of chewing gum."

Jaybird had been more cautious. "L-T you didn't let me get in on the planning of this one. You got some secrets for us?"

Murdock had grinned and waved at him and closed his eyes. He'd been ready for a three-hour ride out Highway 8 past Boulevard to where it swept within a mile of the Mexican border at Jucumba, and on to Ocotillo and into the desert town of El Centro. From there it was a short run due north to Niland and the Navy's Chocolate Mountain Gunnery Range.

Three hours later the bus stopped at the small headquarters building, and the L-T went inside to check in and confirm the time of stay. Then the bus moved out to the far end of the long bombing range and parked. This would be their home base for the next two days.

The desert was the same. A little scrub growth, sagebrush, cacti all over the place, and a dusky range of low rolling hills called the Chocolate Mountains eastward from the Coachilla Canal. The SEALs wore their desert cammies, and now put on their American Body Armor operations vests with pouches for ammo and radio and grenade pouches on the web belt. There was no bullet-proofing body armor as such on the webbing.

Each man had ammo to fit his issue weapon. Today all carried the H&K MP-5SD, except for the specialists. One HW man in each squad had a McMilan M-88 .50-caliber sniper rifle that could knock down a man from two kilometers away. The other HW men had the new-issue Heckler & Kock 21A1 machine gun. It fires the 7.62 NATO round at nine hundred rounds per minute. Two vest pouches held rounds. Range was up to 1,100 meters. And it would take any of the NATO loads from AP incendiary to tracers and ball.

Doc Ellsworth carried his favorite, a Remington 870 12-gauge pump shotgun with the barrel cut off at the end of the magazine and only a pistol grip instead of a stock. It held five deadly rounds of double-aught buck that could cut a man in half at twenty feet.

All had as backup the new Heckler & Koch Mark 23 Model O Special Operation Offensive handgun system. This double-action pistol had a twelve-round magazine of .45-caliber, and a decocking lever that silently lowered a fully cocked hammer. A screw-on Knight sound suppressor hushed the rounds, but added seven inches of length to the stock weapon, making it 16.6 inches long with a weight of four pounds.

It was big and heavy and extra long with the silencer on. Part of that could be solved by attaching the suppressor only when it was time to use the weapon.

Each man carried 50% more than the regular ammo issue for his weapon and one canteen of water.

Murdock had the men fall in, and put Jaybird in charge of the Second Squad.

"We'll start out with a casual little two-mile run. I know it's early and the place hasn't even started to heat up. It can't be more than about eighty degrees out, so it'll be a walk in the park for you guys. We'll all carry the new H&K forty-fives, so get used to them. What's another four pounds for tough guys like us? Let's move out."

They did a mile out on a marked cross-country course,

and a mile back to the bus. Their time was a ragged eight minutes a mile.

Murdock shook his head. "You pack rats are out of shape. Too much garrison life."

"Yeah, we been back all of four days now," Scotty Frazier popped off. They all laughed.

"One drink. Remember that canteen has to last you one hell of a long time. Next, Ron Holt is going to give us a refresher course on the H&K forty-five hideout we carry. A sixteen-inch hideout. We'll go out to Range A for that little schooling. Ron, move these innocents out to slaughter."

There had been little use of the H&K .45-caliber pistol in their last engagement in Lebanon. It was too easily traced to the U.S. and it had been too heavy along with all of the other large-caliber firepower they had packed along. So they had left it on the ship.

Now was the time to get intimately reacquainted with the little weapon that could be the last line of defense for the SEALs in some combat situation.

They sat in the sand near Range A, field-stripped the weapon, oiled it, and put it back together. Ron Holt walked them through the process and told them the strong points of the weapon and what to be careful of.

"This weapon has more of a recoil than the 9mm jobs we've been used to," he said. "Allow a scosh bit more aiming time. It's going to rise on you no matter how strongly you hold it. Remember, you've got twelve shots, so make each one count.

"Now, let's draw some ammo and see what you can do at twenty yards."

They fired for half an hour. Each man put more than a hundred rounds through his pistol before they all did a final shoot at paper targets with a case of beer on the line for the winner, when they got off duty.

"I'll fire, but I'm not in the competition," Holt said. "But if any of you wildmen can beat my score, I'll make that two cases of beer."

They fired six shots each on the test. Three men got all

the shots in the bull. But Holt's rounds all touched each other to beat the rest. Joe Lampedusa won the contest.

Holt turned the show back to the L-T.

"Gentlemen," Murdock said, "the fun is only beginning. We'll double-time out to the edge of the Coachella Canal, and get in some quality training time."

19

Tuesday, November 25

1134 hours
Chocolate Mountain Gunnery Range
Niland, California

The fifteen men of the Third Platoon of Seal Team Seven struggled out of the Coachella Canal and flopped on the desert sand and rocks. They had just completed a half-mile swim against the six-knot current of the swift-flowing water.

Lieutenant Blake Murdock sat up and winced, then let out a small groan and waved for Doc Ellsworth.

Doc walked over and squatted beside his L-T, then sat down in the sand.

"Looks like you're about due, L-T," Doc said.

"Not so fucking loud, Doc. I could get you a bullhorn."

Doc took out an ampoule of morphine and Murdock rolled back his cammie sleeve for the shot.

Doc rubbed the shot spot with some alcohol and nodded. "Damn good thing you talked Mr. DeWitt out of this picnic. He'd be in Balboa Hospital by now."

"Went to see his family in Seattle." Murdock rolled over on his stomach to relieve the burning in his buttocks and upper thighs. "Doc, how long is it going to take these damn things to heal up?"

"Depends. Some are healed over now. The ones with shrapnel that has to work their way out of your butt are going to take longer, a month at least."

"Oh, damn."

Murdock let the men rest for ten minutes, then hand-signaled for Jaybird to come up.

"You're up, Platoon Chief. Make a call."

"My choice?"

"As long as it's the CQB."

Jaybird sighed. "That's two miles the other direction."

"By then our cammies should be almost dried out and our weapons should be drained. Let's go. A nice easy seven-minutes-to-the-mile run. Easier than double time."

Jaybird heaved up to his feet and bellowed to the frogmen. They lined up in the two squads and moved out with Murdock and Jaybird leading them.

The Close Quarters Battle House was devised by the British in training their elite SAS troops. It provided training in room-to-room fighting.

When troops barge into a room they don't know who or what is inside, and they must have a plan to take down anyone there and neutralize the whole place in only a few seconds. There is no room for mistaking friend for foe, or mixing up who is covering which side of the room or how the hostiles will be handled. Everything must be planned out in advance, practiced and practiced until the procedure is so ingrained in the SEALs' minds that they act automatically with no time to think.

"If you have to stop and think in a combat situation, you're dead." A SEAL truism that has helped save a lot of SEAL lives.

The CQB was more affectionately known as the "Killing House," because that's what SEALs did in such a situation when on a combat mission. It always paid to practice.

The old Killing House at the gunnery range had been made from used tires stacked up and laid out in the shape of roofless rooms and halls. The tires had been filled with sand to help absorb the bullets and prevent them from ricocheting or go zinging off into the rest of the training area.

The new one was more like a real building, with walls of bullet-absorbing material, rooms, halls, even a roof.

The desert sun had half dried out the cammies by the time

the men arrived at the CQB. Jaybird sent four men inside to set up plywood silhouettes of good guys and hostages. The hostages all had hoods over their heads and their hands tied.

The new rooms were better than the old roofless ones, because the roof and lack of windows made most of the rooms almost dark. Since the SEALs did most of their work in the dark, the training was more realistic.

When the British set up the program for the CQB, they worked out a firing stance that presented the shooter facing the target with his legs spread and arms extended in front and elbows locked. The weapon was held in both hands. The British advocated that the shooter not use the weapon sights. Rather the shooter looked over the top of the barrel, picked out a special spot on the target such as the chest, and fired.

The Americans modified the system when they put it into practice. Having the body squared and looking forward left too much of the attacker open to return fire. Like duelers of old, the Americans modified the British stance and stood sideways to the bad guys, leaving the side-view body as a smaller target.

The two-handed grip was used and the shooting arm was straight. The other arm rested against the chest for support.

When the targets were set up, Jaybird let the men divide into fire teams as they logically would entering a targeted room. This depended on where they functioned in the squad combat order.

They would use the rapid-aim fire technique. The submachine gun or pistol would be held with the barrel slightly elevated. When a target was found, the gunman put the front sight on it, centered it on the rear sight, and fired in a fraction of a second. It wasn't quite like firing from the hip, but much of the same eye-hand-target coordination was used.

Jaybird set up the first run through the three room with three-man teams. As usual, each man would take a third of the room. They burst through the door one at a time in quick succession.

Jaybird was on the first team, and he led them into the

first room. He burst through the door with his MP-5SD sub-machine gun at the ready and visually swept the left one third of the room. He found three terrorists near one hostage.

He had his MG set on three-round bursts, and blasted each of the three terrs with a burst without touching the hooded hostage.

Right behind him came Ron Holt, who had the center one third of the room. Before Jaybird had fired his second burst, Holt had found two terrorists holding automatic weapons. He fired two bursts into each one.

At the same time he fired, Magic Brown stormed in and checked the right one third. Only one terr was there, with a knife, about to kill a hostage. Magic put six rounds into the cutout and blasted it across the small room.

"Clear here," Jaybird said.

"Yeah, clear," Holt said.

"Clear and easy," Magic said.

Jaybird snapped on an electric light recessed in the ceiling. All of the terrs had been killed. He waved and turned off the light.

"Let's move to room number two."

Each team went through the three rooms five times with their MP-5's. Then Jaybird changed the signals.

"Now we do it with the H&K forty-fives. Unstrap them and let's do it with the fucking long silencer. Remember that it's going to be different than using your H&K Five."

Murdock had made the runs with two other men. He nodded as Jaybird made the change. It was a good idea. The more actual firing time they had with the new offensive little ass-kicker, the better. But it was going to be different.

Firing the new .45 was a disaster. On the first three men through, one of them shot a hostage, and one of them had the silencer on wrong and the silencer fell off. The third man hit one of his three targets and missed the other two.

"What the hell is the matter?" Holt bellowed at the men. He took them outside, and all of the SEALs practiced quick-aim firing for twenty rounds into the side of the CQB mockup.

"Now, let's see if you can at least kill a few terrs before they blow your asses into the Chocolate Mountains."

The second try, the men hit 80% of the targets.

Holt growled at them. "We'll have more work on the forty-five. I told you it takes a little more time to counter the recoil. This ain't no machine gun. You got to pull the fucking trigger every time you want it to go bang and get a chunk of hot lead to rotate itself out the end of the fucking barrel."

After five rotations through the three rooms, the platoon had reached a 95% rate of kills. Holt growled at them. "Yeah, ninety-five percent. So only three of you mother-fuckers got yourselves killed. Ain't you damn proud of your little asses. I give up, L-T, they all yours."

Murdock sent three men back to the bus to pick up the two .50-caliber sniper rifles and four hundred rounds of ball ammo. The bus was only half a mile away. When the three came back, Murdock marched them another half mile beyond the Kill House to Range B. The targets were a thousand yards away, well over half a mile.

"Every man is going to fire twenty-five rounds on the McMillan M-88. I want you proficient with it, not just making noise. You'll each have a spotter with a twenty-power scope. I want to see the last ten shots at least hits on those man-sized targets out there.

"This weapon is lethal at two kilometers. That's over a mile and a quarter. If you can see it, you can kill it with this eighty-eight. This is your party, Magic. You work with Ronson first and I'll clue in on the second gun. When you get Ronson up to speed, he can tutor the rest of the squad. Let's do some shooting."

"I've done fifty rounds on the eighty-eight," Ronson said.

"Show me," Magic said.

Ronson settled down with the fifty and adjusted the bipod, then the Leupold Ulra MK4 16-power telescopic sight. He asked for the two-power converter, and screwed it on the end of the telescope moving the sight to 32-power.

He put five rounds into the magazine, inserted it into the weapon, and chambered a round.

Then he settled down to aiming, and a moment later the big round went off. Jaybird held the spotting scope beside him and he saw the hit.

"Miss. A yard to the right. Watch that windage."

Ronson sighted in again and fired. Jaybird saw the hit in the permanent target.

"Hit," he said.

Magic cuffed Ronson on the shoulder. "Get out of there and let the homeboys have a turn. I'll use my weapon with the Second Squad."

Ken Ching, the new man, fired the big weapon four times and shook his head. "This is not an easy popgun to make go bang. Almost tore my shoulder off."

Jaybird put on his serious face. "Mr. Ching. That's because you held it too close to your shoulder. Allow about a half inch between your shoulder and the stock to absorb some of the recoil."

"Really?" Ching asked.

"Oh, yeah," Red Nicholson chimed in. "Helps a bunch."

Ching laughed at them. "Not a chance. Learned about that from my grandpa when I was twelve and he had a ten-gauge shotgun."

Murdock took his turn with the big fifty, and was impressed with the telescopic sight and how well it zeroed in on a man-sized target over half a mile away. He got his twenty-five rounds in in two sessions. It was easier on the shoulder that way.

It was nearly 1400 when they finished firing. They double-timed it back to the bus and Jaybird broke out the rations.

"Not those damned MRE horse turds," Ross Lincoln bleated.

"You don't want any, you don't get any," Jaybird said. "You should have tried the old C rations they used in WW Two and in Korea. Those were not the best. These rations are ten times as good."

Each man took one of the dark brown plastic pouches about a foot long and seven inches wide. They were marked: "MEAL, READY-TO-EAT, INDIVIDUAL." These were all the same: "MENU NO. 6, CHICKEN ALA KING, ACCES-SORY PACK C, CINPAC INC. CINCINNATI, OHIO."

The men cut open the pouches and looked at the familiar contents. Most of them had eaten more than their share of the MREs on combat missions and field exercises.

"How they expect us to make coffee when they don't give us no damned canned heat?" Al Adams asked. "Hear the old C rations had a little can of jellied gasoline you lit and it burned damned hot."

"Yeah, if you had time and nobody was shooting your ass off," Joe Douglas chirped.

The men dug through the contents. The chicken à la king came in a brown plastic package inside a slender cardboard box.

"We supposed to eat this chicken stuff cold?" Scotty Frazier asked.

"Yeah, cold, or I'll take it away from you and stuff it up your ass," Magic Brown bellowed.

The rest of them guffawed at the crack and settled down to eat. One envelope had crackers in it, and another was filled with peanut butter. All of the plastic envelopes had tear slots so they could be opened easily.

"Wow, I got Taster's Choice Instant Coffee," Jaybird said. He had opened the accessory packet B that bragged of having coffee, sugar, dry creamer, salt, chewing gum, an inch-high bottle of Tabasco sauce, and a wet-wipe towelette.

In the main envelope there were also a cocoa beverage powder for a hot or cold drink and a beverage base powder to mix with half a canteen cup of water. Most of the men used the beverage powder and discarded the cocoa and coffee mixes.

Murdock was surprised to see many of the men eating the crackers and peanut butter. He ate the cold chicken à la king. It wasn't half bad. It would have been better hot, but they didn't want to take the time. They had plenty of water in the water cans they had brought with them from Coronado.

Then Jaybird brought out the capper, large chocolate bars he'd had stashed in a cooler loaded with dry ice.

Murdock found Ron Holt.

"Your PRC come through the swim in its watertight with no problems?"

"Haven't checked."

"Better. I want you to send a message to Command Master Chief MacKenzie back in Coronado."

Holt stared at him in confusion for a minute.

"That's not SATCOM. It's not line out of sight and we ain't talking to no aircraft." He frowned for a minute. "This damned thing can do so much sometimes I forget all it can do. Oh, yeah, hook into the worldwide cellular telephone system. Piece of cake."

He snapped two switches, and saw the power come on for the warmup. Then another light blinked and he hit the cell-phone circuit.

"We have a phone number, sir?"

Murdock gave him a number, and Holt punched it into the keyboard. A moment later Holt nodded and passed the hand set to Murdock.

"Master Chief MacKenzie. Murdock here."

"Indeed it is, sir. How goes the Hell Days?"

"Fine, so far. Wanted to remind you that I won't be able to have that dinner out with you tonight. Unless you want MREs."

"No, thanks. This man Holt getting the knack on the new radio? At least new to him?"

"Seems to be working out. Thanks, Master Chief. We're off on a fun hike."

He hung up and looked back at Holt. "Now set up the unit to contact SATCOM and get me through to the CIA."

Holt frowned for a minute, then hit two switches and unfolded the satellite's small antenna. It was collapsible, and when extended looked like a small dish. He attached the antenna and turned it slowly and watched the readout dial. When the antenna was in line with the communications satellite many miles overhead in orbit, the readout told him it was in the correct position.

"Let's send a data burst, so nobody can get a fix on our position, Holt. You know how to do that?"

"Yes, sir. Write out your message and I'll type it on the keypad."

Murdock looked at his code book and wrote out this message:

"Zebra Two Oscar [Third Platoon's code word for the day] training mission under way. No casualties. On schedule. No air extraction needed. Cancel previous request. End."

"What now?" Murdock asked the new radio man.

"Now I type it on the keypad, check for accuracy, and then set the broadcast band to the SATCOM." Murdock checked the message on the liquid crystal display screen and approved. Holt touched another button, and the message was automatically encoded. He looked at his L-T.

"What would come next if we really wanted to send the message, Holt?"

"I'd push the send button and it would jolt out of here in a compressed burst of less than a millisecond of time."

"Right, good. Now shut it down. No transmission. That exercise is through. I want you to have this procedure down so you can do it in the dark, in your sleep with both hands tied behind your back and while having great sex with a blonde. Understand?"

"That's a Roger, sir."

"And stop calling me sir."

"Fine with me. I mean, sure. That's cool, sir."

Murdock shook his head and went to talk to Jaybird. He told him what he wanted and went back to the bus. He found the box of fraggers and half-a-dozen WP grenades.

By the time he got outside the bus, the men had finished the MREs and were sprawled in the shade of the big rig. Jaybird walked back to the bus after having set up the .50-caliber ammo boxes out from the bus at twenty yards, thirty yards, and forty yards.

Jaybird stopped a dozen feet from Murdock. The L-T took out one of the smooth and round M-67 hand grenades with the spoon handle and held it up. "You men know what these little sweethearts are. Sometimes they can save your ass. If you know how to use them right. Harmless as a newborn babe until the damn spoon is popped."

Murdock pulled the ring and jerked the safety pin out of the grenade. He held it a moment, then let the arming spoon pop off the grenade and tossed it underhand toward Jaybird.

20

Tuesday, November 25

1448 hours
Chocolate Mountain Gunnery Range
Niland, California

Jaybird's eyes widened just a moment. Then he reached out, caught the 4.2-second-fused fragmentation grenade, spun, and threw it as far as he could toward the boxes he had just set up as targets. At once, Jaybird dropped to the desert sand and turned his head away from the coming blast.

The grenade exploded just as it hit the ground between the thirty- and forty-yard targets. The men heard some shrapnel whistling through the air over their heads.

"Anybody hit?" Murdock asked. The SEALs shook their heads, and there were a couple of audible negatives. Jaybird got up, dusted off his cammies, and walked on up to the group.

"Jaybird didn't know I was going to do that," Murdock said. "He reacted properly under an extreme stress situation. As SEALs we always have to be ready for the unexpected. That's how we stay alive and make sure the other guys die. For the next half hour or so we're going to throw live grenades. No horsing around. These little bombs kill people."

The SEALs sat up and then stood.

"Fernandez, go into the bus and bring out another case of fraggers. The rest of you line up and get ready to throw

151

some. Those cardboard boxes out there are open on the top. Whoever puts a grenade inside any of them gets a three-day pass.

"You'll each throw three times, one M-67 at each of the three boxes. Better hit the deck after that first twenty-yarder."

Jaybird led off the line. He was long on the twenty-yard box, came within six feet of the thirty-yard one, and was short on the forty.

The shrapnel kept flying. Jaybird moved all the men but the thrower back another twenty yards as a precaution.

One of the new men, Harry "Horse" Ronson, was the only one to drop a grenade into a box. He hit the thirty-yarder and blew it into pieces. They were nearly finished throwing. Jaybird sent a man out to replace the shrapnel-torn box.

Murdock was the last man to throw. He picked out one of the WP grenades and threw it as far as he could. It sailed five yards beyond the last box and burst into a star pattern of fiercely burning white phosphorus trails. When the smoke blew away, Jaybird led the SEALs out to make sure there were no smoldering fires in the sparse grass and shrubs of this far end of the Mojave Desert. White phosphorus burns so hot it will burn right through anything flammable. That includes an arm or a leg if the sticky WP hits a person. When the SEALs came back, Murdock was ready for them.

It was 1537. The sun burned down with an attitude and the men had finished their canteens, filled them, and drained them again. Someone said a working man in the desert needed seven quarts of water a day to survive. At this point Murdock believed the figure.

"Now the fun stuff begins," Murdock told his troops. "Grab your TO weapon and a spare canteen of water. We'll take the usual load of issue ammo, and our blessed H&K forty-five hideouts. Get the gear from the trailer and report back here on the double."

Murdock got his own load. He carried the MP-5 and six

loaded magazines. He filled a canteen to join its brother on the other side of his utility vest and hit the desert again.

This was the outback of the armpits of the far end of the desert. Nobody complained about some booms or auto-weapon firing out here. There was nobody to complain. The village of Niland at one time had had 1,200 people. He didn't know how many were there now. It was six miles away to the south and west. There was a numbing, vacant area of sage and hills and sand across the Chocolate Mountains to the northwest for forty miles before a hiker would find another road, Interstate 10, running between Blythe and Indio. There were a lot of miles of wilderness to get lost in.

One dirt track of a road crossed about in the middle of the parcel, but it was seldom used. Murdock turned and looked at Lion Head Mountain, the highest point in the Chocolates. It rose only 2,090 feet. The low mountain range was close to the Salton Sea, which is 235 feet below sea level. Might be interesting climbing the peak in the dark.

When the men assembled, Murdock put Jaybird in control of Second Squad and laid out the general plan.

"We usually march around at four miles an hour. Fifteen minutes to the mile. This afternoon, after that big meal, we'll be moving out at six miles an hour or exactly a mile in ten minutes. To do this we'll start with a half mile hiking and a half mile jogging at a smart pace. At the end of the first two miles, we'll check our watches and see how we're doing."

Murdock looked his men over. There were no questions. Nobody griped about the training run or the hot weather which had resulted in their cammies showing dark sweat splotches. These men were the professionals. They knew that to stay alive they had to be in top shape every day. A mission might grab them tomorrow. Besides, as every SEAL knew, "The only easy day was yesterday."

"Let's go. Combat spacing, five yards between men. Let's do it."

He didn't tell them anything about the mountain. He'd have a surprise for them on that score. The hill itself was about ten miles from where the bus sat. A nice little twenty-mile jaunt, plus some other goodies.

Before they started the march, Murdock asked them a question. "How many of you have a compass?"

Four or five men called out "Yo-o-o-o-o." A batch of hands went into the air.

Murdock nodded. He had taken a sighting on the mountain before, and now headed across country for the spire. They hiked the first twenty minutes, then jogged for the next twenty. There was a lot of grumbling and adjusting equipment and lashing down gear that tended to bounce around as they ran.

The two HW men groaned under the twenty-five-pound H&K M-88, but they all kept going.

There was no bantering now, no good-natured insults or jabs or barbs. Now they were professionals doing their job, staying in shape and enduring another hike that could be a long one. The mile in ten minutes didn't faze the SEALs. That speed was drastically slow for a track-and-field man. Many marathoners ran twenty-six miles at slightly over five minutes to the mile, but they weren't packing along forty pounds of gear on their backs.

Murdock kept up the pace. His butt hurt again and his legs started to burn in back where the shrapnel shards still had to work their way to the surface. He gulped three Motrins without the aid of water and kept going.

After the first half hour, the sun was still beating down on them like the messenger of doom. The desert wouldn't start to cool off until an hour or two after sundown. Murdock looked at the bright orb up in the cloudless sky. The sun would be with them for at least two hours yet.

They alternated the running and walking. Then, just as they came up a small rise, Murdock pulled out a fragger and pitched it thirty feet to the side well out of range and with no chance of hurting anyone.

The moment the grenade went off the SEALs as a man flopped into the dirt and chambered a live round in their weapons.

Murdock flipped the fire selector on his MP-5 to three-round bursts, swung the barrel down, and jolted off two three-round bursts into the area where he had thrown the grenade.

Taking their cue from their leader, the SEALs on that side of the line immediately fired into the same area. The men on the far side faced outward acting as security.

Murdock stopped shooting. "Clear!" he shouted. The word was repeated down the line and the men ceased fire.

The squads changed now from a garrison-type march to a combat order. They did it silently as Murdock gave hand signals. First in each squad came the point man, then the Squad Leader. For the Second Squad Jaybird filled in for Ed DeWitt. Next in line was the radioman dogging the L-T's heels. The AW man with the heavy M-88 was next. The fifth man was the grenadier, who often carried a CAR-15 with a grenade launcher attached. In this case the medic for the platoon walked with the First Squad as the grenadier.

The sixth man in a squad combat march was the second AW man, with an M-88 on this training run. The seventh man was normally the Platoon Chief, and the last man was the rear guard who watched to the rear and did a lot of walking backwards to cover the rear on a 180-degree arc.

Murdock kept up the pace. They passed through some sharp arroyos where desert cloudbursts sent sudden floods of water down every gully digging them deeper and sweeping everything in front of them. The water, much needed, often came so fast, little of it could soak into the parched land and it ran off into temporary streams.

An hour out, Murdock called a halt. The HW men leaned their M-88's butt-down in the sand and wiped sweat.

"How the hell hot is it?" Jaybird asked.

"My thermo shows a hundred and eleven," somebody called out.

"Got to be hotter than that," Jaybird answered.

Murdock called Jaybird over. "See that nubbin up there on the skyline?"

"Lion Head Mountain, about twenty-one hundred feet high?"

"That's the one. Here's where we split up. We're about

four miles from the top. You take a compass bearing to a point a mile due north of it. I'll go due south. Should take you about an hour to get in position. We don't have our radios, so we'll have to do it by timing.

"We start to close the pincer at exactly 1800. It's now a little after 1630. Gives us an hour to move to our initial point and then a half hour to get to the top."

"No live firing," Jaybird said

"Absolutely. We don't want to blow away half our platoon on an exercise. We'll take ten minutes here, then move out."

An hour later, Murdock brought his First Squad into position. The sun was down at last, but the heat still shimmered over the sand and desert rocks. They had kicked out two rattlesnakes and a desert jackrabbit on their way.

Now, Murdock checked the top of the low peak. He'd been there before. Half the SEALs in the platoon had done this one. They had another ten minutes to wait for the timing. At 1800 they packed up and started for the top. It was a series of small rises, then a last slant up a slope with loose rocks. It was more of a walk than a mountain climb.

When they got within fifty yards of the top, somebody bellowed at them.

"Halt! Who goes there?"

"Your mutha!" Magic Brown bellowed back.

"You're a friend, come on up."

Jaybird met them from behind a pair of boulders near the top.

"Make a fine defensive area," he said.

"Exactly what it's going to be," Murdock said. "Spread your men out in a perimeter on that side. I'll take this side. When everyone's in place, throw a WP grenade as far down your side of the mountain as you can. Then put up defensive fire on the WP."

They did.

Murdock threw a WP on his side, then moved from one of his men to the next. The M-88's barked with their heavy voices. The MP-5's chattered off three-round bursts. Doc got off his five rounds of double-aught buck from his beloved shotgun.

After four minutes Murdock called a cease-fire and the weapons trailed off firing into silence.

Jaybird dropped down beside Murdock where he lay in the sand looking down the mountain at the last wisps of smoke from the WP grenade.

"Make a fire check on both those WPs," Murdock said. "Then we'll assemble below and head for the bus. Hope that we have plenty of the MREs left." Before they left the top of the hill, Murdock called over Doc for another shot of his joy juice. Murdock had felt the damn shrapnel every step up the mountain, but he wasn't about to let anyone know it.

It was cool and nearly dark two hours later when they arrived back at the bus. Jaybird passed out a different kind of MREs to the men, and then talked to Murdock.

"This a no-sleep operation?"

"Started out to be. How are your men holding up?"

"Tired. No urgency to push them, like running for their lives. But they'll keep going."

"Good. Half hour to eat, then we get moving again. Oh, get some boy scout to build a fire so we can make some coffee. Go damn good about now."

It was forty-five minutes later before the troops left the bus, just after 2100. It was fully dark by this time. The HW men now carried their more standard H&K M-89 sniper rifles with the 7.62mm NATO round. It cut the weight by ten pounds. The other men had either MP-5's or M-4A1's, the CAR in .223-caliber with the M-203 grenade launcher under the barrel.

Six of the men packed the CARs. Two men carried sacks of 40mm grenades. Each man in the platoon would be firing the grenades.

"Let's say we're holed up in Libya," Murdock said, "a desert country we're not on friendly terms with. We've accomplished our mission and now all we have to do is get out. We can't risk world opinion with a chopper retrieve, which could prompt some air battles. So we have to walk out. We hide by day and move at night. The coast and our contact with a sub is eighty miles away across the desert. How long does it take us to walk to the coast?"

"Dark for about eleven hours," Red Nicholson said. "At four miles an hour through that damn desert sand, we can do forty miles a night. I bid two days in spades."

"Sounds good," Murdock said. "I'd allow another night's travel just in case we ran into some minor skirmishes with Libyan forces hunting us."

"You mean we have forty more miles to go tonight?" a voice piped up.

"Anybody got blisters?" Doc shouted.

Nobody had. Most of them had calluses an inch thick on their feet.

"No, we won't go forty miles tonight," Murdock said. "But we will take another hike and blow up some 40mm grenades. Let's move out."

They hiked to the canal and along it for two miles, then came back and stopped outside the old Kill House made of old rubber tires filled with sand.

They set up two hundred yards away and began firing. The first rounds hit short. The men with the CARs lined up and fired one after the other to keep track of hits. Murdock fired a flare high over the old Kill House tire rooms, and the hits began to come as long as the flare lasted.

When each man had fired his three rounds of the 40mm grenades, Murdock headed the men back to the bus. Once there, he grouped them around him.

"I had big plans for the rest of the night, but I think we've done enough for one day and a half. Flake out where you want to. No blankets, no sleeping bags. The bus seats might work out best. Somebody raid Jaybird's cold chest and see if we ate up all those chocolate bars." They hadn't. The SEALs took care of the rest of them, and Murdock looked around for a place to sleep.

Doc moved over and watched him.

"Moving a little slow there, L-T."

"True."

"One more shot of juice?"

"No. Had enough. Hell, I'm a SEAL. See you in the morning."

They were all awake when the sun came up a little after six. They had another MRE and made coffee and chocolate, and even ate the entrée. Then Murdock surprised them.

"Load up and let's get out of here. We've done what I wanted to do. Now we're heading back to Coronado."

"Yeah, and a shower!" somebody called.

"Why now? You ain't had one in two months," someone answered him.

It went that way for the first half hour. Then most of the SEALs went to sleep for the last two hours of the ride back to Coronado.

21

Saturday, May 16

1324 hours
USS *Intrepid*
Taiwan Strait

Murdock luxuriated in his clean, dry cammies and tilted the cold can of Coke. The sub had picked them up slightly after 0400 hours, and an hour later they were on board the supercarrier *Intrepid* steaming south from the Foochow area toward the Chinese port city of Amoy.

He'd been first on board with Greg Johnson's body, and had seen that it was properly taken care of. His next of kin would be notified with the visitation by two officers. Murdock would write a letter to his people with a believable lie about how Johnson had died in a tragic training accident at sea. His coffin would be closed.

Murdock had seen that his men were given dry uniforms and fed, then had Jaybird make sure their new-issue weapons were cleaned and oiled and ready to go. By 0700 hours most of the SEALs had sacked out for much-needed rest.

Murdock had taken a sleep period as well. He'd set his mental alarm clock to wake him up after six hours, and had come to promptly at 1300 refreshed. He'd had a can of orange juice, then gone to find Jaybird and Magic Brown.

Both had been up. He'd taken them back to his quarters, and now they sat down and worked over the rough plans they had made for the second phase of their attack on the Chinese mainland the day before.

Murdock popped for soft drinks in his quarters, and the SEALs relaxed.

"We've got the poison gas and the troop transports for tonight," Jaybird said.

Murdock looked at the notes he had made and left on the carrier from the first planning session.

"We talked about neutralizing the gas or the delivery vehicles. The gas was set to be delivered by Navy missile-launchers. We need to take out the merchandise before it gets loaded on those ships."

"We have any intel where the damned poison-gas missiles are kept?" Brown asked.

Murdock got on a ship's phone and found Don Stroh. The CIA man was in Murdock's room in three minutes. He carried two file folders.

"You want to know what we know about the poison gas?" he said. "The quick answer is not one hell of a lot. There are two places where our satellite printouts show that they store that class of missile. One is right on the docks, the other a half mile inland, where we suspect that they do the final assembly and loading the buckets with their share of the deadly gas. Right now we're not even sure what kind of gas they plan to use. Whatever it is, it will be airborne and deadly."

Magic Brown grinned at him. "Hell, Don, all we wanted to know was if you had a nice birthday."

Stroh laughed. "Hear you boys kicked ass good at that airport. That takes out the paratroops and any chance they might use those planes to drop the missiles with the gas. We should have some satellite pics in another two or three hours showing how many of those planes you destroyed."

"All of them," Jaybird said. "Every damned one of them. We can tell you that right now."

Stroh looked at him. He lifted his brows, then spread out the printouts he'd brought on the bunk, and they all looked at them.

"So the loaded missiles about to be used should be in the port warehouse," Jaybird said.

"Should be, but we can't count on it."

"Could split up for two attacks," Murdock said. "First Squad takes out the port facility, and Second Squad drives inland and hits the plant and storage area."

Jaybird shook his head. "Not a chance, L-T. A half mile through Amoy where they have a million damn Chinese? We don't even have any transport and no way to get much in there except those damn bicycles they ride. We might get in and blow the plane or burn it down without releasing any gas, but we damn well would never get out. There must be four or five thousand Army and Marines around this base."

Stroh rubbed his face and nodded. "I'm with Jaybird. I wouldn't want to try a run in there with no transport and no air support."

"So we take out the missiles at the port and hit the two missile ships they used," Murdock said. "Do we know what ships they would use for the delivery?"

Stroh brought out more prints of the Amoy port area. They were in perfect focus and so detailed the SEALs could see a rowboat on the shore near the missile sheds.

"Here are the two ships we think they would use," Stroh said. "They are tied up a block or so from the missile warehouse. They're not as big as a cruiser. I'm not sure what their designation is, but our boat people tell us that these ships are rigged for missile-launching. They can handle up to twenty missiles each. They aren't huge missiles. Don't have to be with a poison-gas payload."

"So now we take out the storage and the two destroyer types?" Brown asked.

"You don't need to sink them," Stroh said. "Just mess up the time schedule so they don't have any time to repair the damage you do and still load the missiles at the storage area."

"What about the three troop transports?" Murdock asked.

Jaybird shrugged. "Probably should be our lowest priority, Skipper. If the paratroopers didn't land on Taiwan, those troops won't have any secure docks to come into. They must not be set up to do an amphibious landing, and don't reckon they're too damn good at swimming."

Murdock lifted his brows and agreed. "I'm with you. That means we have two main targets and a secondary if we have the time. What about transport?"

"Our ships routinely stay at least fifteen miles off shore so we don't antagonize the Chinese," Stroh said. "Any deviation from that would throw up alarms."

"So we use the sub again and move in to a mile offshore," Murdock said. "Probably be best to stick to an underwater approach since we have to breach their harbor security. Don't know what they have, but there must be something, at least patrol boats. We'll use our rebreathers in and out."

"Depending on the situation and the terrain, we'll have to play your retrieve by ear," Stroh said. "I know it's best to plan it all, but we don't know when you'll be coming out or what shape you'll be in."

Brown snorted. "Damn right. We could get cut up bad in there. They must have a whole fucking shit-pot of troops and guards around those missiles."

"We know that for sure from the movement of men and vehicles around that building we looked at. It's right on the dock with gantry tracks on the pier so they can load the missiles."

"Sounds spooky," Jaybird said. "Wish to hell we had some schematics of that warehouse. We have any people on shore?"

"Lost the only man we had there, as you know," Stroh said. "No time to get a new man in there and working."

"So we go with what we know," Murdock said. He looked at the photo printouts of the warehouse where the missiles should be. "Not a chance we can take that place down with seven men," Murdock said. "We won't split up. We do the missiles themselves first; then we all go get those two warships. Then if we have time and gear, we take on the three troop transports."

Jaybird gave a big sigh. "Yes, L-T, like that. We can have some security around the warehouse for the guys doing the work inside."

They talked over the options for retrieval. There was the sub a mile offshore, but by then there would be patrol boats and maybe some small warships working over the close-in areas.

"Three miles out we could do an easier submarine pickup, or even a chopper lift," Stroh said. "If it's still dark we could send a launch out for you."

"We'll leave it open. We'll have our radio, the big SATCOM type, and we'll make sure we have it cued in to your frequency here before we leave. Oh, the blessed wireless might get shot up. So we make contingency plans. That would be the sub, one to three miles offshore, and contact with the sonar beeper."

Stroh made notes on a pad. "Captain Victor has his orders. He'll give us anything we need. His only restriction is against engaging in any overt action against Chinese armed forces unless it's well beyond the twelve-mile limit and his ship is in imminent danger of attack."

"We'll need more ordnance than I figured before, and quite a lot of TNAZ explosives," Murdock said. "We'll go for the longer-range weapons this time. We'll have a list of what we need in half an hour. Jaybird, let's see that preliminary list we made yesterday."

"Decided on the timing?" Stroh asked.

"We're steaming south at twenty knots," Murdock said. "It'll be dark here when? About 1900? I'd like to be swimming to shore at 2300. Gets them when they're tired and sleepy. We want to catch the guards with their britches down."

"We've been moving south now for a little over eight hours at twenty knots," Stroh said. "The captain says he can have you positioned off Amoy in about two hours."

"Tell him to slow us down so we arrive off Amoy no earlier than nightfall," Murdock said. "We'll be at least twelve miles offshore and over the horizon, but we don't want to be caught loitering out there. Let's say we'll rendezvous with the sub at 2200, move in, and exit the sub at 2300 and start our swim. We should be in the harbor by 2330."

Stroh continued making notes. When Murdock finished, Stroh looked up and nodded. "Roger. I'll get up to the captain and tell him what you need. He'll contact the sub and have him on station at the right time." He stood and moved for the door.

"Stroh, be sure to talk about our extraction. It could get hairy as hell. Remind him we might need another way of exfiltration beside the sub if the Chinese Navy gets frisky."

"Yeah, I remember. Maybe a fast launch from the carrier, maybe the sub, maybe a chopper and some rope lifts or a ladder climb. We'll be ready with all of them."

Stroh waved at them and left.

"Now, let's get the individual weapons spelled out," Murdock said. "We'll need more long-range weapons. Only two MP-5's. The rest with CARs and grenade launchers. The two HW men will have the H&K 21A1 machine gun and twelve hundred rounds. Doc can keep his shotgun. That will give us some firepower. We'll want each man with a CAR to carry ten forty-millimeter rounds including three WP."

Jaybird wrote in his notebook. "What about the warships? Limpet mines just below the waterline?"

"Heavy bastards," Brown said. "Need three for each ship. Maybe we can get some buoyancy device to float them suckers along with us instead of dragging them."

"Yes, good idea," Murdock said. "The Navy should have something that will work. We'll want plenty of TNAZ as well and detonator timers."

"Might come in handy to take a few claymores and PDMs in case they send a whole damn company of ground-pounders at us on the dock," Jaybird said.

"Do it," Murdock said. "We're going to need enough explosives to do the job. See what kind of neutral flotation devices you can find to equalize the weight with buoyancy. Shouldn't be hard. Save a lot of dragging all that weight."

They kept on planning out the details of the arms, ammunition, and explosives. When they all agreed they had it right, they went their various ways to gather the material.

By the time they drew the equipment from the carrier's

stores and selected weapons and explosives from their own supply they had brought along, it was after 1500. Each SEAL checked his own weapons, ammunition, special gear, and the extra loads he would carry into the fight. The men with the limpets had special flotation packaging that would give the heavy mines neutral buoyancy. That would make it easier to move them through the water.

Each squad had its share of the extra explosives, limpets, claymores, and PDMs—pursuit-deterrent munitions.

"We'll move out in our black wet suits with hoods, Draegers, boots, and fingerless gloves. We'll have our cammies in one of the waterproof pouches in case we get landlocked. Then we'll be ready."

The men kept checking their gear.

"We'll have time for a good meal, then a nap, before we move down to where we get on board the sub. Each of you is responsible for your own gear and the unit gear assigned you. Any questions?"

"Which target first, Skipper?"

"We'll go in through the bay to the pier beside the poison-gas missiles. They're our first target. We'll take it down as we planned without rupturing any of the containers. We don't want to wipe out half a million Chinese with their own gas."

"Why not?" somebody jabbed. Everyone laughed. It broke the tension.

"This is going to be the tough part, so get ready. Jaybird will send us to the food. We'll be back here rested up and ready to roll at 2230."

"Aye, aye, sir," two of the men said. The rest nodded and kept on checking their gear. They would go over it a dozen times before they were satisfied they had everything in place. Then they would load it all in their waterproof gear bags and secure them by nylon straps to their load-bearing equipment vests.

The transfer from the carrier to the submarine went smoothly. Then they were in the underwater craft moving cautiously toward shore. When they came to their point of departure a mile off the Amoy harbor, the sub came up to periscope depth and the captain checked all around. He clanged the handles together. "Down scope," he barked. A periscope makes a positive radar reflector, and if the Chinese had a surface-search radar working and set for such a small target, they could be spotted.

"No sign of any silhouettes out there," the captain said. "Looks like you're free to move."

"We'll be locking out," Murdock told the men. "You've done it before. No big deal. Everyone who goes out first, wait on the surface so we can form up. Go in the chamber with your roped-together buddy. Take it easy. I'll be the last one up. Let's move."

Jaybird had never liked this way of getting off a sub. The boat was forty feet underwater. The men would cram together five at a time in a phone-booth-sized chamber, flood it, open the hatch, and slide out into the sea. Then they would close the hatch and the water inside would be pumped out and the inside hatch opened so the next men could come in and flood it.

It would take fifteen minutes to get all thirteen men to the surface. Jaybird took a deep breath and stepped into the chamber. He pulled in his two gear bags and moved over.

"Make room in here, we got two more coming. Push it over, let's go."

The fifth man climbed in, stowed his gear bag at his flippered feet, and pushed his face mask up on his forehead. Jaybird closed the hatch, then hit the valve to let the water come in. He took another deep breath as the water rose, put on his face mask, and slipped the Draeger rebreather mouthpiece in place. Damnit, let the fucking water come!

22

Saturday, May 16

2312 hours
Near Amoy, China
Taiwan Strait

Jaybird Sterling was not claustrophobic. He kept telling himself that as the water surged over his head and at last filled the exit chamber so the exterior hatch could be opened. He swam out with his two equipment packs and moved slowly to the surface. It was always a relief to be out of that damn sardine can. But he was not claustrophobic.

On the surface of the dark Taiwan Strait, he looked toward shore and saw the lights of the port city. Around him he saw and heard the rest of the platoon surfacing. He counted. Ten up. Three still to come. They were down to thirteen fit fighting men now in the platoon, including the two L-Ts. One dead and two wounded. They would be lucky if they came out without any more wounded.

Two minutes later Murdock surfaced with the other two men. Each of the SEALs quickly tied his six-foot buddy line with the man he had been teamed with. It helped them stay together and each would know if the other man was in any trouble.

Murdock pointed at the glow in the sky. "That's Amoy," he said in a normal tone. Everyone could hear him. "Take a compass bearing on it and let's move out. We'll work at fifteen feet. Try to stay in visual if you can. See you close to shore."

169

They dove and leveled off at fifteen feet. Murdock adjusted the compass board that some of the men called the attack board. It was a black plastic housing or frame with a large compass in the center. The frame was about a foot wide with handhold slots on both sides and a depth gauge at the front. It had a Cyalume chemical light, with a twist knob to open a lengthwise slit in a holder to regulate the amount of light coming out. That light was essential to see the bubble compass at night but it could be regulated so as not to give away a SEALs position.

Murdock settled in at fifteen feet and lined up the compass arrow at the bearing he had chosen and began his steady and even kick. He could tell the distance he traveled through the water by the number of kicks. After years of practice he found he could think about something else while still counting the rhythmical kicks in his head. It worked out to so many kicks per hundred yards, and he could come out within inches of his target every time in practice.

He felt a tug on the buddy line and looked through the dank waters at Radioman Ron Holt. The SEAL came closer and gave him a thumbs-up sign and they kicked forward.

The cammies in the waterproof pouches were a precaution. They needed to be prepared in case they did get cut off from the water or had to go inland to that other facility. The cammies were much easier to fight in on land than the restrictive wet suits.

Murdock went over and over their plans for the poison-gas missiles. They had to be disabled without letting any of the gas escape. They didn't want to kill a hundred thousand Chinese. Besides, if they ruptured the containers, the thirteen SEALs on-site would be the first to die.

Murdock heard motors in the water. They sounded close. He turned the light on his attack board up high and pointed it around him in a signal to the others. It meant come to the light. Soon he had all the men close by. Murdock signaled that he was going up for a sneak and peek.

He lifted to the surface and pushed out his face so he could see around. He pulled back his mask. Not fifty yards to starboard he saw a Chinese patrol craft. It idled in the

water. He could hear the crew chattering. For a moment he
thought about simply ignoring it and going back to depth
and proceeding. He changed his mind and he and Holt went
back down to the men. He found Willy Bishop. With hand
signals he told the men to stay at depth and wait. He untied
himself from Holt, then took Bishop to the surface. They
pulled out their rebreather mouthpieces and talked.

"You have some TNAZ handy?"

Bishop nodded.

Murdock pointed to the idling patrol boat. "Let's give
them a small blast. Enough to blow it out of the water with
a ten-minute fuse."

Murdock lifted Bishop far enough out of the water that he
could unzip a waterproof pocket on his vest and take out
half of a quarter-pound chunk of TNAZ. He took a timer
detonator from another pocket, and then Murdock let him
down. He held both out of the water and inserted the
detonator into the chunk of explosive and set the timer for
ten minutes. They both swam silently toward the boat.
There were no lookouts.

Bishop wedged the explosive into a fitting on the boat
about two feet above the waterline. He pushed the timer to
activate it, and they dove down and swam back to where the
rest waited. Jaybird was waving the attack board with its
light fifteen feet underwater, and they found the rest easily.

Murdock checked his watch. They swam toward their
objective for seven minutes. Then he motioned the others to
the surface. They watched behind them. The boat had
moved farther away from shore. They could see its running
lights. A minute later the sky flashed with a bright blue-
white flame and a rolling thunder of the explosion rocketed
across the water at them. The patrol boat shattered into a
hundred pieces and the fuel on board caught fire, and for a
moment a bright light cut into the darkness. Then it faded.

Murdock motioned down and the men went to fifteen feet
and resumed their swim toward the shore.

Before long Murdock could hear engines powering above
them. They must have sent out more patrol boats to find out
what had happened to the first one. Nobody would ever

know. It would give the Chinese something to wonder about. For a moment Murdock thought it might put the Chinese on a higher alert. He was sure the whole country was alerted after what had happened at the atomic island and at the air base. This explosion sinking a patrol boat wouldn't help. The Chinese had too much coastline to really seal it off to invaders. That was one military problem China would always have.

Murdock and Holt, tied together again, swam for another twenty minutes. They should be close to shore. He and Holt worked up to the surface for a look.

They could see the lights of the town now. It was a big place. Ahead they spotted the entrance to the harbor marked by a row of lighted buoys. Convenient. As they watched, they saw a pair of boats larger than the patrol craft. The two boats worked back and forth across the channel leading into the harbor like a pair of Prussian guards. They must have sonar and radar, but neither would show the swimmers. The only way the boats could find them would be with some frogmen of their own.

They all swam again. Soon they were under the guard boats near the channel. They kept swimming forward, the sound of the guard boats faded, and they were inside the bay. A hundred yards farther inside, Murdock lifted to the surface again to check, and found the channel marker buoys where they should be. The SEALs hugged the left side of the entrance and worked along close to the shore. They were at less than fifteen feet now as the water became more shallow in this undeveloped part of the harbor.

They almost swam into a point of land inside the bay, and Murdock surfaced for a moment to check his position. Yes. Around this point and then along the side of the bay for maybe a half mile. The Chinese Navy docks should be in that area. They moved cautiously now, past some warehouses, some shallow water docks, then a boatyard.

Murdock took one more quick peek. They were just outside the Navy's restricted area. He saw docks, warships, and the part he was interested in—Pier 12. It was clearly marked. On Pier 12 was the warehouse where the loaded gas missiles were supposed to be held prior to loading on the Luda-class destroyers.

From the dark waters of the bay a hundred yards offshore, the SEALs checked out the dock and its security. It had much more protection than they could see from the satellite photos.

The building itself was set twenty feet back from the edge of the pier, evidently to facilitate loading. There were two chain-link fences around this end and side of the warehouse. They spotted a roving guard on foot. Inside the fences Murdock pinpointed four stationary guards. The fences could be electrified.

Behind the fences he could see big double truck-type doors and a smaller one to the side. Just getting into the building would be a fight.

He sent word back to Bishop to come up front.

"The wire," Murdock whispered to him.

"No problem. Use primer cord and cut a man-sized hole in the first one and then the second one. Need some fire support. Have to have those sentries and guards eliminated first."

"Are the fences electrically charged?"

Bishop took another look at the setup and shook his head. "No, sir. No juice in them. Be a snap to cut through."

Murdock used hand signals to the clustered SEALs, and Red Nicholson and Kenneth Ching moved out as scouts to get under the dock and then on-site and take out the roving guard.

They swam underwater to the pier, went under the wooden supports to some dry land, and took off their rebreathers and fins. Then they went up the ladder to the dock. The roving guard outside the wire moved toward them unaware. Red cut him down with a three-round silenced burst from an MP-5. At that point none of the stationary guards could see them. The two SEALs pulled the body off the dock and dropped him into the bay. They kept his AK-47 and four magazines of ammo.

The two SEALs waited out of sight from the dock on the ladder, and Murdock couldn't figure out why. Then he spotted a second roving guard riding a bicycle up the dock. When he was almost beside them, Ching jumped up and said something in Chinese. The man turned his way. Ching grabbed him, applied a choke hold from the back, and lifted the man off his feet and let him fall, a foot breaking his neck.

Chin dropped the dead guard into the bay and sent his bike in after him.

Now they looked for the fixed guard posts. Ching stayed where he was, and Nicholson went back to the ground under the edge of the pier and ran down to the second ladder up from the water. It was fifty feet down the dock and gave him a better view of the side of the building. Nicholson now used a silenced M-4A1, the old CAR-15 with its .223 screamer rounds. He lifted just over the edge of the dock and checked his field of fire. Just the two fences. He'd have to hope one of his rounds would get through.

The guard on his end was in a small shelter at that end of the building. Nicholson braced on the ladder, leaned on the dock, and set up his shot. He tried for a chest hit. Red fired twice and the guard slumped in his guard station.

Red heard a soft *chuff, chuff* from down the dock. Ching must have found a target. Red quickly sighted in on the second guard, who'd come out of his post and stretched. Red put two rounds into his chest and watched him go down in a heap.

Two more coughing rounds from Ching were heard. Nicholson dropped down the ladder and met Ching on the dirt under the pier near his ladder.

Murdock watched through his NVG from his spot, now about fifty yards off the pier. The night-vision device gave him a lime-green view of the scene and outlined the situation in a glance. He saw the four guards inside the fence go down and then his two scouts drop down the ladders.

"Let's go," he said softly to the remaining ten men around him, and they swam for the pier. Three minutes later all were onshore and had dropped their breathers and fins. They drained the water from their weapons, opened watertight pouches and put on their Motorola MX-300 communications radios. They each had a headset, an earpiece inside the left ear, and a wire down the back of the neck, through a slit in a shirt, and plugged into the battery and transceiver on each man's belt. A filament mike perched below each man's lower lip. It provided no-hands-on instant communication for about two hundred yards.

"Bishop, get up there and do the fences. Fernandez and Lincoln, go along to cover him. As soon as the fences both are blown, First Squad is on the assault. The rest of the Second Squad spread out in defensive positions in case we have some company. Go, go, go."

The three SEALs rushed up the ladder with Bishop in front pulling out the tools he would need, including the primer cord, really a heavy string of pliable explosive that burned so fast it was deadly. Wrap it around a man's neck and set it off and it will blow the man's head off. The SEALs used it for cutting holes in things like fences, doors, and walls.

Bishop sprinted to the first fence while the other two SEALs dropped to the tarmac both facing outward, both with CAR-15's set on full automatic and ready to fire.

Bishop worked quickly, weaving the ends of the primer cord in and out of the chain-link fence, tying it in place here and there with strips of plastic. He soon had a man-sized hole outlined. He inserted a detonator timer, set it at fifteen seconds, and pushed the lever to activate it. Then he ran back twenty yards and went to ground facing outward with his hands over his ears.

The cracking explosion sounded like a stick of dynamite hung on a string from a tree limb had exploded. A sharp cracking detonation cut through the chain-link wire and blew the "doorway" out of the fence and against the next one ten feet away.

Bishop jolted up as soon as the explosion hit and ran for the hole, through it to the next fence. He repeated the routine there and blew the second hole.

By that time, the seven men of the First Squad came up to the first fence and waited. When the second one blew, they surged through the opening in a flash and charged the small door to the left of the center of the warehouse. The door was locked.

Six rounds from Murdock's MP-5 smashed the lock and the door swung open inward.

The first three men went through the way they did in a Kill House. Murdock went first and took the right-hand third. Jaybird was second through, and handled the left third of the room. Holt came through a fraction of a second later ready to hose down the center of the room.

All three wore NVGs. It was a small office-type room with a desk, two chairs, and a bookcase. No one was there, it seemed. Then a man lifted up from behind the desk, a pistol in his left hand. Holt put two rounds from his CAR-15 into his chest and one in his head, and he slammed backwards out of sight.

"Clear here," Holt said.

"Clear," said Jaybird.

"Clear," Murdock echoed.

A small nightlight burned to one side. The SEALs lifted their NVGs and checked the place again. Holt looked at the Chinese and made sure he was dead.

Two doors led off the room. Murdock unlatched one as silently as he could by turning the knob, then cracked it open so he could see through. It was the inside of the warehouse, brightly lighted. It was full of missiles, some in slings, some standing in mounts to be worked on, others in a rack next to the wall. Murdock could see more than a dozen.

He heard some men talking loudly to each other, and he motioned Ching up to the doorway. He listened for a minute.

"Bragging about the women they're going to have when their twelve-hour shift is over."

Murdock edged the door open an inch wider. Now he and Ching could see two Chinese soldiers on a catwalk at the far end of the building. They had rifles slung and seemed to be walking a fixed post.

The rest of the First Squad crowded into the room. They were weapon-ready for a fight.

Jaybird and Murdock had MP-5's, Ron Holt had a CAR-15 carbine with a grenade launcher, Magic Brown had his M-89 sniper rifle, Red Nicholson had another CAR-15 with launcher, Harry Ronson toted the H&K 21A1 machine gun with NATO rounds, and Doc Ellsworth carried his favorite, a Remington five-shot sawed-off shotgun with the pistol grip instead of a stock. He kept it slung around his neck to leave his hands free.

They checked the other door from the room. It also opened into the main warehouse area.

Murdock pointed to three men and at both doors. "Take out the two men on the catwalk first. Then we charge in and see who else is in there."

Two SEALs with long guns moved to the cracked-open doors and sighted in.

"Now," Murdock said. The coughs of the two silenced weapons sounded and the SEALs burst through both doors. The sentries overhead were dead or dying. Two more Chinese Murdock hadn't seen on the floor stepped out from behind a stack of missiles and began firing at the SEALs.

23

Sunday, May 17

0052 hours
Naval yards
Amoy, China

Four SEALs dove behind heavy wooden boxes to avoid the rounds from the two Chinese soldiers ahead. Murdock rolled once and came to his feet behind some crates.

"Watch your fire," Murdock said into his mike. "Don't hit any of the missiles."

They had been cautioned to use single shots, not burst fire, while inside. Murdock looked out from his protection and saw that the Chinese had taken cover as well. Murdock nodded at Holt, who was beside him. Holt leaned around the boxes and blasted down the aisle as Murdock jolted ten feet ahead to another set of wooden boxes. He passed a missile and hoped that none of their shots ricocheted and penetrated the warheads holding the poison gas.

He made it, then laid down fire toward the place where they saw the Chinese, as Holt moved up on this side and Magic Brown surged forward on the other side of the eight-foot-wide aisle.

There had been no more firing from the Chinese.

"Ching, talk to them," Murdock said to his mike.

All firing stopped. Ching's voice bellowed into the open space of the warehouse with its three-story ceiling.

"Soldiers. You are surrounded. Come out with your

weapons held over your heads. You can't escape." There
was no response. Ching repeated the lines in his best
Mandarin.

A moment later a roar came from down the aisle. Three
Chinese soldiers surged from behind wooden crates, firing
automatic weapons and charged forward.

Murdock and Magic Brown chopped down the three
before they ran twenty feet.

"Clear here," Murdock said. "Check the rest of the
facility."

Murdock and Holt worked the right side of the hundred-
by-hundred-foot complex. They found no more defenders.

"Clear left," Murdock heard in his earpiece. Ronson.

"Clear center," Doc Ellsworth reported by radio.

"Clear right," Holt said.

Quickly they checked the far front and then the back.
There had been only five defenders, all accounted for.

Ching checked the Chinese casualties. "One is still alive,"
he reported on his radio.

"Question him," Murdock said. Murdock went up to
where Ching knelt by one of the three soldiers. Blood came
from the man's nose and mouth. His eyes were glazed, but
Ching shook him and he spoke slowly.

Ching asked him several questions in Mandarin. The man
answered them, then almost lost consciousness, but Ching
shook him and he went on talking. Then his eyes glazed
again and a long deep breath came out of him and he died.

Ching looked up. "These are all regular DF-15 missiles in
this building, with a range of nearly four hundred miles.
They go on the Luda-class destroyers. These do not have
poison gas. The poison-gas missiles are the smaller DF-11.
He said they won't come from the assembly plant until
tomorrow night. The gas missiles make the workers and the
soldiers extremely nervous."

Murdock sent outside for Bishop. He checked the missiles and confirmed the dead soldier's words.

"Just plain old HE type, Skipper. No room for any poison
gas in these babies. They sure will make a big bang,
though."

"You're certain?"

"Yes. As certain as I can be without exploding one of them."

"Check every one of them. do it now and quickly. If they all are HE, then rig enough of them with TNAZ so the whole complex will go up with one big bang. Use two-hour timers so we'll be long gone. Get with it."

They checked the dead men again. SEALs don't take prisoners. They made sure they were dead with a quick, silenced shot to the head of each of the five Chinese.

Murdock could hear firing outside. He hit his send button.

"DeWitt. What's going on out there?"

"Company. Four guys drove up in a funny little rig that looks like a rip-off of a jeep. We nailed three of them. One got away. The jeep looks good for transport if we need any."

"We'll need some. The gas missiles aren't here. Hide the rig somewhere and dump the bodies in the bay. We'll be out soon."

Murdock watched Bishop working the TNAZ.

"Know what we used to do for sport on the Fourth of July back in Tennessee?" Bishop asked.

Murdock shook his head.

"We'd take sticks of twenty percent dynamite and blow up outhouses. Mostly outside of town a ways. Lots of folks in the country still used outhouses. Damn, you could just see the shit flying all over the place."

Bishop taped the last of the TNAZ onto the nose of a missile and set a timer.

"Should do it, L-T. Primed four of them. The explosions inside here will trigger sympathetic detonations of all the missiles in the place. Be a damn nice bang."

Murdock led his men out of the building. They paused at the small door and checked. Murdock couldn't see the men of Second Squad. Then he found them. Three were behind the jeep rip-off. Two more were by some wooden boxes on the dock. The others scattered in defensive positions and behind cover.

He started to go out when he heard the whine of a motor

and an Army truck that looked like a six-by-six ground around the corner and troops spilled from it.

"Save the truck, take out the men," Murdock whispered into his lip mike.

Murdock let four men from First Squad slip out the door and hide just behind the fence. All had their weapons aimed at the eight men who had dropped off the truck.

"Magic, take out the driver," Murdock whispered into his mike. Five seconds later Magic's silenced weapon fired. Then all the SEALs cut loose with their silenced weapons.

Four of the Chinese soldiers died in the first volley of shots. The others dove to the ground, not sure where the deadly rounds came from. Lieutenant DeWitt's men smashed the life from the last four Chinese in seconds. The driver of the truck had fallen half out of the cab, and the rig had stopped.

"Save the truck," Murdock radioed. "Drive it behind the far end of the building. We'll get it later."

Ross Lincoln was their truck, jeep, motor, and transport expert. He ran to the truck, pulled the driver out, and climbed aboard. It took him a few moments to find the switches and accelerator. Then he started the truck and drove it out of sight behind the end of the missile building.

The SEALs dropped the dead Chinese into the bay and then grouped on Murdock, who led them back down the ladders to their rebreathers, fins, and gear bags.

"Time to swim," Murdock said. "The two Luda-class destroyers that launch their missiles are down the dock about four hundred yards. Let's suit up and get down that way. Pick-up those drag packs with the limpets. If we can't find the poison-gas missiles, at least we can take out their delivery system."

Jaybird frowned in the Chinese darkness. "Skipper, these little poison-gas missiles still have over a hundred miles of range. Taiwan is only ninety miles away. Why don't they just fire them from here? They don't need the ships to launch them."

Bishop snorted. "Jaybird, it's a safety factor. They launch them poison-gas bangers from land, and one of them misfires or blows up on the pad and that one sets off a few others, they could wipe out half a million of their own people. If they launch at sea and there's an accident, they lose only one destroyer and a few hundred men."

The SEALs swam just below the surface staying in close contact with each other. By the time they were halfway there, they knew that the destroyers had lots of security around them.

At two hundred yards the SEALs surfaced and checked out the targets. Floodlights blazed from several points lighting up both the destroyers and the water thirty meters out on the water side. There were six walking sentries on the dock guarding each ship. The whole area was fenced off with a chain-link eight feet high. The SEALs saw two dogs on leash walking the area next to the fence.

They stowed their Motorola radios in their watertight compartments, and had to rely on whispers and hand signals.

"Wonder how good their security is in the water?" Murdock said to Jaybird, who treaded water beside him.

"I'd bet there's little to none," Jaybird said. "The same attack plan we worked out?"

Murdock nodded. "Get them moving."

Jaybird signaled to four men with the limpet mines. They swam away. Two men would place two of the big magnetic mines on the hull of the destroyers three feet under water.

Murdock had thought of shooting out the floodlights, but decided that would only alert the Chinese. The men with the mines would plant them, then set timers for twenty minutes, and the SEALs would swim like crazy to get out of the area before the blasts sent shock waves through the water that could seriously injure anyone close enough to them.

Murdock looked at his watch. He allowed them ten minutes to swim in and place the limpets, and then five minutes to swim back. They came back right on time, and the platoon turned and swam back toward the missile warehouse.

They swam silently on top of the bay while waiting for the explosions to go off. The explosions were late. Murdock looked at the men who had set the timers. They hand-signaled that they were set for twenty minutes.

Then a deep rumbling explosion shattered the night. It sent shock waves through the water that the SEALs could feel. Then the blast blew out of the water into the air, and they heard a shattering roar. The same thing happened three times more, and the SEALs gave a silent cheer and swam faster toward their dock.

This time they kept on their rebreathers and all of their gear and carried their fins and equipment bags. They hoped to be back in the water as soon as they blew up the missile-assembly building.

"Where the fuck was that warehouse, Jaybird?" Murdock asked as they climbed the ladders up to the dock, then ran across the open area to where the big six-by-six Chinese Army truck sat.

"Half a klick right up this main drag out in front of the warehouse," Jaybird said.

The men crawled into the truck, found bench seats along each side, and dropped their gear on to the floor and primed their weapons for a fight.

"The place is a large warehouse with a fence all the way around it," Jaybird said. "Leastwise, that's the way it looked in the satellite photos."

They could hear sirens now. A car with a flashing red light on it tore past the warehouse heading down the dock toward the damaged destroyers.

"Let's go," Murdock called to Lincoln in the cab. Horse Ronson had set up his H&K machine gun so it aimed out the back of the truck just over a low tailgate. The other men had their weapons free of water and with a round in the chamber, locked and loaded.

Murdock sat beside the tailgate. They were still in an industrial section. The street was narrow, and here and there trucks were parked along it next to buildings.

A small truck with siren wailing and red light flashing came racing down the street toward them. Lincoln pulled to the side and let the rig go by.

"Seems to be an emergency down at the docks," Jaybird said. The men laughed.

"Coming up on what looks to be a checkpoint of some kind," Lincoln yelled through a sliding panel into the cab. "What the hell do I do?"

"Turn right at the next street," Murdock said. He leaned around the side of the truck and saw the floodlights and two Army rigs pulled up across the street a block ahead. He felt the big truck turn and careen down a side street barely wide enough to let it scrape through between buildings. Just as they turned, Murdock saw one of the small rigs at the roadblock jolt forward. Was it going to chase them? he wondered.

"Go up two blocks and then to the left for two more blocks and then left again," Murdock yelled. "Maybe we can get around the roadblock that way."

Before they turned the second time, the Army rig from the roadblock raced up behind them. Its headlights blinked and then a siren gave a short angry snarl.

"Do it," Murdock said to Ronson. He triggered his 21A1 and sent a stream of 7.62mm NATO smashing into the Army rig's windshield and engine. Four five-round bursts sent the small truck slewing sideways into a thin wall and out of sight crashing through the front of a business building.

The SEALs' truck rumbled on, made the next two corners, and surged back onto the main avenue they had left before when they saw the roadblock.

Murdock looked down the street behind them and saw where the roadblock was. Now there was only one rig there, and no one seemed to be looking their way.

"How much farther?" Murdock called to Ross Lincoln.

"Just ahead, Skipper. Maybe fifty yards. What the hell do you want me to do with this rig? I can't just drive up in front."

"Turn down the first cross street next to it and get us away from any street lights. We work best in the dark."

Murdock looked around the side of the truck. He saw the warehouse ahead. It was lit by floodlights. The one fence they had seen in the photos turned into two fences. The place looked like Fort Knox. There seemed to be one layer of security after another. The only thing he didn't see were tanks and a regiment of Chinese infantry ready to defend the place.

Then Lincoln called out again.

"Trouble, L-T. Looks like some kind of a half-track weapons carrier coming around the far corner of the warehouse. What the shit am I supposed to do now?"

24

Sunday, May 17

0154 hours
Missile assembly building
Amoy, China

"Stop the truck," Murdock shouted to the driver in the front of the Chinese six-by-six. He waved to the two closest SEALs in the back of the rig who had CAR-15s with grenade launchers.

"Both of you, two HE rounds each at that weapons carrier. Wherever he goes, shoot him up. Do it now."

Scotty Frazier jerked the pouch open that held his grenades and loaded one. He had one round off before the other man had his grenades out. Al Adams got his weapon up to use just as the first grenade hit in front of the slowly moving weapons carrier. Adams's first round hit the rig in the middle and exploded with a roar. Two men went flying out of the troop compartment.

Frazier adjusted his aim and put his second round into the carrier as well, stalling it. Adams's second shot hit just behind the rig where half-a-dozen Chinese soldiers had just evacuated the burning weapons carrier. Four of them went down screaming.

"Take it down," Murdock, shouted, and the SEALs jumped from the truck and found firing positions. With their silenced weapons at a range of only forty yards, they chopped up the remaining Chinese soldiers. Then a round

187

generated a spark that hit vaporizing gasoline, and the whole
rig blew up in one shuddering explosion as the weapons on
board went off in the fireball.

They were taking fire now from guards around the target.
Murdock put his men in a long line of attackers wherever
they could find cover.

Magic Brown, with his sniper rifle and scope, began
picking off the outside security.

Murdock and Jaybird checked out the protection around
the building. Concrete barriers in front of the place prevented a truck from crashing through the fences. There were
barriers inside the fences as well. The fences were chain-
link with razor wire on top. As they watched the firefight,
they saw two machine guns blasting from the second-floor
windows. Magic Brown and Miguel Fernandez, with the
other M-89 sniper rifle, concentrated their fire on the chatter
guns and soon silenced them.

Murdock didn't know if they'd wiped out the weapons or
gunners, or if the fire had been too hot for them and they'd
simply pulled back from the window. He'd remember the
potential up there. But first came the fences.

"Frazier, put two forty rounds on that chain-link fence
gate to the right, the man-sized one. Blow it the hell open."

Frazier heard the orders in his earpiece and loaded a
grenade. He had to move to get a shot at the target. He
rushed from a stalled truck to an old car of uncertain vintage
and bellied down behind it. The shot was easy but would it
blast open the door? He aimed, and triggered the launcher.
The round hit short and exploded with a roar. His second
round hit the gate in the middle and detonated. It blew a
foot-wide hole in the chain link but didn't make the gate
open. He fired again to the left. This round hit the frame of
the gate and blew it off its locks and hinges.

The Platoon Leader grinned and used hand signals as he
and three of his First Squad stormed through the gate to the
next chain-link fence. Jaybird wrapped primer cord around
the gate lock and set a detonator for ten seconds. He jolted
away from the spot and the primer cord exploded with a

roar. It blew the gate open and Murdock and his First Squad stormed through it to the side of the warehouse.

Ed DeWitt and the Second Squad quickly positioned themselves outside in a defensive formation to provide security for the men inside. They would be needed. Murdock could hear sirens wailing away, and some sounded like they were on rigs moving his way.

Two side doors to the big building were steel, but a small man-sized door in the side of one looked like a possible entry place. Another look changed Murdock's mind. It had sliding steel security bars on this side, and probably inside as well.

To the left was the main entrance, with standard doors. They looked to be wooden with door handles.

Magic Brown shook his head. "Not a chance in hell to go in there," he said. "Fucking doors will be booby-trapped and covered by at least two machine guns inside. They know we're out here now."

Murdock agreed. "Let's try around the corner, a side or back door."

The squad moved with Red out front and the L-T coming next and then the usual combat formation. They took no fire as they went around the corner. There were no doors or windows on this side. The squad sprinted to the back of the building. Two truck doors stood open beside a truck-high loading dock.

Murdock motioned the men to get to each side of the doors. They went in with a rush, weapons at assault-firing positions. They stormed through the doors and met no resistance. They flattened against the sides of the concrete room. One door showed at the end, twenty feet away. The L-T went forward and turned the knob. He eased the door open a crack and looked through.

He saw a long lighted hallway with two doors leading off it. No windows. He swung the door open and motioned his men forward. They spread out at five-yard intervals.

The first door down the hall was locked. Jaybird opened the second door carefully. Inside they found a kitchen with two men working over a stove. Jaybird's MP-5 dropped

them with chest shots. The SEALs saw two more doors
leading off the kitchen. They checked both. One led into a
dormitory of some type. It was dark and they could hear
men moving around in it, and one man snoring.

Murdock motioned for them to close the door. He found
a wooden chair, pushed the back of it under the door handle,
and kicked the rear legs firmly on the floor. To open the
door anyone would have to break the chair legs. It was a
stopgap operation.

They looked out the other door. It led into the main
assembly room. Murdock studied the place from beside the
door. He spotted four guards. Two were on balconies that
looked as if they were made for protection. Two more
roving guards worked the floor.

He stared at the missiles. They looked like the ones they
had seen at the docks. They were about the same size.

Ken Ching pushed up where he could see the missiles.
"Same damn ones we saw in the other building," he said.
"Where are the smaller ones?"

One of the guards noticed the open door and walked that
way. Magic Brown cut him down with his silenced sniper
rifle. Murdock gave the sign to open fire, and six weapons
at the door quickly put down the two men on the second-
floor guard posts.

"Let's take a look," Murdock said in his mike. He
directed the seven men. Two went on each side and three
down the middle of the room. Most of the sleek rocket
weapons were on work stands, upright as if ready to fire.
Others lay in boxes for transport. Some looked as if they had
a lot of assembly work to be done.

Shots came from ahead. They were not silenced. Murdock ducked behind a stack of wooden crates that would
soon hold the missiles and looked around the corner. One
Chinese with an old rifle steadied his weapon as he aimed
over a closed box halfway across the room.

Murdock lifted his MP-5 and sent a three-round burst at
the soldier. Two of the rounds caught him in the side and the
chest and he fell backwards, his rifle still on the wooden boxes.

"Clear right," Ron Holt said into his mike.

"Clear left," Harry Ronson said.

Murdock ran down through the center of the big room until he was sure there were no more men there.

"Clear center," Murdock said. "Ching, check the four Chinese. See if any of them can be questioned."

He looked around the complex. The other missiles had to be there somewhere. He remembered the dormitory. Too many men in there could ruin his whole night.

He waved at Jaybird and Magic Brown and called for Ronson on his Motorola. They crouched behind some missile boxes.

"That dormitory sleeping area. We've got to clear it before they surprise us. We'll use half-a-dozen fraggers and then our NVGs for the rest. It's got to be quick. Let's go."

They ran back to the kitchen. The chair was still braced under the door. Horse took it out. They each held three fragger grenades, the trusty M-67's. Magic found a light switch and turned off the kitchen lights. They all pulled down their NVGs.

"Horse and Magic, throw deep. Jaybird, middle. Then get back out the door here and I'll do the short ones. Go, go, go."

Magic opened the door and stepped into the semidarkness. He threw his three grenades as did Horse behind him. They surged back into the kitchen as Jaybird and Murdock threw their middle and short ones.

The 4.2-second fuses on the first grenade went off before Murdock finished his tosses. He and Jaybird bumped into each other getting out the door. They surged to the walls beside the door as the inside of the barracks room exploded with the roar of the grenades and the screams of the Chinese troops.

When the last grenade exploded nearby, the SEALs could hear the shrapnel singing through the door. Then they stepped into the open doorway. Horse was in front of his H&K 21A1 machine gun. He chattered five-round bursts wherever his green scope showed Chinese defenders. Magic went down the other side of the aisle and began chopping down soldiers wherever he saw them.

"Magic and Horse take the right," Murdock said into his mike. The four messengers of death began working down the rows of bunks. Now they could see there were about thirty bunks in the room arranged two-high. One shot came from halfway down the right-hand side, and Horse hosed down the area with a nine-round burst.

Murdock saw a figure rise up from behind a metal bunk. He jolted three rounds into the man's chest area, the easiest body mass on a target to hit, and the Chinese slammed backward and didn't move.

Jaybird worked ahead slowly, checking under the bunks and on top of them.

"Clear right," Magic said.

A moment later Jaybird fired a three-round burst and then Murdock heard his words. "Clear left."

They worked back up the aisle between the bunks and hurried through the kitchen. Once in the main room they lifted their night-vision goggles, and Murdock heard a voice in his earpiece.

"L-T, I've got a live Chinese who's able to talk. Could you come up here and give me a hand. He's a tough little guy."

"Right, Ching. Be right there."

Murdock's earplug came alive again. It was Lieutenant DeWitt. "Murdock, we've got trouble out here. Looks like half a company of Chinese regulars. They know how to fight. We're in good defensive positions but we could use that other MG and Magic out here."

"Copy that," Murdock said. "Horse, Magic, Red, and Doc get outside and lend a hand. Use those forty-millimeter rounds. Move."

"Thanks, Skipper," DeWitt said. "We'll hold the fort."

The four SEALs sent outside went to the rear door quietly. Magic shook his head. "Nobody home," he said. They left the back door and hurried around the side of the building like four black shadows. At once they heard the sharp crack of the rifles out front, then the stuttering sound of a Chinese burp gun.

Magic was surprised that they still used them. The only

ones he knew about were the .45-caliber squirt guns the Chinese had used in Korea fifty years ago. They couldn't still have those old weapons, could they?

Back inside the building, Murdock found Ching halfway down the center aisle. A Chinese soldier lay on his back. His right side was soaked with blood. His right arm was shattered and bloody from his shoulder down.

"He's tough and still alive, but he doesn't want to talk," Ching said.

"Ask where he lives." Murdock said.

Ching chattered at him in Mandarin, and the man looked surprised and mumbled something.

"See if he has a family," Murdock said.

Ching talked to the man again. He seemed to relax a little.

Ching pointed to the missile next to them and asked if it was a Dongfeng DF-15. The wounded man said all of them were. High explosives, blow up half of Taiwanese town, he told Ching.

Ching asked him about the smaller missiles, the ones with the poison gas in them.

The wounded soldier's eyes went wild for a moment. He chattered and waved his arm and talked again. Ching had to stop him.

"He says he knows nothing of the poison-gas missiles. 'They don't have any here. Never did have any.' Then he snorted and said, 'all lies.' That's what the generals tell them to say. The Chinese people are afraid of the poison-gas missiles. So afraid they move from a place where they are kept."

Ching asked him if the small missiles were there, the Dongfeng DF-11. The Chinese soldier didn't answer for a moment. Then he nodded. "Yes, here, right here, but you will never find them," he told Ching in Mandarin. Ching translated for Murdock.

"Why never find them?" Ching asked the man. He shrugged and gasped in pain from his wound. He said again that the Western devils would never find China's number-one weapon. His left hand worked under his left leg slowly.

Murdock stepped on his wrist and the Chinese screamed in pain.

Murdock reached down and brought out a small-caliber handgun loaded and ready to fire.

Ching talked to the man for another five minutes, but that was all he would say. The missiles were there, but the Western devils would never find them. The Chinese grew weaker as he talked. At last he shook his head, laughed at his questioner, and took a deep breath and died.

Murdock stared at the lifeless body a moment. "So the missiles are here, but we'll never find them. I've got a hunch we'd better soon. DeWitt out front could run into more trouble than he was now."

Murdock touched his lip mike. "Everyone on the inside. The missiles we're hunting are here someplace. They can't be in the second story, so maybe they're in a basement. Everyone get busy looking for any hint of an opening into a basement. Secret panel, stairwell, elevator, anything. Let's move."

Outside, Magic and his three SEALs came to the front corner of the building. They were only four dark shadows. They saw a Chinese six-by-six drawn up fifty yards down the street. Rifle fire came from the protection of the truck. Other Chinese weapons sounded from the buildings on the far side of the street.

Horse Ronson set up his machine gun and fed in a new belt of NATO rounds.

"The damn truck," he said. Magic nodded. Magic faded along the front of the building to a concrete barrier that prevented any trucks from crashing into the place. It also served as a protected firing position.

Red moved next to him, and Doc shared the same twelve-foot concrete barricade.

Ronson opened up on the truck with five-round bursts. The sound of the machine gun brought immediate return fire. Magic and Red concentrated on the fire coming at Ronson. Four bursts later, the truck's gasoline tank blew and the truck billowed into a raging ball of flames. Chinese soldiers rushed away from the rig. It highlighted them for good targets, and half of them never made it into the darkness.

Toward the center of the string of concrete barricades, Ed DeWitt touched his mike. "Good shooting, Ronson. We didn't have a good angle from here. Looks like some of them are getting discouraged."

Those with NVGs used them, and here and there a silenced round drove a Chinese soldier to the ground wounded and hurting. Down the line two SEALs fired 40mm grenades where they saw three or more Chinese in a group. In the distance the SEALs heard sirens, but they didn't seem to be coming toward them.

"Looks like they're pulling back," DeWitt said into his mike. "Let's hold steady and see if they regroup."

Inside the factory warehouse, Murdock stood with his hands on his hips. "If I were a Chinese, where the hell would I hide missiles I filled with poison gas so they wouldn't scare half the population?" The only place he could think of was underground.

"Let's do it again, guys. Go over this floor like it was your bank vault. There has to be something here somewhere to tip us off how to get into the fucking basement."

25

Sunday, May 17

It took the SEALs five minutes to find any hint of a basement. Then Ron Holt realized that one section of the floor was made of wooden planks.

"Could be something down there, L-T," Holt said. They checked how big the wooden area was. It covered nearly a third of the floor.

"Scour the whole section of the plank floor," Murdock said. "Look for anything that might be able to move."

Five minutes later, Magic Brown stumbled on it. There was a slot in the floor against the far wall and next to it an open space. Against the wall was a panel that Ching said read "Lights." They opened it and found a series of buttons. Ching read the markings under them and began pushing green buttons.

At once a section of the floor detached and swung downward. The part of the plank floor that moved was twelve by fifteen feet. It swung down on hinges, and at once an elevator platform filled the void, rising into the place where the floor had been.

"Let's take a ride," Lieutenant Murdock said, and the four men stepped on the elevator. Ching pushed another button and they were lowered into the basement area. It had a twelve-foot ceiling and was brightly lit. They saw no workers, no guards.

At once they saw the missiles, the smaller ones.

"These are the Dongfeng DF-11," Ching said. He read the markings on them. "They also don't look like HE rounds. The nose cones are different. These are larger and with silver and green streaks of paint down them."

"Careful down here," Murdock barked. "No shooting unless absolutely necessary to save your life. Now, Ching, what can we do to disable these babies?"

Ching frowned, then shook his head. "Damned if I know. We need Scotty Frazier in here." Murdock used his Motorola and called Frazier off the security detail.

Ching rode the elevator up, and brought him down two minutes later. Frazier looked at the missiles.

"They loaded with the bad juice?" Frazier asked.

"We have to assume they are," Murdock said. "How do we disable them?"

"We don't blow them up, burn them down, or shoot them full of holes, that's for damn sure. We try that and we all fucking die along with half of Amoy. Mechanical. There must be something I can do to the propulsion." He started at the closest missile and began tinkering with it. He pulled out a pair of pliers, a crescent wrench, and a screwdriver and went to work.

Murdock hovered over him, saw it bothered Frazier, and walked away.

"That's one of them, L-T, but we ain't got time to do them all," Frazier said. "Take three or four hours. Up topside Mister DeWitt said he thought some more troops were coming. My suggestion is to lift up the elevator and disable it, so they can't get the fucking missiles out of this cave."

Murdock nodded, but kept looking around. His gaze swept over a coiled fire hose against the wall. He grinned.

"Maybe we turn this place into a swimming pool. That wouldn't do the missiles any good at all, would it? They we jam the elevator. Turn on every fire hose you can find down here full blast."

The SEALs scurried to the hoses, strung them out, and

turned them on. There were no keys or safety measures.
Soon water began to cover the floor.

"Let's move it, guys," Murdock said. They ran to the
elevator platform and Ching hit the buttons to move them
up. At the top, he studied the panel a minute, then took out
his Sig-Sauer .45-caliber P-266 pistol and put six of the big
rounds into the control panel. He didn't have the silencer on
the heavy weapon, and the crashing sounds of the six shots
billowed through the building.

"Let's get out of Dodge," Murdock said, and the five men
trotted toward the door and the hallway to the back entrance.
They went outside and came around the side of the building
into a firefight.

Murdock used his radio. "Lincoln, where the hell's that
Chinese truck?"

"Half a block down," Lincoln said. "I can get to it from
here. Where do you want me to pick up you guys?"

Murdock had been thinking about that. There was an
alley along the side of the building across a thin wooden
fence.

"Alley down this side of the building, the right-hand side
if you're facing the way we drove up here. Got it?"

"Yes, sir. Be right with you."

DeWitt spoke into the net. "Skipper, want us to make a
slow withdrawal to the right side of the building?"

"Roger that. Start to pull some men over. Be at least five
minutes before Lincoln gets here. Don't let them know
you're moving."

"Right. I've got one wounded. Doesn't seem to be too
bad. See you soon."

Murdock sent Horse Ronson up to the corner of the
building to help lay down machine-gun fire to help the
SEALs pull back. He spotted half-a-dozen fire points and
began raking them with five-round bursts. Two SEALs
moved past him and around the corner. One of them was
limping.

Ronson kept up his chattering fire. He spaced out the
bursts, conserving his ammo now so he could last through
this fight and any others.

Another SEAL came past, turned, fired a final 40mm grenade, and darted around the corner before the round hit a hundred yards down the street.

Al Adams with his CAR-15 dropped beside Ronson.

"Holding them off. Thanks for the help." He started to load a 40mm grenade.

"Better save it, mate," Ronson said. "We ain't back in the bay yet. Might need some more firepower."

Adams waved and ran around the corner of the building.

The rest of the SEALs came back singly until Lieutenant DeWitt dropped down beside Ronson.

"That's all of us, Ronson. Heard the truck yet?"

"No, sir."

"We better give the Chinese something else to think about."

Just then three figures jumped up from thirty feet away and charged the corner of the building.

Ronson cut down two of them with two five-round bursts. Lieutenant DeWitt lifted his MP-5 and sent six rounds into the last Chinese, who staggered and fell only a dozen feet away.

"Let's move back halfway," DeWitt said.

They heard a truck coming, and saw it as a black shadow as it rolled down the alley twenty feet across the wooden fence.

"Yeah," Ronson said. "Moving time."

They both set up as rear guard as they heard the fence smashed down and the SEALs stomping over it. Jaybird ran up to them and motioned them back. He stayed where they had been and sent a burst of rounds from his MP-5 toward the far corner the rear guard had just left. He kept the curious Chinese soldiers from firing around the corner. A horn honked once, and Jaybird sent another six rounds screaming toward where the Chinese must be coming. Then he turned and ran for the truck.

As he climbed on board, Magic Brown was slamming one round after another over the tailgate of the truck and into the spot where Jaybird had just been. The truck lurched ahead and they rolled down the alley and into the street.

That was when they heard the sirens. Murdock sat in the front seat beside the driver Ross Lincoln.

"Which way, L-T?"

The sirens came from the bay side. "Wanted to go back the way we came, but those sirens must be bringing more troops. We better head the other way for a mile or so. Then we'll cut back to the east and then south again and hope we can find the bay. I'd love to get back to the water as soon as we can.

The street they were on was narrow, a side street of some kind with mostly industrial buildings on both sides. They had turned left from the warehouse, and soon came to a wider avenue heading south the way they wanted to go.

Lincoln paused at the intersection. They looked right and saw two sets of blinking red lights racing toward them. They waited. One Army car and an ambulance went screaming past with sirens wailing.

"Straight across," Murdock said. "No other choice. We still need to go left when we can."

"What about the troop transports, sir?" Lincoln asked.

Murdock frowned and rubbed his face. "We ignore them. If the planes don't drop the paratroops to secure the dock areas, the troops can't land. If the missiles don't fly, they won't wipe out the Taiwan military. I think the troops on those transports are moot right now. They don't mean a fucking thing."

Two blocks later they came to a wider street heading south.

"Take it," Murdock said.

They swung that way, and another block down they saw a roadblock ahead. Two military rigs sat crossways in the street closing it. Murdock reached into the back of the truck through the back window of the cab.

"Give me a machine gun." He barked. He got one in his hands at once and pulled it into the cab. There was a belt of ammo hanging from the receiver.

"Keep going, then slow down as if you're going to stop," Murdock said. "I'll fire and you ram us right through hitting the center of the barricade."

When they were forty yards from the two Chinese Army cars, Murdock rammed the H&K chatter gun out the passenger's-side window, leaned out, and sprayed a five-round burst into each of the two cars. Then he concentrated on four soldiers standing behind the cars. In a moment they took return fire.

One round cracked the windshield. Murdock fired across the hood and scattered three shooters. Then he saw the collision coming and held on to the door frame and the weapon.

The heavy truck hit the two smaller rigs and drove them forward with scraping and tearing of metal. Then the much heavier truck pushed the small rigs aside and was through the barricade. The SEALs in the back of the truck poured out deadly fire at the defenders of the fort, who were now exposed and too dazed even to fire back.

Half a block later they were free and clear.

"Good driving, Lincoln. You ever been in a destruction derby at your local racecourse?"

"Just once, sir. Lost my radiator and my engine on the first crash. Nobody told me you had to back up into everyone."

The street they drove down was less industrial now and showed an occasional business and a house or two. The street swung slowly to the left.

"Sir, looks like we're heading right back toward that main drag we came up to the missiles place. We want to do that?"

"No, take a right on the next good-looking street. We don't want to hit any more roadblocks."

The next street was wider than any they had been on. Here the buildings were all retail firms, and only a few had two stories. They drove half a mile, and then Lincoln pointed.

"Looks like another barricade ahead, sir, about three blocks. Three or four rigs and some flashing reds."

"Right next street," Murdock said. "We don't want to get lost, but we can't take a lucky round into the radiator which would stop us dead in half a mile. We need to get out of town. Let's keep on this street as long as we can. At best we're going parallel to the coast. Then all we have to do is cut cross country and find Mother Ocean."

Murdock hoped it would be that simple. He touched his radio mike. "Casualty report," he said.

DeWitt came on. "Frazier has a slight side wound. Not critical. He's fit for duty. Doc tied it up and gave him a shot. The other problem is Fernandez. Nasty hit in his right forearm. Might have touched a bone. He says he can still manage his M-89. Doc looked at it and wrapped it and gave him a shot of morphine. I'll watch them both."

Murdock acknowledged the report. So far all of his men were fit to fight. It might not last. All they had to do was get back to the water. But how in hell did they do that? A good road map would help.

"Ching," Murdock called. Ching poked his head through the opening between cab and truck body.

"Yes, sir."

"We need to get to the coast. Are there any road signs that could help us? Poke your head out and check every cross street and road we see. We're fucking lost."

They drove another fifteen minutes without spotting any signs to help them. The buildings had gradually given way to empty lots and then an open field, and now they were at the ragged edge of the city. They could see the glow of the lights behind them and a darkness that spelled safety ahead.

"We're in the fucking country all right," Lincoln said, "but just where in the hell are we?"

Murdock had Lincoln stop the rig. He and Ching got out and stared at the lights.

"We're south of Amoy," Ching said. "We have to be. If we turn left we should be heading for the coast."

"If we can find a road going in that direction," Murdock growled. "Ching, sit up front with us and see if you can find out how to get us to the coast. These Chinese don't waste much money on road signs, do they?"

They rolled again. Lincoln tried to read the fuel gauge. Ching told him the tank was half full. The headlights worked and he was pleased about that.

"Ahead, some lights," Ching said. "Maybe a small village."

"Maybe a roadblock," Murdock said. "No reason they should have one way out here, so they probably do."

They drove closer, and the lights showed three vehicles parked across the road. One rig blinked its lights at their truck.

"Blink back," Murdock said. "They blinked three times. Blink back three times."

Lincoln did, and a moment later they felt bullets slamming into the hood, radiator, and windshield. Glass shattered over the three in the front seat, and Lincoln swore as the Chinese engine coughed twice and went dead. The truck rolled to a stop a hundred yards from the bright lights of the roadblock.

"Out, everyone," Murdock barked. "We'll see if you guys remember your land-warfare training. We knock out that roadblock and take one of their vehicles. Let's go now. The right side of the road. Go, go, go."

26

Sunday, May 17

0313 hours
China countryside
Near Amoy, China

As the SEALs bailed out of the six-by-six they saw a rocket coming. They scattered and flattened on the road and in the ditches. The RPG went off with a cracking explosion as it hit the cab of the truck and shattered it. Fuel vapors exploded a second later blasting the truck into small pieces. The SEALs crawled away from the burning hulk as fast as they could.

Small-arms fire tore into the ground around them, but all the men made it to the right-hand side of the road and into a field that held a long row of brush and row crops beyond.

"Red, out front. We'll be crawling until we get away from that damned fire light. Combat formation, let's go."

Red led the crawling force, with Lieutenant Murdock right behind him shadowed by Ron Holt. He still had the radio that could be zeroed in on the satellite and give them communications with anyone in the world.

"Yeah, I got it," Holt groused when somebody asked him. "The damn thing weighs a ton and I got to keep lugging it around. I know, I know, it could save our butts this time. Yeah. Right. You want to carry the fucking radio?"

Nobody did.

The thirteen SEALs worked slowly out of range of the

light then rose to a bent-over position and moved cautiously toward the roadblock. It would have been better to attack it from both sides, but now they had no chance to get men on the other side of the road.

"We go with what we've got," Murdock told Red when he came back to say that the Chinese had set up a barricade behind the two army cars and a light truck.

"We get there and put half our shooters on the far side of the barricade and half on this side, so we'll have them in a kind of cross fire."

He sent DeWitt ahead with five men, and he kept six. Each squad had an MG and a sniper rifle. It should work.

Murdock found his firing position less than fifty yards from the roadblock. He settled his men in a small ditch that probably was for irrigation. DeWitt had to circle around the roadblock by two hundred yards and then get back into position at the road. When DeWitt was ready he'd give three clicks on the radio.

They waited. Murdock wondered if he should get the men out of their wet suits and into cammies. It would take some time. They'd have to find a secure place. He hesitated. He hoped that they soon would be back in the water, and the wet suits would give them the insulation they needed for a long swim.

He heard three clicks on his earpiece, and fired one three-round burst from his MP-5. It was almost out of range, but it was the signal for the rest of them to start shooting.

By prearrangement, Murdock's men fired first. That brought return fire from the roadblock and pinpointed the shooters for DeWitt and his crew who had filtered in behind them.

Magic fired with his sniper rifle, and grinned now and then when he laid in a perfect shot and a defender screamed and went down.

Then DeWitt opened up with his men and after a two-minute burst of fire from Second Squad, Murdock could hear no fire of any kind coming from the roadblock.

"They bluffing or are they down?" Murdock said into his lip mike.

"Looks like they're all down. I see only one man moving."

There was one more round from the Second Squad.

"Skip, I'd say they're all down. Only five or six of them. Want us to move in?"

"That's a Roger," Murdock said. His squad had heard the exchange, and now he stood. The rest of First Squad did as well, and they charged the fifty yards to the roadblock. The Chinese were all down. One wounded man tried to crawl away, and took a round in the head.

"Lincoln, check the vehicles," Murdock said into his lip mike. "The rest of you see what we can use of their weapons. Look for any more of those rocket-propelled-grenades. We need them. The AK-47's will be a good backup. Gather them up and find all the ammo for them you can."

Lincoln ran up and checked out the two cars and the small truck, all Chinese Army-issue. He came back to Murdock.

"All of them run. Looks like the truck would suit us best. Be crowded, but we put three in front and get the rest of us in the back."

"Do it," Murdock said.

Doc came up with three RPGs. "Red found two more. These mothers could come in handy."

"Give three to the Second Squad, we'll keep two," Murdock said. "You have an AK-47?"

Doc shook his head and went hunting.

Lincoln fired up the truck and they climbed on board. Murdock made a wick from an old shirt he found and stuffed it into the fuel tank of one of the cars. It came out soaked with gasoline. He stuffed it halfway back in the gas filler tube and told Lincoln to get the truck moving. When it was out of the blast zone, Murdock lit the gas-soaked rag and ran like hell for the truck.

It was thirty seconds later before the car's gas tank blew up with a whooshing roar. It set the second car on fire, and Murdock and his crew rolled down the road, south for a change. He just hoped this rig didn't run out of gasoline.

The paved road ahead of them was dark. Ching said they

must be heading south according to the stars. "No lights
down there so it can't be Amoy. We should be ten klicks
south and west of the town by now."

As they drove, Murdock told his men to get out of their
wet suits and into their cammies. "Second Squad change
first, then the First Squad. Do it fast." They pulled out of the
wet suits and dug out the cammies from the waterproof
pouches.

They pulled onto a side road and parked while Lincoln
changed, then went back to driving.

"Now we're better set up for a land war," Murdock said.
"I'd much rather that we can run this sweetheart right into
the surf and we can float out of it into Mother Ocean and
take a swim."

"Not likely," Lincoln said. "Headlights coming at us,
maybe a mile off."

"Find a place to pull off the road and out of sight,"
Murdock said. "First damn traffic we've met. Out here it
must be military. Not one hell of a lot of cars or trucks on
these roads at night at least."

They were in a flat area with no hills, no trees. Lincoln
waited as long as he figured he could. Then he took a small
dirt road to the right, cut his lights, and drove along the
twisting road for a quarter of a mile. He shut down the engine, and they waited for the headlights to come along the
road. Murdock sent Red Nicholson to get close to the road
and check out the rig.

Headlights showed down the road five minutes later.
From the growl of the engine, Murdock knew it was some
kind of a truck, maybe a six-by-six like they used to have.
If so, it could carry twenty troopers. The truck slowed when
it came to the road where they had turned off. It stopped for
a moment, then moved on, and was soon out of sight down
the road.

Red came back laughing. "Now that's the kind of army to
be in. There were six soldiers in the back of the six-by-six
with a lantern hanging on the inside, and there were four or
five naked women with them just loving up a storm."

"Wish more of these Chinese were lovers and not fighters," Murdock said. "Let's get back on the road."

A mile down the paved highway they came to an intersection with road signs. Ching got out and read them. He came back nodding. "We're on the right road. The sign says the coastal town of Hiwang is ten kilometers straight ahead."

Murdock wanted to relax a little, but ten klicks were a long way in kilometers or miles. A damn lot could happen between here and there.

Ten minutes later it happened.

The road had changed from paving to gravel. It was fairly well maintained, but the truck had slowed down to thirty miles an hour to stay on the road. They had just made a forty-five-degree turn when they saw and heard a tank directly in front of them no more than a hundred yards ahead.

Lincoln hit the brakes. Murdock's jaw dropped. Ching swore.

"One of their older models," Ching said. "Has a cannon about seventy-five millimeters and twin machine guns. My suggestion would be that we exit this target as fast as possible."

"Everyone out!" Murdock bellowed. Men jolted out of the three-quarter-ton rig and charged for each side of the road. The tank had paused. Now it rolled forward on its metal tracks making enough noise to rouse a seriously hungover college freshman the morning after a frat rush.

Murdock used his radio. "The tracks. When he gets close enough we use two of those RPGs for the tracks. One man on each side of the road. Sound off."

Doc Ellsworth chimed in first. "Doc for one on the right-hand side of the road facing the beast."

"Adams on the left. I'll take a shot."

They waited. The tank was naked. No platoon of foot soldiers followed it along the road. Murdock wondered if it was simply moving from one area to another or was it out hunting them?

A minute later his answer came with a single shot from

the cannon that sent an HE round into the medium-sized truck they had just left, blowing it into three thousand pieces. Little was left to burn.

The tank kept coming, its great metal treads clanking and creaking as it dug up the road moving at a walking pace. Murdock still could see no troops behind it.

The machine gun on the front opened up splattering the land on both sides of the roadway. Murdock lunged behind a sizable tree and the rest of his men bored into the ground, behind whatever cover they could find.

"Sound off if you get hit," Murdock said in his lip mike.

"Yeah, and if you wind up dead be sure to tell us right away so we keep our records straight."

Murdock grinned, not sure who had cracked the joke. It helped right then. Nobody reported being hit.

The tank was almost even with them. He and his men had gone to ground thirty yards from the roadway. They were ten yards apart from each other in good combat disposal. Murdock heard an RPG fire off. He saw a swoosh of smoke behind the rocket and then the trail as it slanted up a little, then down, and hit the left side of the tank's track and exploded with a punishing snarl.

The big tank shuddered and rolled on for a moment. Then a great grinding and screeching of metal on metal sounded, and the tank chewed up many tank parts before it came to a stop. The motor still roared.

"He's down," Murdock said. "Adams, you have any fraggers?"

"Roger that."

"Get up on top of that sucker and if he pops his hatch, feed him three fraggers and then get the hell off that thing."

"Aye, sir."

Murdock waited. The tank made two tries to get moving. One track kept turning, and spun the tank around in a small circle since the other track wouldn't move at all. As the tank came around, Murdock saw a shadow jump on the back of it and work forward. That would be Adams.

The tank stopped. The machine gun chattered firing down the road and to the side well away from the SEALs.

Nothing happened for three or four minutes. Murdock was getting ready to haul ass when he heard a clank and the top hatch of the tank lifted up, then swung backwards. Murdock saw the shadow on the back of the tank stand up near the hatch. Then it leaned in and dumped something down the hatch opening. At once Adams jumped off the rear of the rig and stormed for the trees on the other side of the road with his arms pumping like a hundred-yard-dash winner.

One grenade went off with a mild thump, then two more went off, followed by what must have been the rest of the 75mm rounds in the tank. Fire and smoke belched out the tank turret and from view slots at the front.

Murdock nodded. "Men, it looks like we're down to shank's mares. Let's see if those twenty-mile training hikes did you any good. We'll use the road unless we meet headlights or troops. Then we hit the boonies and decide what to do. Let's form up on the road fifty yards beyond the tank and get moving. We're on the road to water. The sooner the damn better."

Murdock called DeWitt and Jaybird up and they worried it.

"That tank was looking for us, I'd bet a sawbuck," Jaybird said.

"He could have been a probe, to try to draw our fire," DeWitt said. "Then he'd report us by radio and wait for help."

"Only he don't need help anymore," Murdock said. "He must have got a message off. So we can expect company. Right up this road. Which means we move off the road now a half mile to the right and keep it in our sights as we head for the beach."

"How far, L-T?"

"Jaybird, wish I knew. Last estimate about eight klicks. Let's get an ammo count. How many of those AK-47's and rounds we have left. How are the casualties?"

"Frazier is up to speed," DeWitt said. "Fernandez has his arm in a sling. He can't use the eighty-nine. Lincoln has it. Fernandez can fire his Sig .45 if we get in trouble."

"We'll find trouble. They know where we are now. They must be sending in a regiment in trucks to cut us off. They know we're moving toward the coast."

"So hello, Mother," Jaybird said. "Gonna be a hot time on the old China coast tonight."

"Yeah, and maybe tomorrow if we don't get out of here in the next three hours," Murdock said. "Daylight is not our best friend right now."

Murdock led them off the road to the right, moved out a half mile so he could still see the track of a road, and then continued on south.

The moon was three-quarters full. The moonlight came as a big help. Murdock could see a half mile and keep on course. At five miles an hour it would still take them two hours to get anywhere near the water. If nobody objected.

Again someone did object.

Murdock could hear them. He never did see them. Airplanes, big and slow, the ideal kind for dropping paratroops. He shook his head in disbelief. Who else would they throw into this fight to save Chinese face?

He didn't see any of the parachutes open, but by the sound of the three planes he knew when the troops had jumped. Each time the craft's engines speeded up, Murdock could tell by the sound that the troops were away. Three planes, he was sure. How big? Twenty men in a stick? Or more? At least sixty heavily armed Chinese soldiers would soon be up front somewhere watching, waiting, and actively hunting them down like small foxes at an English fenced-in hunt club.

Murdock wasn't sure why he looked up. When he did he saw six white parachutes drifting down directly toward his men. Murdock said: "Right above us. Do it."

He lifted his MP-5 and fired at the parachutists.

27

Sunday, May 17

0353 hours
Near the coast
Amoy, China

The Chinese paratroops above began firing automatic weapons, but they were at a terrible disadvantage. Three of them were shot dead in the first volley from the SEALs. The other three survived for another twenty seconds before they died in a murderous cross fire from the men on the ground.

Murdock waved his men to the side. "Let's get away from here as fast as we can," he called. "Our firing will be zeroed in on by every Chinese soldier within miles. They'll rush to this spot like a pack of hyenas after a fresh-killed antelope."

They jogged to the left, away from the sound of the planes. After a quarter of a mile, Murdock slowed it to a fast walk. He touched his lip mike. "Fernandez, Frazier, how are you holding up?"

"Frazier here. Damn good. Got me one of them paratroops back there."

"Fernandez?"

"Not the best, Skipper. Damn arm hurts like fire. Got off some shots with my Sig. I'm not holding anybody back. Just hope we find that water before long."

"Me too, Fernandez. You hang in there."

Murdock checked the landscape. They were coming into a small range of hills now that had some cover. Not tall

213

timber, but scrub trees of some kind, heavy brush here and there. A few of the hills looked to rise three hundred feet off the level land the platoon had been on.

He aimed at the heaviest part of the cover and kept moving.

Somebody clicked twice on the mike, and the SEALs dropped to the ground. The whispered message came into earpieces.

"We got company. Eight to ten soldiers out front a hundred yards folding up parachutes. Damn white chutes stand out like beacons."

Murdock knew it was Red's voice. He lifted up and sprinted out thirty yards to where Red should be. Red was just past that a ways and flat on the ground behind some brush.

"Get the snipers and MGs up here," Murdock said in his radio mike. "Everyone up thirty yards front in a line of skirmishers. We'll take them out before they set up."

It took four minutes to get the troops in line and ready. Then Murdock aimed in with the AK-47 he carried and fired off three rounds.

That was the signal for the rest to start firing. The two machine guns blasted five-round bursts and the sniper rifles jolted. Murdock put on his NVG, but it didn't help much at this range. He saw one parachuter go down, then another one. He figured on eight of them by the number of white chutes. The SEALs took some return fire, but it was not organized. He guessed that the officer or noncom in charge had been one to feel the wrath of SEAL lead early.

"Cease fire," Murdock said into his radio, and the fire from the rise slowed and then stopped. Below they saw two men running away from them.

Murdock frowned as he realized this meant the Chinese now would have another fix on their location. He checked with Ching, who studied the stars a minute, then angled the SEALs just past the dead Chinese jumpers on a due-east course. The damn water had to be over there somewhere. Murdock knew it.

"Where the fuck are the rest of those jump troops?" Jaybird asked Murdock.

The platoon leader shook his head. "Scattered. Maybe not by design, could have been tricky winds. Night jumps are always a hazard for us. It must have been for them. I've got Red hunting a spot we can hole up for a while and make a radio call. It's time we ask our uncle for some help."

"Didn't think he could do that."

"Won't hurt a hell of a lot to ask. We've got no more than two hours of darkness left. Something's got to happen pretty soon or we're stuck in the middle of goddamned China in the daylight."

They found a small hill with heavy woods, and Murdock had Holt break out the AN/PRC-117D SATCOM radio. He removed the disc antenna, folded it out, and lined it up with a satellite in synchronous orbit with the earth and 22,300 miles overhead.

They had agreed to talk in the encrypted frequency that the carrier could pick up offshore. On the second try the carrier answered.

"Captain, we've run into some trouble. We're about five miles inland maybe five klicks south of Amoy. Could use some air support and a pickup by a pair of Blackhawks."

There was a pause. Then the speaker came on.

"Yes, understand your problem. As we talked before, such operations are absolutely prohibited by the Chief himself. Any chance you can get to the coast?"

"Not in the two hours of darkness we have left. At night who will know what aircraft come in here for us? You can key in on our position from this signal. We have wounded. We need air support right now while we're not under attack."

Don Stroh's voice came over the speaker.

"Murdock, you know we can't do that. Why the hell you so far inland? Don't answer. Tell you what. We'll ask the Taiwanese Air Force to give you some support. It's their damn war. We'll get back to you. Find a hide-hole and crawl in. This could take some time. We don't even have direct radio contact with Taipei. Hold on there, man. I'll move mountains for you if I can. Oh, did you take care of those ships and the missiles?"

"That's a Roger, sir, to both. No gas on Taiwan. Our situation is that right now we need some air support or a miracle, and I'm about fresh out of miracles."

"Go to ground. Find a good hide-hole. I'll talk with the folks in Taipei."

"I don't like the idea, but looks like we have no choice. We'll do what we can and give you another call once we're situated. Murdock out." He put down the mike and scowled. The platoon had heard the conversation.

"We've got two hours to find a place to hole up that will keep us out of sight during the daylight. Not a chance any of our people or any rescue planes are going to come looking for us tonight or in the sunshine tomorrow."

"Hide where?" Jaybird asked. "This is fucking China, remember?"

"We could dig individual holes if we had entrenching tools," Murdock said. "We don't, so that's out."

"Maybe find a briar patch like we did in Lebanon," Jaybird said.

"Wrong kind of vegetation here," Magic said.

"So we keep moving toward the ocean," Murdock said. "Maybe we can luck out and miss the rest of the patrols and get to water in two hours."

"Yeah, maybe," Jaybird said. "Don't count on it."

They formed up in their usual combat order and kept on moving to the south and east. They topped a small rise and Red came back and talked to the L-T.

"We've got something up there, but I'm not sure what it is. Looks like a small village, but it could be an army camp. Seems like a lot of noise for a village."

Murdock went up and took a look. They stared down a gentle slope at lights four hundred yards ahead.

"Yeah" Murdock said, looking through the Starlight scope on Magic's 89 sniper rifle. "Military all right. Take a look. A damned Chinese company or maybe two companies. Must be three hundred men down there."

"So they'll have out security and ambush patrols and the whole damned routine."

"Probably," Murdock said. "We go around them. Which side?" They checked both sides of the quarter-mile-wide camp. On one side they saw a small stream, and on the other a low row of hills slanting down from the ridgeline they had been following.

"Ridge?"

"Yep. Looks like these troops have just been trucked in here or marched in and they're setting up their camp before they sack out for a few hours. Then they come look for us with sunup."

"We better move."

They told the platoon what was ahead of them. The men kept their weapons ready to fire, moved into single file, and took Red Nicholson's lead along the far side of the ridge and, they hoped, past the Chinese.

They hiked silently for ten minutes. Then Red stopped them with two clicks on the mike. Everyone hit the dirt. They waited.

Murdock moved silently forward. Red hovered behind a tree looking ahead.

The Platoon Leader couldn't see a thing through the darkness. Murdock heard one silenced round from Red's CAR-15, then a soft groan and silence. Red darted forward, his K-Bar out in his right hand.

The radio clicked once and Murdock hurried forward. A dead Chinese soldier lay in the trail. Red had just finished relieving him of his AK-47 ammo and rolled him down a small slope.

"Might be some more sentries out here," Red said. "We best move our tails around these puppies in a rush."

The platoon moved faster then, around the Chinese camp and on to the east. Gradually the row of hills became lower and lower until they were in a wide river valley. They saw no river.

Ching checked the stars through the clear night and angled them a little to the right to keep on their easterly route.

"Hope to hell we're going the right direction," Magic Brown growled at Ching.

"You and me both, brother," Ching said, his grin showing in the pale moonlight.

They worked ahead slower now. There were buildings here and there. They were in fields now—rice, row crops, Murdock couldn't figure out what it was. At least there were no flooded rice paddies to wade through.

They found a road and moved along it in a nearly eastern direction. Murdock sniffed trying to see if he could smell the salty tang of ocean air. Nothing.

The sound came from behind them and grew and grew until Murdock hit his mike button twice to put the men on the ground. Overhead two jets slammed past them at no more than three hundred feet. They made a thunderous roar as they flashed past, their jet engines showing that their tails were on fire.

"Chinese SU-27's, probably," Ching said. "Russian-built with 2.3-mach speed. But even at six hundred miles per hour that's ten miles a minute. With seventeen hundred and sixty yards in a mile, times ten, that's seventeen thousand six hundred yards they travel in a minute. Breaking that down in yards per second, the plane is moving over the ground at nearly three hundred yards every second. Not a hell of a lot of time to give close ground support for the Chinese troops."

"Just the idea of the jets being here is not good news for our team," Murdock said. "You sure of those figures?"

"I don't have my calculator with me, but if memory serves, that was a problem in a class I had on aircraft recognition."

"Let's keep moving. What are these buildings?"

"Mostly farms," Ching said. "The farmers live in small villages, then come out to their land to work it during the day. The buildings are for tools, machinery, storing crops. No people in them, usually."

Headlights flared in the night ahead of them. They broke into two groups, faded off the road thirty yards into the fields, and lay down.

Two trucks came by, both military. One had a machine gun mounted on the front with a gunner draped over his weapon. Murdock figured he was sleeping and would be awake the moment the truck stopped. Both rigs kept going down the road.

Ahead and to the right, Murdock made out a new ridge of low hills working generally eastward. He shifted his men that way, leaving the road. They were less than a hundred yards away from the road when they heard someone coming.

There was low chattering in Chinese and some shouts. Murdock's men flattened out in a line that would give them maximum firepower on the targets.

They waited.

Five minutes later the first of the group came in sight. Magic Brown swore softly. "Hold fire," Brown said. "L-T. I got them in the scope. They're civilians. Looks like they're farmers coming out to start a long day's work."

"Hold fire," Murdock said in the mike. They lay there as about twenty men and boys tramped past. They were almost ready to get up and move when another band came behind the first. These were women, Magic Brown informed the SEALs.

It was another five minutes before they could lift up and move toward the low hills.

"We better get out of here damn fast or we're gonna be in the middle of a whole swarm of farmers," Ching said. Murdock agreed, and they double-timed down a path between fields, used a road for a half mile, then cut across a field that led into a smattering of brush and trees that were on the first of the row of hills.

By the time they were inside the trees with enough cover to make Murdock happy, there was less than an hour to sunrise.

"We've got to find someplace to hole up during daylight," Murdock said.

"Like where?" Ron Holt asked.

"So what the hell are we supposed to do?" It was Ronson.

"In those other hills I saw what I thought was a cave,"

Red Nicholson said. "We could look for one around here."

"Yes," Murdock said. "We'll move higher and into the thickest growth of trees we can find. Keep on the lookout for any kind of hiding spot, including caves. Let's go."

They worked higher.

The darkness began to recede. There was a slow lightening of the sky ahead of them in the east.

Murdock didn't want to hide his men behind trees for fourteen hours. The Chinese troops would be all over this area come sunup.

Red touched his shoulder. "Sir, down there, that small valley that leads to the east. See that black area almost at the base of the hill?"

"A cave?"

"I can tell you for sure in about ten minutes."

"Go, Red. Run the whole damn way. It's past time we had these troops out of the hot sun."

Red Nicholson took off at a lope down the hill toward the small valley a quarter of a mile over. Murdock watched him run, then looked at the brightening sky to the east and frowned.

28
Sunday, May 17

0513 hours
Hills near coast
Amoy, China

Murdock checked his watch and then the sky to the east. It was going to be daylight well before 0600 hours. He hoped they would have time. They damn well better have time to go to ground before some Chinese hardcases found them.

He watched Red vanish into some trees, then work through them and come to the spot he had thought might be a cave. Red looked at it, then vanished. He was back in view a minute later, held his rifle over his head with both hands, and pumped it up and down.

"Move it," Murdock snapped. "Red's found our hide-hole. We have about ten minutes to get there and save our fucking SEAL hides."

They jogged and ran down the slope, across a small open place, and into the brush and trees where they had last seen Red. He came out of a hole and grinned.

"We found ourselves a fucking mine tunnel. Not a big one, but big enough and long enough for us to use. Welcome to SEAL House."

Murdock looked at the hole. It *had been* a mine tunnel. Rocks and dirt had fallen around the opening, reducing it to no more than two by three feet. Trees and brush had grown up around it. There was no sign of a road or even a trail leading away from it. Good.

He pushed inside and in the dim light saw the remains of animal droppings, and some small bones, probably from creatures that had been an evening meal for a wolf or a coyote or a fox. Did they have those animals in China? He had no idea.

"Yes, this will work. Everyone get in here and we'll get the place cleaned up a little. Who has the candles?"

Three men brought out candles and lit them. It was surprising how much light they produced in the closed-in area.

"Magic, you and Ronson go out and cut a couple armsful of brush an inch thick and ten feet high and bring it back and plant it in front of our hole so no one can tell it's here. Get back before it gets light. Go."

They hurried out the hole.

"Now, push all the animal shit and bones over into one corner. Then stake out spots and sack out. It's been a long day and we might just not be through with it yet. If any of you have anything to eat, now is the time. No fire, no smoke, no noise." He watched the men settling down along the tunnel. It was eight feet high and about ten feet wide. There were no rail tracks on the floor or any sign that there ever had been.

He moved toward the opening. "I'm going to see if I can find a lookout. No way are we going to be trapped inside here blind and fucked up. Stay here, stay quiet. Jaybird, with me."

They left the hole and checked around them. They could see fifty yards now as the night began to fade into dawn.

"Up to the left," Murdock said. They worked through some trees and light brush to a spot fifty yards above the tunnel. Murdock settled down behind a fallen log. There were trees and brush in front and behind him. There also was a good view of the valley in front of them.

"Good cover and concealment," Jaybird said. "I'll take the first watch. We can get here and back to the tunnel without being seen. Keep your Motorola turned on."

"Right. Come daylight we should be able to see east for

four or five miles. Hope to hell we can see the surf out there somewhere."

They both stared through the half-dawn, but could see no more than a quarter of a mile. They spotted their two woodcutters moving back to the tunnel with branches. By the time Murdock got down to the tunnel, the two men had half the brush jammed into the ground and woven together so it would stand up. It was two feet in front of the opening, and tied in with some other trees and brush to look natural from the front.

Murdock nodded. "Yeah, that will do it. Thanks. Inside now and get some shut-eye. No telling when we'll be up and moving again."

"If it's before dark tonight you can count me out," Magic said. "I'll have my butler take care of it for me."

Ronson took a swing at him, missed, and they stepped into the tunnel.

When Murdock got inside, he found Holt near the opening. He had the SATCOM radio set up and held the dish antenna. Murdock waved at him.

"Yeah, Holt. Good idea. Set up that dish outside the hole. We can work behind the screen out there. About time we check in with Don Stroh and see how he's coming along with our Taipei friends."

Three minutes later, he sent an encrypted message by the burst technique so if the Chinese had radio locators, they wouldn't have time to triangulate on their position.

"This is Afterburner calling Stroh land. Anybody home?"

"Afterburner, we're hot and ready. Only thing is, our friends in Taipei aren't exactly welcoming the idea of helping you."

"They know the whole China plan to take over their island?"

"They do, have for two days."

"Talk tough to them, Stroh. You know the territory here. You know how these people think. Find a handle on them and start yanking it around."

"Love to. If you have any suggestions they will be appreciated. We got through to Langley and they have no help. Right now I'm burning up the telephone trying to find somebody in Taipei I can trust. Will let you know when I learn anything."

"We're in a secure area here. Should be good for the next fourteen to fifteen hours of daylight. By then I hope you have some great news for us. Otherwise all we can do is run for the beach and hope to hell we can find it. Murdock, out."

He gave the handset back to Holt. "Keep the receiver turned on. We should have plenty of battery. They might just try to contact us. Camouflage it somehow so it won't show up in the daylight."

Murdock looked around. It *was* daylight. Only the screen of brush and small trees brought back by his men kept him from being a target for any Chinese soldier looking this way. He stepped through the hole inside and felt a little better.

Lieutenant DeWitt rose up from where he had stretched out on the dry tunnel floor.

"Maybe no news is good news, Skipper. Doc has tended to Fernandez and Frazier. Both are comfortable. Fernandez is the worst hurt. He needs some real medical treatment. If we don't get out of here for two days, he could lose his arm."

"We'll be out of this tunnel and charging for the beach as soon as it gets dark tonight, Lieutenant, I guarantee you that."

Murdock hoped that was true. Guarantees were easy to give. He didn't have the least idea how he was going to make good on his promise.

29

Sunday, May 17

0658 hours
On board the USS *Intrepid*
Taiwan Strait

Don Stroh had long ago stripped off his tie and discarded his suit coat. He had been talking to CIA headquarters in Langley, Virginia. They had exchanged more than a dozen encrypted rapid-burst transmissions via the satellite. He had forgotten what time it was in D.C., but it didn't matter. Nobody slept or ate when a crisis like this was underfoot.

His last message came through from the director:

```
STROH. I WON'T TALK TO THE PRESI-
DENT ABOUT MAKING AN EXCEPTION TO
USE U.S. AIRPOWER TO RESCUE YOUR
TEAM INSIDE CHINA. HE MADE THE
POINT CLEAR. NO CONFRONTATION
WITH CHINA, AND NO USE OF U.S.
ARMS AGAINST CHINA'S LAND MASS OR
HER PEOPLE FOR ANY REASON WHAT-
SOEVER.
    THE ANSWER IS NO. YOU MENTIONED
THE TAIWANESE AIR FORCE. SUGGEST
YOU PURSUE THAT ROUTE. WE KNOW
THAT TIME IS ESSENTIAL. TRY
TAIPEI WITH YOUR PROPOSAL. AS YOU
```

SAID, IT'S THEIR NECKS WE'RE
SAVING. OUT.

Don Stroh read the message again. He'd been staring at
it for ten minutes. What the hell. He'd have to call on every
favor he ever built up in Taiwan when he was stationed there
for three years.

First he used the cellular ability of the electronics on
board the carrier and called the top Agency man in Taipei.
Tom Morton was not pleased to be roused out of bed before
noon. Tom knew about the invasion plans for Taiwan, and
had talked with the President of Taiwan, Lee Teng-hui. Both
of them were up to date on the invasion plans and the U.S.
attempt to thwart them.

"Tom, it's done. The invasion is stopped cold. Now we
need some help to get our team out of China."

"How in hell can I help do that?"

"Talk to Lee. We need some Taiwan air support and a
chopper pickup for our thirteen SEALs. They've been in
firefights in there for the last ten hours."

"Whoa. You want Lee to attack Mother China with his
jets to save the skin of thirteen men? He'd laugh at you.
Thirteen men are nothing. He has millions of men."

"That's your job, Tom. Convince him that these thirteen
men have saved his island more than ten million dead and a
sure takeover by China. Show him that he would have been
dead by now of poison gas if these SEALs hadn't attacked
the missile sites, the bombers, the destroyers, even the
atomic center up north. He damn well *owes these men*."

"Oh, damn. I hate it when you get logical and emotional.
I'll call and try to get to see him this morning. No promise."

"Too late to do a rescue today. We'll try to get them out
to the coast tonight. We'd need his jets for close ground
support and maybe some choppers to go in and get the men
after dark. We don't know where they'll be by that time.
They might even make it to the strait where our people can
pick them up. You've got to try."

"I'll try, I'll try."

"So wake up and make some phone calls. It could take a

day to set up everything. We only have about fourteen hours."

Don Stroh hung up the phone. He was sweating. He hated it when he did that. He used to sweat every time he did something wrong or made a mistake. Now he sweated when he got excited or emotional about some issue or project. He hated that too.

He sent another message, this one to Langley about his move to get to the Taiwanese Air Force to help. He hoped it worked.

He sent a short-burst message to Murdock telling him what he was working on. No way to know if Murdock got the message or not. He might have left the SATCOM on receive only, maybe not. Murdock had probably turned off the radio. Damn.

"Chief, call me immediately if you get any transmissions from Murdock or from Tom Morton," Stroh told the enlisted man in charge of the radio room.

Stroh waited. It was nearly two hours before Morton called back. Both ends of the conversation were encrypted, then turned back into regular speech.

"You trying to get me killed, Stroh? I brought up the idea of using a pair of jet fighters and a chopper to go in and rescue the guys who saved their whole damn country, and President Lee blew his stack. He said that would be risking war with China. I pointed out that China had already declared war on Taiwan, had actively tried to murder ten million of his people. He threw me out of the place. Had his guards lift me up and carry me out to the fucking street."

"Lee is a show-off. Go right back in there and remind him of the plans he's seen for the invasion of Taiwan. Remind him that sixteen U.S. Navy SEALs have saved his fucking ass. Then tell him he owes us this much. Three aircraft against ten million of his people? Sounds like a damn good business deal to me. Get back in there and make him understand."

Morton swore for two minutes, then gave up. "Okay, okay. I'll give it another try. I can't promise anything. I did give him golf lessons for two months. Every fucking morning. Maybe I can play on that somehow. You never know what's going to work with these goddamned presidents."

Don Stroh told him good-bye and hung up the hand set. Stroh paced the commo room. He stared at the radios and all the communications gear. None of it did him any good unless it talked to him. He had been thinking about asking the U.S. President to call Lee Teng-hui. Chat with him President-to-President.

Stroh pounded his fist into his palm. Nothing to lose. Give it a try.

He sent an encrypted message through directly to the President requesting an urgent talk about the Taiwan situation. He had no way of knowing if the President would respond or not. He checked the time. It was 9:30 A.M. in Taiwan. D.C. was thirteen hours behind them. That would make it 8:30 P.M. yesterday in the Capital. At least it wasn't the middle of the night.

Now all he had to do was sit around and hope that the President thought this incident important enough to call him back about it.

30

Sunday, May 17

0935 hours
On board the USS *Intrepid*
Taiwan Strait

Don Stroh sat in the communications room of the giant carrier and held his head in his hands. He had sent the message directly to the President at 0930. It was logged. How long should he wait hoping there might be an answer? An hour? Two hours? Six hours? He heard one of the machines chattering. Something was always chirping away in the commo room.

Someone tapped his shoulder. He looked up.

"Mr. Stroh. A message for you, from the White House."

Stroh leaped up and knocked over the chair he sat in.

"No shit?"

"Honest, sir. Right over here."

It was coming off the encrypting machine. Stroh read the print out.

```
PRESIDENT    VITALLY    CONCERNED
ABOUT    THE    THIRTEEN    SEALS    IN
CHINA.   HE'S   TALKING   WITH   HIS
ADVISORS.  MAKE  YOURSELF  AVAIL-
ABLE AT 1000 HOURS YOUR TIME FOR
DIRECT TALK WITH THE PRESIDENT.
STANDING BY.
```

Stroh looked at the sailor, who had a big grin.

"That's it?"

"No, sir. The President himself will talk to you on a handset directly at ten hundred. That's about twenty-two minutes from now, sir."

"Yes, yes. Thanks." Stroh looked at a pad and ballpoint pen on the desk. He righted the chair and sat and put down in order what had happened, where the SEALs were, and what could be done if the Taiwanese Air Force would do it, if the Taiwan President ordered them to. He thought he was ready. He had met the U.S. President twice, but he was sure the man wouldn't remember him. Damn, what else should he be doing? He didn't know. He felt drained, used up, as limp as yesterday's washcloth.

He'd close his eyes for just a minute. He leaned back in the chair and tried to relax. Just for a minute he'd rest his eyes and then he'd go over his list for the President.

Someone touched his shoulder again.

"Mr. Stroh. Mr. Stroh. The President is on the line for you."

Stroh came out of the chair, barely avoiding a tip-over, and went to the console the sailor directed him to.

He picked up the handset. "Yes, Mr. President, this is Don Stroh."

"Mr. Stroh. Good to talk with you again. How did your wife do in that art exhibit she was having? Sorry I didn't get there. Maybe next time. Now about those SEALs."

"We have thirteen inside China, sir. Right now they are about four to five miles from the coast east and south of Amoy. They have singlehandedly prevented the invasion of Taiwan by the Chinese. I understand you have prohibited any U.S. airpower to go to these men's aid."

"Yes, that would provoke an incident that could be far reaching. We just can't risk that if there's any other way."

"There may be, Mr. President. What about the Taiwanese Air Force? We helped build it, supplied them for years. Our men have just prevented up to ten million deaths on the island. I'd say they owe us. Could you call the President of Taiwan and ask him to help us? We'd need two jets for nighttime close ground support and maybe a chopper for an extraction of the thirteen men."

There was a moment of silence. Don Stroh's eyes went wide as he waited.

"Yes, that seems like a fair request. What time is it there?"

"Just after ten A.M. sir."

"I've talked with Lee Teng-hui before. Yes, I'll get right on it. I'll call you back one way or the other. Yes, Stroh, good idea. They owe us, and we owe those SEALs to get them out of there. They've done a tremendous deed for Taiwan. I'm going to make sure that Lee appreciates that. You stand by, Stroh. I'll be back in touch with you."

"Will do, Mr. President. Thank you."

They signed off, and Stroh leaned back in the chair and mopped sweat off his forehead.

The sailor came up.

"Mr. Stroh. We have a printout of that conversation if you need one for your files."

"Yes, thank you. He's going to call the Taiwan President. Isn't that great?"

Stroh thought of something else then. The President had remembered him. He'd asked about Barbara's art exhibit. He did remember. What a man. That does it, Stroh decided. If the man ran for President again, he had the Stroh family vote.

Saturday, May 16

2118 hours
Oval Office, White House
Washington, D.C.

William Hawthorne, President of the United States, picked up the red phone in his office, his face a little on the grim side. "Mr. President, Hawthorne here. It's good to talk to you again."

"President Hawthorne, I am pleased to speak with you and to thank you and your countrymen for their invaluable aid to Taiwan." President Lee was proud of his command of English and never used a translator with the Americans.

"Good, good, Mr. President. Since we talked two days ago, the threat to Taiwan has been beaten back and, we think, eliminated. We have one small problem."

"What's that, Mr. President?"

"The small band of fighters that has prevented this attack and invasion of Taiwan is still in Mainland China and in extreme danger. We need the help of some of your military aircraft to aid them."

"Us attack China? That, sir, is not possible. We are a small beetle here beside a giant who can squash us at any time it chooses. We can do nothing to irritate the beast."

"Mr. President. These thirteen men have saved the island of Taiwan. They have saved the lives of up to ten million of your people. They have prevented massive destruction of your armed forces and the deaths of most of your military personnel. We think that you owe these men a great deal."

"That may be true, but to send our warplanes into China . . . it could provoke all kinds of retaliation."

"If it were done at night, China wouldn't know what aircraft they were. They would have no way of determining who had entered their airspace. You have been violated. It is perfectly natural for you to respond in kind."

"Yes, I understand your thinking, Mr. President. Is there a time factor?"

"Our men are safe for the daylight hours. It's morning there, as I understand it. By nightfall we would hope that there could be some rescue attempt or at least some jets for close ground support to help these SEALs stay alive."

"Mr. President, I will talk with my cabinet and my military leaders. I will convey your viewpoint and your suggestion. I must have agreement here before I can do anything. I will let you know what my people decide within eight hours."

"Thank you, Mr. President. We have done all we could to help continue the existence of Taiwan. We hope that now you can repay that assistance with some aid of your own so we can rescue these thirteen heroes now trapped in Mainland China."

"Yes, Mr. President. I understand. Thank you and good-bye."

The U.S. President put down the handset and frowned. He had no idea which way President Lee Teng-hui would go. He was a politician, a skilled one, and he would act in accord with what was best for his career and then best for Taiwan. It was a toss-up. The President rubbed his hand over his face.

One of his aides came in reminding him about a reception he was due to attend. He sighed and stood. He wondered if those thirteen SEALs in China would be dying while he smiled and made polite conversation at some damned reception. He wished that he knew one way or the other.

31

Sunday, May 17

0824 hours
Old mine tunnel
Near Amoy, China

Murdock had sat at the mouth of the mine tunnel and watched day come to China. It was the first time he'd seen it—and, he hoped, the last. He stared out through the concealment of the brush in front of the opening. He could see what he figured was five miles to the east. There was no sign of the Taiwan Strait. How far were they from the water?

He wished he could push aside the ground mist and some haze as the day brightened. Some of it would burn off or blow away. Maybe then he could see the strait shimmering to the east.

Now he concentrated on the mission at hand. He had his men safe for the time being. He had spotted no military traffic below. Jaybird up in the lookout had seen nothing to alarm them. Only one truck had been spotted, and it had appeared to be a farm vehicle of some kind. It had driven into the valley about three miles out and stopped at a pair of low buildings.

Murdock wished he had a 20-power scope. Usually a SEAL had little use for one, but right now in this ground war phase of the mission, a long-range scope would be handy. As he watched, he saw a three-truck convoy roll from the left side of his view into the middle of the valley and stop. He could see figures leaving the trucks. They seemed to be talking about something. Then they all got back in the rigs and drove away past the rest of the valley and out of sight to the north.

The SEALs' luck was holding so far. All they needed was another ten hours of good fortune and they could head for the beach.

Two hours later, Murdock called Jaybird.

"Nothing doing, Skipper. All quiet out in front."

"Good. I'm sending Red up to replace you. Time for some shut-eye for you. He'll be up directly. Nothing new on the big radio so we don't know about any help coming."

Red woke up when Murdock shook his shoulder. He came awake at once ready for action. No warmup required.

"Yeah?"

"Take the lookout from Jaybird. I'll show you where it is. Keep your Motorola on and your eyes open. If we get any visitors who look like they will overrun this spot, get your ass back down here without being seen."

Red nodded and headed up the hill to where Murdock pointed.

Jaybird came back, waved at Murdock, and sacked out. Murdock called DeWitt over.

"You had any sleep?"

"Some."

"Good. My turn. If I'm out more than three hours, wake me. If any troops head this way, give me a yell. I'm due for a nap."

DeWitt said he'd handle it, and went to the front to look out at the valley.

It was almost 1400 when DeWitt awoke Murdock.

"We got some company. Not sure how far they'll come this direction. Near as I can tell, there's about a hundred of them. A Chinese infantry company maybe."

Murdock came to his feet at once and went to the front of the tunnel.

At least a hundred, he decided as he watched the line of green-clad figures working slowly up the valley. They were spread thin over the mile-wide opening, but it was narrowing as they came forward. He saw four big trucks a mile behind the figures. They must be rushing men to every possible spot where the enemy could be and letting them sweep forward. Bad news.

The troops looked to be doing a good search job, poking into piles of brush and growth, checking out trees and the one building in the area below. They were still two miles away, but there was no indication they might stop their search.

"What do you think, Skipper?" DeWitt asked.

"Same as you. We wait and see how far they come. If they get here we hope to hell they don't find the opening to this tunnel. If they do we're fish in a barrel."

"But the odds are better staying in here than trying to run for it," DeWitt said.

"Agreed. We've used our skill and talents up to this point. Now we have to sit back and see how our luck is running. We win or lose on one throw of the fucking Chinese dice."

Murdock touched his throat mike. "Red, you still there?"

"That's a Roger."

"Better get your butt down here. Try not to leave any tracks, especially around the entrance. Want to have all of our chicks in one basket here."

"I'm moving. Over a hundred of them soldiers out there. Hope we don't need to tangle with them."

Both the officers watched the Chinese move ahead slowly. They were in a long line of skirmishers. The SEALs could see now that the men had their rifles slung over their shoulders with the muzzles down. They were out on a hike.

They came closer.

Twenty minutes later they were within a half mile of the tunnel. The opening had narrowed as they came up the valley. Murdock counted again and saw no more than fifty troops. Half of them must have split off and taken the valley next to this one. Good. Fifty was a hell of a lot better than a hundred.

Red joined Murdock and DeWitt inside the tunnel.

"Red, wake everyone up and get them ready to travel,"

Murdock said. "All gear stowed, everything set for a firefight. Check all weapons and have them locked and loaded."

"We busting out of here, L-T?"

"If we have to. Odds aren't so bad now, maybe four to one. I want the MP-5 guys first, then the CARs, and the heavy stuff behind."

Jaybird came up rubbing his eyes. "I sleep that long?"

"No, you're still dreaming. Take a look out front."

Jaybird did, then leaned back in. "Less than a quarter of a mile. They gonna make us in here?"

"Hope not. If they do, we crash out of here with the MP-5s chattering and head to the side, across the slant of the hill. See those trees over there maybe eighty yards? We'll make a stand there until we can bug out."

"Bug out?" DeWitt said. "I haven't heard that term for twenty years."

"It still works." Murdock went back to the front of the tunnel and stared through the branches of their handmade blind. The Chinese were closer now. They didn't seem dedicated to their search. He could hear some bantering and laughter. Now and then a sharp command came from someone, but soon the talking started again.

Directly ahead of the tunnel, he saw six Chinese soldiers working their search. They probed into heavy brush, trampled some down, checked a small stream that splashed by.

They worked closer.

Someone yelled at them and they stopped and looked left and right. They were ahead of the line. They waited.

Murdock motioned Jaybird up with his MP-5. With hand signals he told Jaybird to take the left three and he had the right three. The soldiers were still a hundred feet away.

The platoon leader knew that he and Jaybird could waste these six and the rest of the Chinese wouldn't know it for a while. Then they could find the gap and close in and it would be a tough fight. If they hit the six, they would have to be in the process of moving out fast.

They could hear the six men talking now. Murdock

signaled Ching to come up. He listened, but shook his head. "A word here and there. They're too far away."

The three men watched as the soldiers moved closer. Murdock aimed at the three on his side and waited. Sweat popped out on his forehead. He hated waiting. All his years in the Navy had never taught him patience. He remembered the prayer his mother had told him once. "Lord please grant me patience—and do it right now!"

The Chinese were within fifty feet now, and Ching nodded. "They're talking about a leave they went on. Many girls, much wine, and plenty of food."

"Fucking big help," Jaybird said.

Now the soldiers looked left and right and slowed.

Murdock squirmed where he sat looking out from the hole. The Chinese moved again. Now they were within twenty feet of the blind made of cut-off branches rammed into the ground. If they hit it with their rifles, the whole thing might fall down revealing the tunnel.

The Chinese chattered again and Ching nodded. Then one of them held up his hand and the talk stopped. He looked to the left. The soldier laughed and waved at his buddies. He said something and they all cheered.

Murdock looked at Ching.

"Break time," Ching said. "They have a ten-minute rest period and can drink water if they have any."

The six men looked around, then walked forward to within six feet of the blind and sat down in the shade.

Murdock signaled Jaybird to move back. He and Ching sat near the opening watching the Chinese. They drank from canteens, laughed, and talked.

Ching listened, but couldn't even whisper what they were saying. They were so close Murdock could smell their sweat. He looked at his watch. Ten minutes would be an eternity. Then where would the six Chinese soldiers go? If they found the blind and the entrance to the tunnel, it would be time for the SEALs to shoot their way out and get over to that patch of thicker trees. He'd lose some men, he knew. There were just too many Chinese out there.

They waited.

Murdock held up five fingers. Ching nodded.

After nine minutes on Murdock's watch, the Chinese soldier evidently in charge of the others stood, yawned, and stretched. He said something and the others stood. They talked back at him, and he shouted something and they quieted. He waved, and they began walking away from the blind.

Murdock looked at Ching. When the soldiers were twenty feet away he whispered. "He said they were moving back to the trucks. The search here was over."

Murdock took his finger off the trigger of his room broom. It was over for the moment.

Ed DeWitt came up and looked out. He nodded. "About time we got a little good luck for a change. Where will they go when they get in the trucks?"

"They said something about getting back to the trucks and moving down four kilometers," Ching said. "Damn glad they closed off the search right there."

"Anybody who wants to sleep can sack out," Murdock said. "We'll have a long night of it, so better get some rest while you can. Frazier, you'll be on the lookout as soon as it's safe to take a hike up there."

Murdock looked around until he spotted Red Nicholson. "How you doing, sailor?"

"Good. I'm good. What do you need?"

"Soon as it's safe to leave, want you and Magic to go up and over this mountain and see what's on the other side. Also hope you can see the water out to the east."

"Will do."

Ed DeWitt called to Murdock from the opening. "Better come see this."

Murdock bent down and looked out just in time to see two jet fighters go roaring across the valley not more than five hundred feet off the ground.

"The Russian-built jets are back," Murdock said. "Now I wonder what those Chinese are up to this time."

32

Sunday, May 17

1520 hours
Old mine tunnel
Near Amoy, China

The two sleek SU-27 jet fighters made one more low pass over the valley as if they were trying to see how low they could come to the ground, then pulled up and vanished.

"Playing games," DeWitt said. "Probably don't let them fly them all that much, it gets expensive, so they play around when their leash is cut."

"Wouldn't care if they stay away," Murdock said.

It was twenty-five minutes more before the trucks in the valley below pulled out with their Chinese soldiers. Then Red and Magic took their weapons, added more camo streaks to their faces, and headed up the hill.

"Check it out and come back," Murdock told them. "Don't get into a firefight with anybody. We don't want our Chinese brethren to know where we are."

Less than half an hour after the two men left to scout the new route, Jaybird called from the tunnel entrance.

"Might want to check this out, L-T."

Murdock looked down the valley and saw a formation of six medium-sized choppers churning along. Then they turned and the formation fell apart a little as they came straight up the valley toward the tunnel.

"They could be real trouble if they have even ten troops each," Jaybird said.

"Big trouble."

They kept watching, and soon the birds wheeled to the left, did a 360, and headed back the way they had come. A minute later they were out of sight.

"Now what the hell was that all about?" DeWitt asked. "Were they ready to drop off troops to sweep this area?"

"Maybe they got some radio message that this one had been covered and they moved on to another zone," Murdock said. "It's good to remember they have that kind of mobility. They can get troops in faster and where trucks can't go. Which is bad news for us bears."

"I saw that movie," Jaybird said. *"The Bad News Bears."*

"Let's talk," DeWitt said. Murdock and Jaybird settled down near the entrance. "Our main objective is to get to the fucking coast where we can get wet and hope for a U.S. Navy pickup. How do we accomplish that?"

Jaybird shrugged. "Hell, we move east. We move silent at night and not get in any more firefights."

Murdock shook his head. "Ideal but impossible with all of the troops and equipment they have blocking us. We're going to have to go through one of these major units sooner or later to get our asses into the water. I hope it's later when we're on the coast road down there."

"There's a coast road?" DeWitt asked.

"My make-believe map doesn't show it, but there must be a coast road."

"So, just before we hit the water, we use the SATCOM and let Uncle know about where we are and that we want a pickup, and then we start swimming," Jaybird said.

"Without our rebreathers and our fins," Murdock said. "So we don't count on any five-mile swims."

"Don't forget, we've got two wounded," DeWitt said.

"We swim at the pace of our slowest man," Murdock said.

"So, how do we get to the coast?" Jaybird asked.

"I hope Red and Magic can tell us where the fuck it is," Murdock said. "That will help. Then we look over the terrain and make our plans."

"What about our ammo supply?" DeWitt asked.

"Jaybird, make a survey. Find out what ammo every man has left including for the AK-47's."

Murdock tried to remember the sketch maps they had seen of the China coast. He knew they had traveled south some, but mostly west to get away from Amoy. Then they had switched to a southern and easterly route, and now he wasn't sure where the hell they were. Maybe ten klicks from Amoy. But just where the Taiwan Strait was, he couldn't be sure.

Jaybird came back with the report. He'd written it all down in his ever-present notebook, a three-by-five-inch number with a spiral bind on the top. He was never without it.

He gave a rundown. The gist of it was that the men had about half of their ammo left. They had six AK-47's in good working order, had thrown away two that jammed. There were about seventy-five rounds for each of the 47's. Murdock had three magazines for his MP-5, and so did DeWitt. Murdock had an AK-47 as well.

"So, we can punish anybody who gets in our way," Murdock said. "Just which way are we heading?"

Ten minutes later Red and Magic came back. Red was laughing.

"Hell, we been going east all the time. We need to swing southeast. We could see the sun off the water out there. Must be six, maybe seven klicks. Quite a few small hills between us and Mother Water."

Magic got in his say. "Just over the top of the hill toward the south is another valley. Sweeps down maybe two miles. Didn't see nothing in it. No buildings, no people, no army, choppers, trucks, just nada."

"So, looks like we head south and east," Murdock said. "What time is it?"

Jaybird told him. "Almost 1700."

"Be dark in two hours. We move out of here then. Catch a quick nap or blow your nose. Tell the guys we'll be leaving combat ready at 1900."

Two hours later, just before they left, Murdock told them everything he knew.

"We've got water southeast maybe five to seven klicks. That's our route. I'll be dark soon and we should be safe in these woods until then. Usual formation. No firing unless directed. We want to sneak and creep through here so the Chinese don't know where we are and zero in on us again."

They filed out of the tunnel in combat formation. Red led out as point man with Murdock and Holt coming behind. They spread out to five-yard intervals and moved up the hill.

Then minutes later Red sprawled in the grass and weeds looking over the brow of the hill. Murdock went down beside him.

"Anything?"

"Not a fucking thing moving down there. Be totally dark in ten. We wait or go on down?"

Murdock studied the area. There could be troops on both sides of the valley. They could walk into a cross fire.

"We wait for full dark. It looks too easy down there."

When they walked through the valley later, they ran into no opposition. It was empty and quiet.

They were almost at the end of the valley, where it opened on a larger flat area and slanted slightly to the east, when Red gave two clicks on the radio. Everyone hit the dirt. Red came back to Murdock.

"Company up front. Not sure how many. Sounded like a squad, maybe more. I smelled a fire. Might be cooking."

"Let's take a closer look," Murdock said. They worked up slowly, crawling the last twenty yards so they could see. They found two small cooking fires and ten soldiers crowded around. There was no attempt made at security, no effort to hold down noise or light from the fire. Why should they? This was their home turf.

The two SEALs crawled out of hearing range and then hurried back to the platoon. Murdock briefed them and sent the Second Squad to the left. He and the First Squad took the right. They formed in two lines at right angles to each other on the back side of the camp. It gave a cross fire with no danger of hitting friendly flesh.

Murdock gave the Second Squad five minutes to get in position and clear fields of fire. Then he leveled in with his

AK-47 from forty yards out and fired. A soldier standing near the fire went down with a round through his chest. The rest of the SEALs opened up as well.

Murdock saw a second man near the fire take a round in the chest, and another in the head and pitch into the dirt. The soldiers scrambled for cover and their weapons. Only one shot was fired at the SEALs. Two Chinese caught rounds in their backs as they turned and tried to run out of the firelight.

The others huddled under any cover they could find. But cover from one side left them open to fire from the other side.

Thirty seconds after his first shot, Murdock hit his mike three times, a cease-fire order.

The weapons went silent. Murdock and his men moved up cautiously. One Chinese lifted up and fired a machine pistol. He missed the SEAL closest to him. Ron Holt fired his shotgun and the double-aught buck nearly cut off the soldier's head.

Seven of the ten Chinese lay dead on the ground. Nobody had shot at the fire. Jaybird checked the food. There was one large pot filled with rice that had cooked and was cooling.

"Hey, L-T," Doc called. "Look at this. A pair of chickens roasted to a turn. Anybody want to share?"

They tore the chicken apart while it was still hot and licked their fingers when it was gone. Some of the men dug into the rice. They found some hard biscuits of some kind, but passed on them.

"Ammo," Murdock said. "Find any AK-47 magazines you can. We might need them."

They reported fourteen magazines, and distributed them to the men with the AK-47's.

They moved out quickly, aware that their fire and the three men who got away would be spreading the word. Somebody would be on their tail again.

Soon they came to a small stream. "Canteens," Murdock said. "Put the pills in them and let's keep moving." They filled their canteens, added the Halazone tablets, and marched down the valley. It felt better now. They knew where they were

going. They had seen water. Above all else they wanted to
return to the sea from which they had emerged.

Murdock came up to Red twenty minutes later. He stood
beside a dirt road waiting for the rest of them. The road
angled to the right again.

"This angle should put us right back moving southeast,"
Red said. "Do we risk the road?"

"Damn right," Murdock said. "Maybe we can make better
time and get to the water. Keep us moving."

They did make better time for twenty minutes. Then
feeble headlights showed in front of them. Murdock used
the radio to get everyone off the road into the dry ditches.
He and Jaybird lay in the ditch waiting. When the truck
came close enough to see, they could tell it was an older
civilian rig. Murdock ran into the middle of the road holding
his AK-47 over his head. A sequel of brakes sounded and
the old rig shuddered to a stop and the engine stalled.

Jaybird ran up to the driver's side of the rig and jerked the
Chinese out of the seat. He stumbled and fell, and when he
hit the dirt two rounds from Jaybird's MP-5 tore into his
chest.

Ross Lincoln ran up and checked the dashboard. He
found a switch and hit it and the stalled engine turned over,
fired, and caught. It was a farm truck with a stake body on
it.

Murdock looked in back. There were two bales of hay
and some cans and a heavy tarp. They shoved off everything
except the tarp off and the men climbed in.

"This thing is older than I am," Murdock said. Lincoln
drove, and Murdock and Ching rode in the front seat.

They turned the truck around and drove south.

"Bound to be a village here somewhere," Ching said.
"This isn't a bad road for rural China."

Murdock stopped the truck. "Is that tarp big enough to
cover all you bravehearts?" he asked. They opened it up and
tried. It would work. "If we need it, cover up everyone. May
be a village up ahead."

They drove for ten minutes at the outrageous speed of

thirty miles an hour. That was as far ahead as Lincoln could see the road with the faint headlamps.

Around a corner they saw lights ahead.

"A village," Ching said.

"Ching, you drive. Lincoln and I'll be in back. You might run into somebody we don't want to see in this little town. Play it cool as you can. If we have to, we'll shoot and scoot."

They got in back and tucked the tarp around all the SEALs. Murdock was at the driver side with his MP-5 ready and a good-sized hole in the front of the tarp that he could see through.

The village was little more than a collection of thirty or forty houses and a few stores closed for the night. They were almost through the town when a figure walked into the headlights and held up his hand. The man had a pistol on his belt and a garrison-type cap which Murdock guessed made him a local policeman.

Ching stopped the truck and the policeman walked out of the lights and up to the side of the rig.

Ching called a greeting to the man as he came up. The cop didn't answer, and tried to look inside the cab in the faint light. Murdock was sure the man could see little.

The policeman barked something at Ching in Chinese.

Murdock lifted the MP-5 muzzle until it centered on the policeman's back and eased his finger to the trigger.

33

Sunday, May 17

President Lee Teng-hui put the call on his phone speaker and nodded at his advisors. Not all spoke English, but an interpreter was there to translate as the call proceeded.

"Yes, Mr. President Hawthorne. It is good to speak with you again."

"Mr. President Lee, I'm glad you called back. How is our project going to rescue those thirteen Navy SEALs?"

"We are in a quandary, Mr. President. We have heard rumors about some attacks on the mainland, but we have no proof. You say a number of airplanes and missiles were destroyed."

"Absolutely, Mr. President. I'll fax you satellite photographs we took less than two hours ago that show over forty paratroop aircraft that were totally destroyed and two missile warehouses that were ruined or disabled. You can also see two warships that would deliver the poison gas missiles are sunk in the mud in Amoy harbor."

The interpreter listened and talked at the same time. He hurried to catch up with the English conversation.

Lee hesitated, watching his interpreter. "Yes, Mr. President, I would like to see definite proof. Not that we do not believe you. My cabinet is most strict in matters like this that could open us to furious retaliation by China."

"I figured you might be a little slow to come around," President Hawthorne said. "When you get these pictures I'm sure you'll see that these lads have saved your island from attack, invasion, and a terrible loss of life that would be in the millions."

"We will study the fax material carefully."

"Yes. I've had word just now that the photos have been faxed to you and should be coming off your machine any second now. Isn't this modern-day communication wonderful? Do you have the pictures yet?"

"No. I'll send someone to our communications room to check. My staff and cabinet members are all here. We will confer on the situation and let you know what we decide."

"Can't stress it enough, President Lee. We here in the U.S. would be terribly disappointed if you don't try your damnedest to get our boys out of China over there by Amoy."

"Thank you, President Hawthorne. You will be hearing from us. We understand that time is short. You will hear. Good-bye for now."

Lee broke the connection and stared at his staff and cabinet. The door behind them opened and a man rushed in with six sheets of paper. He laid them out on the President's desk. They were the faxes the U.S. President had sent.

At once the President and his people studied the photos.

"Can these be real photos of China?" the Minister of Foreign Affairs asked.

"Oh, yes, they have the satellites, the capability," the Minister of Defense said. "They would not send fake photos. It's Amoy Bay in this photo, and look at one part of the naval yard area that is totally flattened."

The rest of the men crowded around to study the photos.

President Lee Teng-hui sat back in his chair and watched his advisors. No matter what they said, it was up to him to make the final decisions. He frowned at the photos on his desk and heaved a long sigh.

34

Sunday, May 17

1945 hours
Small village
Near Amoy, China

Murdock's finger eased on the trigger as the Chinese cop's tone became less formal. He chatted with Ching for a moment through the open window of the farm truck. Then both men laughed. After a little more talk, the policeman stepped back and waved.

Murdock saw him through the faint light and let out a breath he hadn't known he'd been holding. Ching shifted the truck into gear and pulled slowly away from the spot where the cop stood beside the road watching the rig. It took only two or three minutes rolling down the main street of the tiny village before they were through it and back in the countryside. Their travel direction was roughly southeast, heading for the coast.

The road continued flat and straight. Murdock wanted to get back in the front seat, but he made no move. Don't change things when we're winning, he told himself.

Ten minutes and maybe four miles down the road later, Ching yelled that there were lights showing.

"Looks like headlights, L-T," Ching said. "That could mean a roadblock. What the hell are we supposed to do?"

"Cut our lights and keep moving," Murdock said. "Might be another farm truck."

They continued down the road for another quarter of a mile. Then they heard rifle shots ahead and sensed hot lead slugs zinging around them. Nobody was hit.

"That cop must have called ahead," Ching shouted. "Didn't really trust him, but he did let us go. Curfew along here at night, the cop told me. Nobody in a vehicle on the road after dark."

"Stop this thing," Murdock called. "Everyone out and in the ditch on both sides fast."

As the others scattered, he talked to Ching at the driver's-side door. "Keep it running. We'll tie down the steering wheel and put a stick on the accelerator to keep it running and head it straight down the road with the lights on. We hit the ditch and hope that the truck keeps their attention."

It worked to a degree, Murdock thought as he watched the truck roll down the road toward the barricade ahead. The rig stayed on the road for two hundred yards, then angled into the ditch on the left side and stalled. Moments after it stopped, Murdock saw something fired from the roadblock. He guessed it was a rocket-propelled grenade.

The grenade hit the truck and it exploded into a mass of flames as the fuel tank blew. The SEALs had gone to ground in the ditch.

"What now, L-T?" Jaybird asked from where he lay in the weeds watching the truck burn.

"They know where we are by now. We better take out the roadblock and keep moving southeast," Murdock said. "One squad on each side of the road for a small cross fire."

"We can use the fields as cover to get up there," DeWitt said. "I'll take the left and pull my men around the far side. You take the near side and we'll squeeze them."

"Sounds good," Murdock said. "No noise. Let's move."

They were almost opposite where the burning truck still smoldered when Jaybird spotted a four-man detail moving up the road toward the truck. Murdock gave a signal to ignore them, and the SEALs kept working silently forward through the fields toward the roadblock.

The headlights still illuminated the barricade. They could

see men now and then in back of the three small utility
vehicles that were parked there.

"They ain't expecting us," Jaybird whispered to Murdock, who only nodded. True, they looked like they were on
garrison duty or on a night training run. They'd get some
first-class instruction in how not to be a soldier tonight.

The First Squad settled into firing positions fifty yards
away from the trucks. Murdock looked at his watch and
waited. Soon he heard a single click on his radio earpiece.
DeWitt and his squad were ready.

Murdock nodded at Jaybird through the Chinese night
and sighted in with his AK-47. His first unsilenced round
sounded like a cannon shot in the quietness of the countryside. It brought the immediate crashing and belching of
twelve other firearms as the rest of the SEALs opened fire
on his signal shot. Murdock watched his target jolt backwards from where he had been leaning against the first
jeeplike rig.

The AKs and the other long guns blasted again and again.
Half the Chinese troops were down and dead on the first
volley, and another thirty seconds of gunfire flattened the
rest of them. Murdock saw one man limp away into the
darkness.

Murdock gave three clicks on his mike and the shooting
stopped. There had been no return fire at all from the
Chinese. He didn't worry about the four who had gone up to
the burning truck. They would not be a problem.

Murdock watched the death scene for half a minute, then
touched his lip mike.

"Let's move in. If any of those jeep rigs are working we
can take another ride."

Murdock ran toward the roadblock with the other SEALs.
There were no live defenders. Lincoln tried all three of the
utility rigs. He got two of them running. The thirteen men
piled in and they moved down the road, southeast again.

"With any luck we could be at the coast in half an hour,"
Jaybird shouted to Murdock where they rode in the back of
the first rig.

"Good luck has been in short supply around here, Jaybird. We'll see how far it holds on this go-round."

Two miles from the roadblock one of the rigs sputtered and ground to a halt.

"Out of gas," Lincoln said. The men crowded onto the other little truck. Two rode on the hood. Two more clung to the sides with one foot for purchase. They slowed down and kept the lights off.

Another five minutes and they came around a small bend and spotted bright lights ahead.

Murdock checked it out through the Starlight scope on the M-89.

"They have a real one this time." Murdock said. "Looks like two tanks, four six-bys, and maybe fifty troops."

"I move we go around this one," DeWitt said.

"Amen," Magic Brown said.

"One of those tanks is moving its turret around to fire," Murdock said, shoving the weapon at Magic. "He can see us. Let's haul ass out of here."

The men piled off the rig and scattered into the field to the left, which had some small brush and a few trees. Doc Ellsworth had just cleared the ditch and run for the trees when a round from the tank slammed into the jeep. It smashed it ten feet back down the road when it hit, but the fuel tank didn't explode.

"Move it," Murdock called. "Those troops won't sit on their hands down there. We've got about a half-mile head start. Let's make it pay off for us."

Before Murdock stopped talking they were taking small-arms fire. The shots were random, and Murdock figured the Chinese were blanketing the whole area hoping to get some return fire that would pinpoint the enemy.

"Move it," Murdock said again. "Straight away from that tank, and then we'll figure out how to get southeast again."

They jogged away from the tank and kept getting an occasional round from behind. Murdock was sure the Chinese didn't know where they were. He wasn't about to give them any clues.

Five minutes later they slowed it to a walk. They passed

a dark building on the edge of a field. Ching said it was a storehouse for the farmland they were going through. They charged through another field and into a blessed grove of trees on a rocky hillside.

Murdock could hear someone behind them. The locals had enough troops that they could have detailed a dozen to take four different directions and try to chase down the enemy. Might work. Any firefight would bring the rest of the Chinese troops in to help and hopefully wipe out the foreign devils. Only, they didn't know who the enemy was. They probably thought the most likely attackers would be the Taiwanese.

Murdock put his men through the trees and came out on the other side near the backside of a village. They hurried along in the field just beyond the houses. He could hear music playing in some of the buildings. Lights showed in most of them. It wasn't even nine o'clock yet. There were lots of people up and moving around. He hoped they didn't run into any kids playing in the fields.

The jogged again. Now they turned south hoping to find the elusive coast of the Taiwan Strait. It had to be over there somewhere.

Five minutes later Murdock heard the Chinese behind them. Evidently this group of hunters had hit the village and turned south as well. Half may have gone north and the other half south. In either case, Murdock knew his men couldn't afford a fight right now that would bring in the rest of the troops.

"Could be some of the Chinese Marines back there," Ching said. He had heard the pursuit as well. "The Marines are the best fighting troops the Chinese Mainland guys have."

"More good luck for our side," Murdock said.

They soon came away from the village into open fields, and then a good-sized hill loomed out of the darkness in front of them.

"Let's go up," Murdock said. He had been rethinking his strategy. As long as the Chinese pursued them, they had to keep running. If they stopped and got into a firefight, it might pull in more troops. Then again, they were now about five miles from the roadblock and the tanks. It could be another sector and there might be no added response. He wanted to shake off the tail.

The hill might do it. The troops behind might be following them with some kind of nightscopes. The Chinese must have brought some. The tracking had been sure so far. If they came up the hill, it would give the SEALs a chance. Murdock moved to the front of the line of men with Red, and together they selected the spot on the ridgeline. The hill was maybe two hundred feet high, with some shrubs and small trees, but not enough for cover and no concealment. Even in the half light of the moon they could see movement on the slope below.

Murdock placed his men along the downslope of the ridge so they could fire over it from a prone position. He set up his machine guns just off center twenty yards, and put the sniper rifles between them. The rest who had long guns spread out on both sides. The Kalashnikovs would come in handy. They could pinpoint the targets fifty yards down the hill in the moonlight.

Murdock brought up his AK-47, chambered a round, aimed the weapon downhill, and waited. The others would hold for his first round before they fired. Murdock had twenty rounds for the AK. When his ammo was gone he'd dump the rifle.

The Chinese came up the hill slowly. There were two point men, but they were doing it wrong. The point scouts should be out at least a hundred yards. These were ten yards ahead. Behind them came a shadowy and ragged line of assault troops. Murdock counted twenty.

They were at seventy-five yards. Closer, they should be closer, especially for the MP-5's.

The lead scouts stopped and knelt down. They started ahead, and Murdock got the idea they were listening. He scraped a metal ammo clip against the AK. The scouts stood at once and angled directly toward the platoon leader.

Yes. Another ten yards. Murdock sighted in on the right-hand scout. He always took the right-hand side and

Holt right beside him with an AK, knew that. Ten seconds
later Murdock fired. Again the other twelve weapons
opened up with a vengeance.

Murdock's man went down with a round through his
heart. The other lead scout took two rounds, spun backwards into the dirt, and never moved. The ragged line of
assault troops suddenly became more ragged. Six went
down in the first SEAL volley. The rest dove for the ground
hunting any kind of cover. There simply wasn't any.

Return fire came from four of the riflemen, but they had
only gun flashes for targets. Their own flashes drew hot
lead. One man screamed. Another leaped up and raced down
the hill. He made it unscratched as far as Murdock could
follow him in the sparse moonlight.

The SEALs fired for twenty seconds. A long fire mission
for most of them. Murdock gave them three clicks on the
Motorola and their weapons fell silent. A few counterfire
rounds came from below. Murdock could see two men
crawling down the hill. A third dragged a wounded man
with him.

"Magic, Fernandez, give us a rear guard. Fire for three
minutes back here, then run to catch us. We'll be straight
south down the hill."

The men moved out. Red took the point as usual, with
Murdock right behind him. They jogged down the hill and
into another series of small fields with dikes around them.
Rice paddies. He was glad they weren't flooded right then.

On the ridgeline, Magic and Fernandez kept up occasional fire into the spot where the Chinese had been, then
aimed farther down the hill. Magic gave a little grunt when
his AK ran dry. He dropped it and waved at Fernandez.
They crawled down the far slope until they could stand with
safety, then jogged south to the bottom of the hill and into
the rice paddies.

Three minutes later they caught up with the platoon as
they slogged on south.

"Where the fuck is the damned coast highway?" Jaybird
said to Murdock.

"Let you know when we find it." A small village showed

a half mile to the left. Far enough away, Murdock decided,
and he kept aiming at the star he had picked to be due south.
South and east. They'd get to the east soon. To the left, he
could see the shadows of some low hills. A few lights
glowed in the area, but no big village. Far to the right he
thought he could see a spray of headlights now and then, but
he couldn't be sure.

Two jets screamed overhead, probably the same two
SU-27's they had seen in daylight. Not a chance they could
be dangerous until morning. However, they did indicate that
the Chinese must be serious about trying to rout out the
raiders still on Chinese soil.

Their route led down a wide valley. They kept to the left
side where there were some woods and barren spots. Well
behind them they saw headlights, and then heard the chatter
and unmistakable sounds of troops getting off transport. The
Marines were on their tail again, and too close for the
SEALs to think too much about collecting Social Security.

They speeded up their march.

Ten minutes later they had neared the end of the low row
of hills when they heard a new sound.

"Choppers," Red said.

Murdock listened. "Yes, larger ones, troop-transporting
birds. More than one."

They saw the running lights first—red, green, and white.
The helicopters came in low from the south almost straight
at Murdock and his platoon. Then they swung in a circle and
a half mile ahead moved into a six-bird front. Then all six
snapped on landing lights and they dropped down to the
ground about fifty feet apart. Murdock and his men could
hear doors opening and troops hitting the ground.

The platoon leader scowled. If each of the birds carried
twenty combat troops that would be 120 fighters ahead of
them.

He looked behind. Now he could see more headlights
with flashes of shadows walking in front of them.

Murdock shook his head. Airborne troops in front of
them, Chinese Marines in back of them. Just what the
fucking hell did they do now?

35

Sunday, May 17

2132 hours
Rural area
Near Amoy, China

"Wish to hell we still had our fifties," Magic Brown said. "We could blow them damn choppers into kindling."

"Roger that, Magic, but we don't," Murdock said. "So what comes next? We've got too fucking many Chinese out there. We can't go forward. No sense going backward and running into those fresh troops off the trucks."

He looked at the terrain. "Tactics depend on the situation and the terrain." He'd had that axiom drilled into him for ten years. He knew the situation. What about the terrain? He stared into the half light of the moon. They were near a small valley that drifted up to the left and into a partly forested hill. It couldn't be over three hundred feet high.

Potential. "Move up that little valley," he told Red, and the rest of them followed. Halfway up, Murdock angled his squad to the left and sent DeWitt with Second Squad to the right. "Find firing positions and cover behind a tree or rock. We'll wait and see if these guys send a detail up here to check it out. If they do we teach them better manners."

"After we let them know where we are, what comes next?" Jaybird asked from where he had settled down behind a foot-thick pine tree.

"Straight over the hill and see what's on the other side. Red is up there now taking a gander."

"Want to talk to the carrier again while we have a chance?" Holt asked.

"Set up the antenna and put it on receive," Murdock said. "If they have any word for us they'll put it on a three-hour repeat. We might catch something. I don't hold much hope that the Taiwanese Air Force will help us. Too political. They haven't raised a hand against China in fifty years. Why should they start now?"

"I'd say they have thirteen good reasons," Holt said. Then he unslung the SATCOM and began hitting switches, unfolded the small dish antenna, and angled it at the right spot in the sky to find the satellite.

When it was aimed, he snapped another switch, but the radio remained quiet.

"Figures," Murdock said.

The SEALs went rock silent then. They had heard something at the mouth of the small valley.

"Incoming," Jaybird whispered.

The Chinese troops were not trying to be quiet. They talked to each other. Equipment jangled, metal scraped against metal. Now and then someone laughed. Murdock tried to see through the nighttime gloom, but couldn't. The nightscope was up the hill. They waited.

The first troops were thirty yards away when Murdock saw them. There were twelve to fifteen men spread out at three-yard intervals across the floor of the valley moving slowly forward. Holt silently folded the SATCOM antenna and stowed it, and buttoned up the radio and slung it over his shoulder. No messages.

Murdock aimed his AK-47 at the man in the center who could be the detail leader. The Chinese soldier looked upward toward him and Murdock fired. The chest shot slammed the trooper backwards into the grass and weeds.

The rest of the platoon fired, and Murdock got off four more rounds before the Chinese troops were either dead or had run into the haze of the darkness.

Red Nicholson slid onto the ground beside Murdock.

"Nothing on the other side I can see, Skipper. No lights,

no people. Another small ridgeline. Looks like we're in a batch of woods that goes on a while."

"Move it," Murdock said into his lip mike, and the SEALs lifted up and trotted behind Red as he led them up the hill, over the top, and down the other side.

"Southeast," Murdock said to Red. They both looked at the stars and Murdock found the one he had been using. "Right about twenty degrees," he said.

"Yeah, about what I'd say too," Red said, and they swung that direction across another small ridge, through more trees, and away from any sign of the Chinese troops that almost had boxed them in.

For a moment Murdock thought he smelled salt air. Then he shook his head. Fantasizing. They pushed hard for half an hour, then came out of the woods and ahead saw a good-sized road with an occasional car or truck rolling along with headlights glaring.

"No curfew here," Magic said.

"Could be trouble to get across," Murdock said. They worked up through a field until they were within a quarter of a mile of the road. It was built up above the level of the fields on each side. A truck labored past, then all was quiet.

Murdock frowned.

"Yeah," Jaybird said. "I heard it again. That's a fucking shovel hitting a rock. Somebody on the other side of the road is digging in. Looks like they're waiting for us."

"Red, go take a look."

Red Nicholson could slip up on an Indian. He knew how to move without making a sound. He was the best point man Murdock had ever seen. The SEALs went to ground and rested.

Murdock worried about the choppers. The men in the trucks he could get away from, for a while. The choppers could rush men in ahead and behind them before they knew which way was up. That worried him. He looked at his watch. The dull glow showed that it was a little after 2230. Maybe eight hours to daylight. There was no chance they would be lucky and find another cave like the one they stayed in during the day. No chance in hell.

He tried to spot Red on his movement forward.

He couldn't.

Red was gone fifteen minutes. When he came back he knelt beside Murdock and touched him on the shoulder. The platoon leader jumped like he'd been given a jolt with a cattle prod.

"Sorry, Skipper. The Chinese are digging in all right. I figure they have a two-hundred-yard front, and beyond that I can't tell. There could be troops all along that road. It's a natural fort for them."

"Hard to get across?"

"Fucking near impossible."

They both heard the choppers about the same time. They came from behind them and to the north.

"The hunting dogs are out," Murdock said. "Red, do you sometimes have the feeling that we're being driven like cattle into the right place that will turn into a killing field?"

"That's what they hope. Never happen."

They listened as the choppers came closer.

"Sounds like the same troop transporters we almost collided with before," Murdock said.

"They must know we dodged them back there," Jaybird said. "Now they're moving up the troops. Maybe we could get a shot or two at them just before they set down."

"Or just before they lift off after dropping off their cargo," Murdock said. "I've a hunch they don't want their precious choppers around where there could be a firefight."

"So where are they going to land?" Red asked.

The sound came closer, then seemed to be right on top of them. The SEALs sprawled in the field hoping the big birds didn't turn on their downward-directed landing lights.

The copters thundered over them, swept to the left, and a half mile away began to form up for a precision landing.

"Let's go get them," Murdock said. The SEALs took off at a fast trot. They saw the Chinese birds turn on their lights and drop down to the ground and the troops pour out of them. Murdock didn't want to count, but he figured at least twenty men per chopper.

The SEALs covered a quarter mile in record time, and

went down behind rice paddy dikes three hundred yards away from the copters.

Murdock went to his Motorola. "Your long guns, anything we've got. Let's see how many of those choppers we can blast into little pieces. If anybody has any M-40 rounds, this is the spot to use them. Let's do it."

He leveled in with his heavy AK-47. He had twelve rounds and was determined to expend all of them. His first shot was slightly high. The rest of the troops opened up. He brought down his sights and nailed the closest chopper with a round through the canopy in front. He got four more shots into the bird before it tried to lift off.

It made it to thirty feet, then the rotors died and it fell like a rock and bust into flames.

Al Adams estimated the range and lofted an M-40 WP at the closest chopper. It landed ten feet short, but the forward surge of the WP streamers caught the grass and the chopper itself on fire and the troops scattered. A minute later the whole helicopter was a mass of flames, and machine gun rounds in the ship began exploding.

DeWitt yelled in delight as his AK-47 rounds punctured another chopper. It spun around as it tried to take off, then made it and lifted into the darkness.

The other birds at last had their landing lights turned off, making them harder targets. Two more were so wounded by the rifle and machine gun fire that they never got off the ground.

The troops on board had spread out, but didn't move forward. Murdock had counted on their attacking, but the platoon's two machine guns must have dissuaded their leader.

When the last choppers were airborne, Murdock hit his mike three times and the SEAL fire stopped.

"We move," Murdock said into the mike. "On me. We parallel the road and get away from all those Chinese troopers. Go, go, go."

They ran a hundred yards to the south parallel with the road. Again they took some rifle fire, but it was random. They were still hidden in the dark.

Murdock started down the road to his right and saw more than a dozen pairs of headlights coming toward them. Trucks, probably, with more ground troops.

He slowed the men to a walk and looked around. The mass of a hill reared to the left. It had some trees and brush that he could see in the soft moonlight.

"Up the hill," he said to Red, who swung that way, found a trail of sorts, and led out at a brisk pace.

More firing came from behind them. Murdock stopped to listen. He could hear and then see elements from the choppers moving toward them. He had no idea how many men. He trotted back to the front of the platoon and picked up the pace.

"No way they can follow us," Red said.

Murdock shook his head. "All they have to do is saturate the possible routes with men and they'll find us. What can we do to slow them down?"

"I've got a claymore," Jaybird said. "I think Doc still has one. We could use them if somebody gets on our trail in some kind of a narrow place."

"Good. Red, hit that gully up there to the left. We'll move up that and see if we have anybody on our ass end."

They hiked for another ten minutes. Now and then they heard troops behind them, but no one close. They were almost at the top of the ravine when they heard someone below them.

Murdock stopped his men and they listened.

"How many?" he asked DeWitt.

"I'd say twenty at least."

"Maybe thirty," Jaybird said.

"Use the claymores," Murdock said. "Go down about halfway in that narrow spot and set them in sequence with trip wires."

Jaybird and Doc ran back down the hill. They set the antipersonnel mines in the faint trail twenty yards apart, one farther up the hill than the other. They were aimed downhill. The trip wire would set off the mine and spew out over two hundred small ball-bearing-like projectiles in a cloud of death. They angled the mines for the best killing effect, set the trip wire on the first one, then on the second.

Jaybird and Doc hurried back up the trail. They could hear the Chinese coming up the slope behind them. They stopped fifty yards from the rest of the platoon to watch the trap.

"I can see some of them coming," Jaybird whispered. "No fucking scout out in front of them. Assholes. Must be twenty of them and all in range. How stupid can they get?"

A moment later a Chinese boot broke the trip wire and the first claymore went off with a roar. Screams of rage and agony echoed through the valley after the sound of the explosion died. Half of the men coming up the hill didn't stand up again.

Someone shouted in Chinese below and the survivors charged up the hill. One man was past the second trip wire when the second Chinese hit it and another belching roar showered the Chinese troops with instant death. The man beyond the death scene turned around and ran down the hill.

Jaybird and Doc grinned in the darkness and hurried up the rest of the SEALs.

Murdock took their report and they trotted over the top of the hill. On the far side they found another hill, higher. They took the downslope at the fast march and started up the other side. A machine gun opened up far to their left. The five-to-nine-round bursts came as a surprise.

"Who the hell they firing at?" Fernandez asked.

"The night ghosts," Ross Lincoln said. "Might mean they got a lot of green troops out there tonight."

Murdock had been thinking the same thing. The Chinese hadn't had a war to fight since Korea, forty-five years ago. New troops, new fears.

"We keep going unless that chatter gun comes closer than a mile," Murdock said. They kept moving up the hill.

"We still heading southeast?" Al Adams asked. "Swear I can smell the ocean."

"You get the imagination award of the mission," Frazier said. "You're probably smelling your armpit."

They kept climbing. There was no path or trail now. The

brush was sparse and the trees few, mostly pine, Murdock decided. They made it to the top, and Red Nicholson stood there looking down.

Murdock moved up beside him. "Goddamn."

"About the size of it. Must be two hundred feet straight down, like somebody sliced the mountain in half with a cleaver. Left or right, L-T?"

They heard the sound of trucks to the right.

"Company to the right," Red said.

"Yeah, lets take this slope down to the left and get around that drop-off as soon as we can. These fucking Chinese know the territory. They know we're stalled up here, so watch them try to plug both sides and the rear."

They hiked down the slope to the left. Murdock called up Doc, who reported that the two walking wounded were not holding them up.

"Frazier is a tough little cookie, sir. His side wound is hurting him, but it ain't serious. Fernandez has that arm wound, but he's still fit for duty. No other casualties so far."

"Keep it that way, Doc."

They hiked along the rim of the drop-off for ten minutes working down the left flank.

Red heard them first.

Murdock was close behind him. "More choppers," he said. "Moving up to block us on this left flank. Damn, told you these fuckers knew the terrain. That gives them a huge killing advantage."

36

Monday, May 18

0100 hours
Sharp cliff
Near Amoy, China

The SEALs kept hiking down the hill beside the sharp cliff. There was still no way down it. They had to go to the left the way they were committed. They heard the helicopters twice more. The birds were flying well to the left of their position. Probably the Chinese aircraft had landed two miles away in what they hoped was a safe spot to discharge their troops.

"They can move straight up this way and cut off our movement to the left," Murdock told Holt. "Then the truck troops from the right begin moving in, and I'm sure they have some men in the rear who can sweep forward to close the fucking trap."

"So what happens next, L-T?" Holt asked.

"We'll get as far down this slope as we can. They probably have two miles or more to hike. Looks like the terrain is flattening out ahead. We should find a spot to get down this cliff along here somewhere."

Five minutes later they heard the water.

"What the hell is that?" Holt asked.

Murdock grinned. "Sounds like running water to me. Not an ocean but the next best thing. It could be a good-sized river."

Jaybird moved up.

"A river?" he asked.

"Sounds like it. If it's big enough it could be a help."

They heard the jets screaming overhead again. The Chinese must be using them to fire up their troops on the ground. Strange psychology, but this was China.

Another quarter mile and the cliff faded away, the ground leveled out, and they found themselves beside a river.

"Must be a hundred yards across," Red said.

Murdock grinned again. "Yeah, and our Chinese friends are going to close the trap and find absolutely nothing at all inside it that they're looking for . . . namely us."

Red motioned them to be quiet. He pointed up the side of the river. They could see along it for a quarter mile upstream. In the faint moonlight they spotted six shadows moving slowly forward. They were on the bank of the river where the walking was easy.

Murdock motioned to Horse Ronson to set up his machine gun. He flipped out the bipod and bellied down behind it. Quietly as possible he chambered the first round of a belt of the NATO rounds and looked at Murdock.

The platoon leader held up his hand as he watched the soldiers come closer. When the six were two hundred yards away, Murdock slashed down his hand and the H&K 21A1 belched out a nine-round burst of the 7.2mm NATO rounds. After a pause, another five-round burst slanted at the confused Chinese.

Two had gone down from the first rounds. Another stumbled and fell on the second burst. Magic Brown got off two rounds from his M-89 sniper rifle, and another Chinese died in the sand. The last two charged into the brush along the riverbank and out of sight.

"Time for us to take a swim," Murdock said. "Get rid of all the weight that won't help you fight. Keep your weapons. Anybody down to two or three rounds for the AKs leave them here and give the rounds to somebody else."

A single chopper came from the south. It snapped on a searchlight and played the powerful beam on the ground. The SEALs scattered into the sparse growth to find enough cover to hide from the light if it came their way. The light paused for a moment when it showed the dead Chinese patrol members. Then it worked a search pattern to the front with the light probing every tree and bush.

Murdock leaned flat against a pine tree to become part of the trunk. The light swept over him and continued. The chopper worked the area a hundred and two hundreds yards away from the bodies, then wheeled and vanished back the way it had come.

"Now it's swim time," Murdock said. "Waterproof the Motorolas and the SATCOM and let's get in the water. It's downstream and away from the bad guys."

"Buddy system without the lines," Murdock added. He pushed into the river with Holt. "Try to stay in contact," he called, then the tug of the current pulled him downstream.

Murdock had not forgotten his two wounded. A shot-up arm and one wound in the side. They were SEALs. They would do better in the water than on land. He tried not to think about it. Jaybird and Doc came moving up to him. They treaded water and floated. Their weapons kept *sinking* them. Murdock had ditched his AK-47 and given his four magazines to Magic.

They drifted down the river. This close to the coast there was only a sluggish current, maybe two knots, Murdock guessed. He figured they had been in the water ten minutes. He let Jaybird and Doc go ahead, and he grabbed Holt and they swam against the current for two minutes. Three pairs of SEALs came up to them. They had three more men somewhere. Murdock stalled another minute and saw the trio coming.

All three were holding hands or holding onto vests. DeWitt had Frazier and Fernandez in tow. They came close.

"Frazier's a little weak, but he says he'll make it. Told me he isn't about to go KIA in fucking China."

Murdock relaxed and he and Holt moved along with the three. Ahead he could see lights.

"Far shore," he said to DeWitt, and he saw the 2IC slant toward the shore. The river here was about a hundred yards wide. The lights were all on one side. As they drifted slowly past the lights, Murdock got the idea that some sort of festival was in progress. There was dancing under outdoor lights, and stalls and booths and fancy costumes.

They didn't catch up with any of the others, but neither was there any disturbance, so they must have gone away from the lights as well.

Murdock and Holt kept up with the trio. They felt an added tug of the current as the river narrowed and dug deeper into the soil of China. He welcomed the increased speed.

DeWitt turned and waved, and Murdock swam over near him.

"We dumped Frazier's 4A1. He's having a hard time. Can I trade you Frazier for Holt for a while?"

Murdock swam up and caught hold of Frazier's arm.

"Which is the bad side?" he asked.

Frazier turned toward him, his eyes glassy, then shook his head. "Sir, right side, sir."

"Easy, Frazier, easy. You're out of Hell Week. All we're doing is getting down this river to the salty Taiwan Strait. You're going to make it fine. Right, Frazier?"

Murdock looked at the man. He was nodding. Murdock shook his arm, and Frazier came back to the present.

"Take it easy, Frazier. We don't leave men behind, remember? You're with us all the way."

Murdock saw what DeWitt meant. It took more effort all the time to hold Frazier up. Murdock called quietly for Holt, who came back and held Frazier from the other side.

"No sweat, sir. We'll get him there."

Ten minutes later Murdock saw big trouble ahead. He figured they had come two, maybe three miles when he heard the rumble of motors. He knew what they were at once. Shallow-draft river patrol boats.

"DeWitt," Murdock called.

He swam over from where he had been and nodded.

"Patrol boats ahead," Murdock said. "Swim up and contact the other men and get them all out of the water on the right-hand side. Looks like more protection on that side. Leave one man close to shore we can spot."

DeWitt waved, and struck out with a crawl stroke that would eat up the distance quickly, taking Fernandez with him.

Murdock and Holt began angling back to the right-hand shore. They hit bottom twice and pushed off. The growl of the patrol boats came sharper now. The river made a bend to the left, and then Murdock could see them.

Six flashing lights showed maybe a quarter of a mile downstream. There were six patrol boats working slowly against the current, searchlights playing over the water and touching both shores, probing through brush and trees.

"Looking for us," Holt said.

"True, let's hit the bank and get into some cover. We'll find the rest of the men later."

They got Frazier to shore, but had to help him walk as they worked up the bank into a thick growth of brush and some trees. Frazier shook his head.

"I can make it. Damn side isn't that bad. I can make it."

Murdock sent Holt running downstream to find Doc and bring him back. He hoped the others weren't too far ahead.

DeWitt swam as strongly as he could while holding onto Fernandez for what he figured was five minutes. He hadn't found the others. Then he heard a cough ahead and stroked hard again. He found them standing neck deep in the water near the shore.

"Out and into the brush," he said. "Murdock is just behind. Doc, you better get back along the bank and see if you can do something to help Frazier. He's not good. They might be near shore or in the brush somewhere. He's hurting pretty bad."

Doc waved and shook the rest of the water off him, made sure his MP-5 was drained, and took off upstream at a jog. DeWitt moved the men deep into the brush. He'd seen the probing searchlight and he wanted to be sure they were out of sight.

Doc ran along the shore. The boats were far enough away so he was not taking any risk staying in the open. He heard someone coming and dropped to his knees, his MP-5 up and ready. A shadow loomed out of the darkness and before he could swing the weapon up, someone slammed into him.

Doc jolted to the ground and rolled over. He started to swing his room broom around when he heard a chuckle.

"Damn, Doc, I nearly wasted you good," Holt said. "How you know I was coming to fetch you?"

"You came within a red cunt hair of getting three slugs up your left nostril. How bad is Frazier?"

By the time Doc got there, Frazier was feeling better. Doc gave him a shot of morphine, a drink of water, and two chocolate bars.

"Don't ask me where I got them," Doc growled.

"We have time to get up to DeWitt before the patrol boats get here?" Murdock asked.

"Not likely, L-T. We best do a hide-hole right here if we can."

They moved deeper into the brush and settled down flat on the ground.

Five minutes later, the patrol boats came chugging by. The powerful searchlight dug through the trees and brush, but revealed nothing unusual to the Chinese men on the boats. They kept on working their way upstream.

"The water again?" Frazier asked.

Murdock made up his mind. "No. Too dangerous. They could come steaming back downstream silently and catch our asses. We'll stick to the land. We should be getting close to the beach."

They went back to the shore and worked up to where DeWitt and the rest of the platoon waited for them.

"How is he?" DeWitt asked.

"Better," Murdock said. "We'll stick to dry land for a while. The beach can't be far away now."

Red came up and checked the stars. "L-T, we need to swing away from the river to get southeast. We ready?"

Murdock sent him out thirty yards ahead and he and Holt followed. All had drained and checked their weapons. All were locked and loaded and ready to fire. Murdock asked Doc about Fernandez.

"His arm is giving him a bad time. I put it in a sling and

gave him a shot of morphine. He should make it. He's one tough cookie."

Their line of march cut across a field, edged around a small village without a single light, and then back on their heading. Murdock kept hoping he would smell salt air. He didn't. Maybe there was an offshore flow of air. Yeah, that must be it. They had to be within a mile of the surf.

They hit a road that went almost in the direction they wanted. They took it and the men eased up a little. The walking was better there than across the uneven fields, jumping rice paddy dikes and wading through unharvested grain.

A truck's lights down the road drove them into the field and they kept there after that. A half mile farther along, Murdock stopped still. He turned his head and grinned. Salt air. At last he could smell the salt air.

He ran up to Red and they checked out what lay ahead. They saw a few lights of what must be one small village to the left maybe a mile off. To the right they saw no lights of any kind.

"Salt air, Red. You smell that?"

Red nodded. "About fucking time. How far?"

"No idea, but our Chinese friends have no clue where we are, which is good for us," Murdock said. "They checked the river and our former position. We vanished into thin air on them. No reason they should think we're down here. Now, all we have to do is find the beach, give a yell on the SATCOM about where we are, let them triangulate the transmission, and come and pick us up."

They stared straight ahead down their star path.

"Let's hit the road again for a half hour. Then we'll see just where that beach is."

Twenty minutes later they slowed and stopped. Murdock moved up beside Red.

"Trucks," Red said. "I can hear them and they are right in front of us somewhere. We need a little rise or a hill or something."

The ground around them was flood plain and flat as a rice paddy.

"Closer," Murdock said.

They walked ahead a hundred yards and came to a slight rise. When they looked over it they saw lights strung along what only could be a road. Trucks rolled both ways. The salt air seemed stronger to Murdock

"Trucks and more trucks," Red said. "The damn Chinese must have a division out looking for us."

"Good, give them something to do while we slip right through their net and into the water. Four hundred yards to the beach. Let's move up as close as we can get without giving away our position. We need a good look at this situation."

The word was passed. No talk, no noise, quiet or dead. They worked up slowly, crawling the last fifty yards through tall grass that gave them perfect concealment.

Murdock and Red eyed the roadway from the grass. It was built up like the other road, only this one had knots of Chinese troops every hundred yards. They were all carrying weapons, each group now and then patrolling halfway to the next group.

"Doesn't look good, Skipper," Red said.

Murdock could hear the faint roar of breakers across the road. He could see no lights beyond the road. It had to be the beach just beyond that thin line of troopers. His only problem was how in hell did he get across that line without losing half his platoon.

37

Monday, May 18

Murdock moved his troops into a dry irrigation ditch three feet deep that ran alongside the roadway. They were still a hundred yards from the Chinese troops.

"We need to find a weak spot," Murdock whispered to Red. The scout nodded. He motioned to the left and they crawled that way. After two hundred yards they could see no change in the placement of the troops along the far side of the road.

"Seems like they expect us to come this way," Red said.

"Yeah, and they might have this many troops along a twenty-mile stretch of the coast road. They must figure the raiders are Taiwanese and they'll try for the coast."

Red checked his watch. "We've got maybe four hours of darkness left. That's to get through the troops here, into the surf, and get picked up before daylight."

"Yeah, don't keep reminding me."

They moved back to the middle of their line of SEALs in the ditch.

"We wipe out the closest guys and make a run for the surf?" Jaybird asked. "I hear breakers not a hundred yards from that road."

"We'd never get wet," Holt said. "They'd cut us down like corncobs in August."

275

Jaybird frowned. "Holt, that makes no sense at all. Corncobs in August? Whoever heard of that?"

"You're not a farmer, Jaybird. Else you'd know."

Jaybird didn't give it up. "Hey, we assault their asses here, all charge across at once, and make a break for the water. Most of us would get through."

"Most. We could lose six men that way," Murdock said. "Not a chance. We all get through, we all get out of fucking China. That's the way it's gonna be. No more talk about casualties."

As Murdock said that, a truck pulled up on the road in front of them and discharged a dozen more soldiers who joined the group directly opposite the SEALs.

"Bad news," Murdock said. He pointed, and moved the SEALs down the ditch two hundred yards to the right where the line of Chinese troops wasn't so thick. Here they were still spread out at one-hundred yard intervals with only six men at each post. The SEALs might have a chance rushing them here.

Murdock and his men lay in the ditch for an hour. He touched Holt's shoulder.

"Wind up that SATCOM and let's see if we can talk to somebody with some clout. Call the damned carrier."

Holt took out the radio, broke open the antenna, and folded it out and aligned it with the satellite. Then he turned it on and listened for a minute. Nothing.

He sent a burst message asking the carrier to reply. A voice message came back almost at once.

"We read you, Murdock. In clear. No results yet with the Taiwanese. Our President talked with their President. We keep hoping. We'll have aircraft in the area south of Amoy just prior to dawn if you can get into the water. Our orders are firm. We can take no direct land action."

"Can you pinpoint our location via this signal?" Murdock asked.

"That's a Roger. We have you nine miles south of Amoy on the coast."

"Good. Sure like to see some Navy out here damn soon."

"Do what we can. Stay healthy."

Murdock shut off the set. He looked at the Chinese troops in front. Be better to get half his men out than none at all. He watched the eastern sky. No hint of dawn yet. It couldn't be far away.

Choppers to the left caught his attention. Three big birds settled down to the ground in their landing-beam islands of light. He saw twenty men jump off each one and form up into a skirmish line.

They were a mile, maybe a little more to the left. If they came straight forward, it would take them fifteen, maybe twenty minutes to get here. If they ran they could make it in ten minutes.

He could shift more to the right, down the irrigation ditch, maybe find some cover somewhere. In the gloom he couldn't see any growth of brush or trees.

They had to move away from that concentration of troops. DeWitt dropped beside him.

"Company," DeWitt said. "We got no fucking place to go."

"Move to the right," Murdock said.

"We're gonna run out of room that way after a while."

"Better than staying here."

Murdock passed the word. They would move to the right again, a thousand yards if there was room. He had a feeling the irrigation ditch wouldn't last that long.

They crawled some places. In others they could bend over and do a poor imitation of a duck walk. Murdock was at the front of the line. When they had come about three hundred yards, he looked ahead and saw that the road turned directly at the irrigation ditch, which ended abruptly. Nowhere to go.

He stopped the line and moved them back fifty yards from the end of the ditch.

"What now?" Jaybird asked.

"We wait and see what happens."

Twenty minutes later they found out.

"Trucks over on the right," Red Nicholson said. Murdock closed his eyes and concentrated. Then he could hear them. More six-bys probably bringing in troops. Did the Chinese know that they were in this little pocket, or were they just hoping?

He checked the soldiers out front. They were still six per post at hundred-yard intervals. Placed that way they could provide fire support for each other, but they'd risk the danger of gunning their own men.

Murdock called in DeWitt and Jaybird.

"Nothing else we can do. We've got to make a try for the beach. No way we're gonna sit here and get clobbered by troops on both flanks. I'm expecting somebody to start marching at us from the rear any minute. Any ideas?"

Jaybird nodded. "How about we do the dirty trick. We straggle out of the dark and we have Ching yell at them that we're coming in and not to fire. It's worked in some combat situations."

"Yeah, with the Germans in U.S. uniforms," DeWitt said. "Back in WW Two."

They passed the word for Ching, who crawled up. He listened to Jaybird lay out the idea.

"Yeah, might work. Could get us close enough to wipe out one pocket, but then they gonna hit us with them six guys on both sides."

"A hundred yards in the dark," Jaybird said. "Surprise. They won't know what the fuck is happening. All we need is to gun those six and turn our guns on the six on each side and run like hell for the surf."

Murdock nodded. If anybody thought that the officers had the only good ideas, they were really fucked up.

"Jaybird, I think you have it. We don't like have a lot of time. You go one way, Ching the other, and brief the guys. We waste the six right ahead, after we get as close as we can on a ruse. Then we gun to the sides and run for the damn surf. Everyone okay with that?"

The other three nodded.

"Tell them. Then, Ching, get back here. We'll come out of the ditch in a ragged line so we don't shoot each other. You stay in the middle of the line and call out when we get within forty yards or so. Your call. If you think we can walk right up to them, do it. You'll be the first man to fire when you think it's right."

Ching nodded and the two men left. Ching was back in three minutes.

"Let's do it," Murdock said.

They stood and stepped over the ditch into a dry rice paddy. They walked forward, a ragged line of thirteen men in cammies, some with soft hats, some bareheaded. They walked with weapons held down, as if returning from some patrol.

Ching held the center of the line, watching the Chinese beyond the roadway. He could see them from the waist up. Most were talking, some laughing. None seemed to be watching across the road.

They moved up to forty yards from the roadway when the first Chinese noticed them. He looked, then pointed. He yelled something in Mandarin.

Ching barked back at him. Saying in Madarin they were coming back from a sweep and tired enough to fall down. The Chinese soldiers seemed to understand that. Then another man beyond the road called something out to Ching.

Ching asked him to repeat it. Then he said quietly, "Now, guys." He lifted his CAR and fired a three-round burst. Up and down the line twelve other weapons joined in. The Chinese, caught unaware, took three casualties. The other three dropped below road level and threw grenades. They popped up and fired single shots, then threw more grenades. Weapons on both sides of the target now joined in firing at the point where they thought there was an attack.

The SEALs hit the dirt. Ching threw a fragger, but it hit short and went off on the roadway. One SEAL bellowed in pain.

Lieutenant Blake Murdock felt something slam into his upper left arm. He spun and sprawled in the dirt. Ching rolled over beside him.

"Won't work, Lieutenant," Ching said. "We better haul ass out of here."

Murdock felt the waves of pain billowing through his

arm, down to his torso, and up to his brain. He gritted his teeth to hold in the moan. Some of it came out.

"You hit, L-T?" Ching asked.

"Yeah, arm. Get us out of here."

"Pull back to the ditch," Ching bellowed. "Crawl, it'll be safer. No more firing."

They moved. Ching helped Murdock crawl. Elbows usually do most of the work pulling the body ahead. Murdock only had one elbow that was contributing. They worked slowly. The fire had slowed, then stopped from the Chinese. They had no targets. They knew their enemy was out there somewhere, but the night and a drift of clouds over the moon had helped to save the SEALs' skins.

By the time Ching and Murdock made it to the irrigation ditch a hundred yards behind the road, Doc was waiting for them.

"We got one more casualty," he said. He looked at Murdock's arm. "Shit, we've got two more casualties, sir." He stripped the cammie back and worked on the wound, wrapping it after dosing it with antibiotic powder. A shot of morphine followed.

Murdock lay there breathing hard. He shook his head. "Who else got hit?"

"Ronson, took one in the thigh. Nasty one. I think it slanted off a bone. He's hurting, but says he can walk, run, and swim to get the hell out of here."

Murdock tried to reason it through. The pain kept crowding out his thoughts. He shook his head again. "No more of that damn morphine, Doc. No more for me. Where's Holt?"

"On the other side, L-T. Want me to crank up the SATCOM?"

"Yeah."

Holt pulled out the folding antenna, and a moment later had sent a message to the carrier.

"On beach. Enemy on three sides, closing in. If we don't get help in a half hour, it won't do us any good. What's the status?"

Don Stroh came on sounding tired. "Damn little help.

We've been twisting balls all night. We . . ." He stopped.

"We got it." His voice broke. "Christ, we got confirmation. The Taiwanese Air Force launched fighters and choppers twenty minutes ago from a base just across the strait from you. They could be on-site any time. Give them a no-shoot red flare to mark your position. We worked that out early on. Hang on, guys, help is coming."

38

Monday, May 18

0427 hours
Coast road
South of Amoy, China

Holt gave a muffled cheer. Doc grinned and gave him a thumbs-up.

"You hear that, sir? The Taiwan folks are coming with jets and choppers could be here anytime. Left Taiwan twenty minutes ago."

Murdock heard it through a haze. Damn morphine. He yawned and blinked, then shook his head. A shiver lanced down his back. His arm hurt like hell.

"Heard. Thanks. Look alive, guys. Security. Pull the line in tighter. Security all around the perimeter. Got a chance to get out of this rat hole, let's not blow it. Damn Chinese could put on an attack any time."

"Red flares, sir. They mentioned red flares."

"Yeah, yeah. Got them here somewhere." Murdock dug out two flares. They were marked red and could be lit and thrown or fired in to the air. "Do them, Holt, when the time comes. Make damn sure it's a Taiwan jet. They'll come from the sea hunting us." Pain washed over him and he grimaced. "Damn, damn it to hell. Fucking damn."

Murdock pushed up with his good arm and looked at Holt. "Flares, they say we should mark our position, or where we want the jets to shoot?"

283

"Our position, L-T. Red is for a no-shoot location, like to spot a downed flyer by air search."

"Yeah, right. Yeah."

Holt looked at Doc in the gloom. Doc shook his head. "He said no more morphine. Have to gut it out. He can do it. Now let's watch for those damn Chinese ground troops."

The Chinese at the highway directly in front of them lifted up and fired over the embankment.

Holt took a quick look. "Must be thirty rifles out there now," he said.

"Don't return fire," Jaybird said. "They don't even know if we're here or not. Keep them in the dark."

The firing from the front continued, but at a slower pace. Soon it was down to a round or two every minute.

DeWitt came and settled in beside Murdock.

"How you doing, Skipper?"

"Damn good. Am I still conscious?"

"Just a little slug in your arm. No sweat. Hear we're to have some Taiwan Air Force company."

"Anytime now. We mark red, they shoot in front."

"Then we charge through the bodies into the surf," DeWitt said. "I like the sound of that. Everyone can walk. Frazier did good on that assault on the highway. He's no worry."

"I'll make it if I have to crawl," Murdock said.

Red tilted his head and looked toward the sea. "We've got friendlies coming in directly in front of us and low."

Murdock couldn't hear them. "When you're damn sure, Holt, throw out that first red flare."

Holt listened, then nodded. A minute later the sound of the jets was unmistakable. Coming right at you they project little sound. He pulled the tape off the flare and held it.

"Jets just changed direction," Red said.

Then they all could hear the whine of the Mach-2 jets. They slammed overhead at two hundred feet and made the ground shake.

"Friendlies, all right," Red said. Holt looked at DeWitt, who nodded.

Holt lit the flare and threw it twenty feet in front of their

ditch. It exploded into a bright red flare that turned the
landscape into a red wonderland for twenty yards around.
The two jets made a wide turn and came back parallel with
the beach. Six rockets streamed from wings of the jets. They
hit in sequence up the highway, then walked down and past
the red flare, smashing into paving and the far side, blowing
the troops there into a mass of screaming bodies.

DeWitt looked at the results. There was no firing from the
Chinese in front.

"One more pass," he said. The jets made another wide
turn and came in from the other direction. Again rockets and
cannon fire blasted the highway in front of the still-burning
red flare.

DeWitt stood and shouted. "On your feet, moving out. Be
ready with assault fire. Go, go, go."

Holt watched Murdock as he pushed up with his right
arm, held the MP-5 in his right hand, and stepped over the
ridge of the ditch and into the paddy field. They ran forward
in a ragged line. They took no fire as they approached the
paved highway. They two Chinese lifted up to fire at them.
Bursts of three rounds from four MP-5's blew them out of
their shoes and dead in the sand.

Murdock lagged behind. Then Holt came beside him and
urged him on. He took the lieutenant's weapon, caught his
shoulder, and helped him to run forward.

"No damn reason I can't run," Murdock brayed in fury.

"It's the morphine," Holt yelled. They heard firing to the
front and kept going. Magic Brown waited at the drop-off
on the other side of the paving. He grabbed Murdock and
lifted him down. Then they all charged into the sand.

Murdock wanted to start singing. He was a terrible singer.
The sand felt so good, so natural under his feet. He heard
DeWitt shouting. What he said wasn't clear.

Holt stayed with his L-T. They took some ragged fire
from well up the beach beyond the rocket attack of the
planes. Then they were wading into the water, the Taiwan
Strait. How long they had yearned to feel its cold kiss.

Holt listened to DeWitt and dropped the CAR he had
been carrying into the surf. He shucked out of his vest

loaded with all the combat goodies, but kept the SATCOM radio over his shoulder. Murdock let him take his combat vest off and drop it in the surf. Then they jumped a breaker, ducked under the next one, and were swimming.

Murdock forgot and tried a stroke with his left arm and screeched in pain.

Holt was there. "Don't worry, L-T, we all gonna make it. The Two-IC has us in control. We're all in a bunch and moving offshore. Feels like the fucking tide is going out. We finally got some good luck on our side."

Murdock tried to sidestroke with one arm. It didn't work. At last he rolled on his back and did a flutter kick. He was surprised how well he floated. Then he remembered all of his combat gear was still in China or on the bottom of the Taiwan Strait.

Rounds started slapping into the sea around them. The Taiwan jets must have seen the ground fire. They came back with cannon roaring and two more rockets and the rifle fire ended abruptly.

DeWitt swam back and helped push them along. Soon all thirteen SEALs were within touching distance of each other.

"Hold it this way," DeWitt boomed into the sudden silence of the still-dark Chinese night. "We stay together. Holt told me he put out two sonar beacons. The sub might pick up the signal and help those Taiwan choppers find us. At any rate, we're out of fucking China."

A cheer went up.

Doc swam over and checked on Murdock's wound. The bandage had come off and he was bleeding again. Too much blood. Doc put on another bandage and kept it in place with two rubber bands.

"L-T, you've got to keep that arm quiet. I'll unbutton one of your shirt buttons and you stuff that hand inside your shirt. A kind of sling. Best we can do right now. You can't loose any more blood. You read me, sir?"

Murdock nodded. Doc looked at Holt, who bobbed his head.

They moved away from the coast slowly. The swimming was at the rate of the slowest man. Murdock was feeling a

little better. Either the morphine was wearing off or dulling
his pain. He didn't know which. He had five or six
wounded. He had no communications, he was a quarter of a
mile from China, which was still fighting mad. How the hell
was anybody going to find them in the fucking Taiwan
Strait?

He asked Holt the question.

"They'll do it, sir. That's their job. We did ours. Now the
pickup guys have to do theirs."

They drifted with the tide, swam a little, drifted again.
DeWitt kept the men together. Doc went from one wounded
man to the next. DeWitt came over to talk to Murdock.

"We're more than a half klick out in the strait now," he
said. "Should be far enough away that Uncle wouldn't mind
getting involved. Did that last message say the Navy was
going to have some aircraft over this way just before
sunrise?"

Murdock said that's what he remembered.

"Take a look to the east," DeWitt said.

Murdock looked and saw the first faint hint of a tinge of
light.

Ten minutes later they heard choppers. Half the men
cheered. Then they were silent to pinpoint where the birds
were coming from. They could be Chinese. They came from
off the coast. That was a good sign. Five minutes more and
they saw a parachute flare blossom to the east and north.

"A flare," Holt screeched. "They must be looking for us."

"Yeah, but we're not sure just who they are," DeWitt said.

A single bird came closer. Another flare, then another one
closer yet. The next flare drifted down slowly about fifty
yards from them. Then they saw four more choppers swing
into line and all five dropped flares as they came forward
directly over the swimmers. They waved and shouted and
waved again.

"Looks like they're the good guys or they'd be shooting
by now," Jaybird said.

The jets snarled down toward the beach again hitting the
Chinese with machine guns and rockets one last time.

The choppers were too high for the swimmers to make

out any identifying marks. They slowed and came around and dropped another series of flares. For a quarter of a mile the ocean was like daylight.

"So they know we're here. How are they going to pick us up?" Murdock asked.

Holt shook his head.

Then they heard another sound, the heavier, deeper, and more familiar *whup, whup, whup* of a big chopper.

"Sounds like a CH-46," Magic Brown said.

It came in slow, ten feet off the gentle swells of the strait. It made one pass over them, then made a wide circle and came back moving no more than five miles an hour.

The tail hatch opened and a rope ladder dropped down. The SEALs cheered again. They had made this pickup at sea dozens of times in practice and training. It was a rough pickup method, but sometimes the only one available. Like now.

The big chopper settled down to ten feet off the water and hovered. Jaybird went up the ladder first. It was tricky work, hard physically to control the swaying ladder. Two men grabbed it in the water to hold it fast, then one more SEAL went up, then another.

A head poked out the hatch door with a bullhorn. "We've got a sling coming down. Understand you have two wounded who can't climb."

DeWitt bellowed that the sailor was right. He moved toward the far side of the ship where another hatch opened and a sling dropped down. They towed Murdock over there and got the sling around his shoulders without hurting his left arm. On signal he was lifted up and away.

Frazier went up on the next drop of the sling, and then Ronson. His leg was bleeding badly again. Holt and DeWitt stroked over to the ladder and climbed it into the glorious interior of the big chopper.

Before DeWitt sat down he made sure that Doc was tending to his patients. Then he sat beside Murdock.

"We made it, Skipper. By God, we got out of fucking China."

Murdock couldn't say a word. All he could do was nod.

39
Monday, May 18

When the CH-46 landed on board the carrier a half hour later, Murdock refused a stretcher and walked with his men following the white shirt across the landing deck.

Two Navy corpsmen met them and ushered the four wounded to sick bay. Murdock made sure that Ronson, Frazier, and Fernandez were all being treated before he let the medics look at his arm. By that time it was dripping blood again.

The doctor shook his head as he cleaned out the wound.

"Slug went all the way through, missed most of the muscle tissue, but you won't be doing any push-ups for a while." The doctor was quiet for a moment. Then he looked at Murdock's buttocks and the backs of his legs.

"Lieutenant, are those shrapnel wound scars?"

"Yes, sir."

"What I thought. I'm new here, haven't seen any from shrapnel before. It all come out yet?"

"Yes, sir."

"You're one of the SEALs?"

"Yes, sir."

"Figures." They both laughed.

When Murdock's arm was patched up, he checked on the

289

other three. Fernandez was out of bed working on a tray full of food.

"They said I could have whatever I wanted," he said between mouthfuls.

Frazier's side wound looked worse, his doctor said. He'd be in sick bay for at least a week before he could be moved.

Horse Ronson sat up in bed and worked on a tray of food. His doctor told Murdock his concern.

"The bullet hit a bone, but didn't break it. Not even a hairline crack. It's going to be painful for at least a month after the bullet wound itself heals. Be sure you keep watch on him."

Murdock said he would.

Don Stroh tracked down Murdock and shook his hand.

"Next time, Don, don't cut it quite so fine. I figured that we had maybe twenty minutes left down there on China soil before those hordes would be all over us."

"I pulled every string I knew of, even some I didn't know about. I think the person-to-person with the two Presidents is what did it. Made old Lee Teng-hui so chagrined that we'd helped out his little island so much he just about had to come around. It was him or nobody."

Stroh brought out an envelope with satellite photos.

"You boys did one hell of a job. Take a look at your recent handiwork."

The photos showed the two Chinese Luda-class destroyers mired almost to their main decks in the mud and slime at dockside. The missile warehouse on the bay had been blown into kindling, and all the buildings for a block around it were flattened or burned to the ground.

"Our shots of the missile-assembly plant show a lot of repair trucks and other rigs around it and not much missile work getting done. What did you do inside that one?"

Murdock told him about disabling the elevator that led to the basement and flooding it with the fire hoses.

"Oh, your old man called about an hour ago. Wants to talk to you when you get here. Said he'd call back."

"How the hell does he know where I am?"

"He's a congressman. He can pull a lot of switches that I can't even touch."

Somebody handed Murdock a phone. "For you, sir," the sailor said.

Murdock took the handset.

"Yes, sir, Murdock reporting sir."

A chuckle came from the other end. "Well, Blake? Aren't these newfangled phones and satellites just the best? How are you? Hear your mission is over and you're back on the U.S. shipping. Good. How did it go?"

"You should know that by now too, Dad."

"I'll get it tomorrow. Nice little picnic, but now it's time you have a leave. I'll talk with your CO out in Coronado. Why not come to D.C. and let that arm heal and you recuperate? You must have at least two months leave time by now.

"Fact is, your mother has a girl she want you to meet. Now, don't say no right away. I sent a picture of her to Don Stroh. He should have it for you. Her name is Ardith. Take a look and then we'll see what you have to say."

"Dad, you know how I feel about Mom trying to pair me off."

"Yep, but she still does it. You'll be home in a couple of days. I'll call you in Coronado. Still hoping to get you into the legislative branch of government. You'll be invaluable on the Hill."

"I'm already in government service, Dad."

"Sure, sure. My job will be open in ten years or so. Want to groom you for it and then move you up to senator. Yes, sir, that would be fine."

Don Stroh came up with another envelope. He gave it to Murdock. He opened it automatically and out fell a picture of the most gorgeous girl Murdock had seen in years.

"Dad, I have Ardith's picture. Pretty."

"Yeah, she is. She's Ardith Manchester, the daughter of Senator Manchester of Oregon. And she's a lawyer, so sharp it makes my head spin. She's his chief of staff but will get snapped up by one of the bureaus or one of the secretaries' offices soon."

Murdock grinned. "Never can tell, Dad. I might be able to get free for a couple of weeks. Not going to do much with this arm for a while."

Jaybird came into the sick bay and looked at the picture. He growled. Murdock told his father good-bye and turned the picture around so Jaybird couldn't see it.

"Get your own girl, swabby," Murdock said.

Jaybird laughed. "Just as soon as we get to San Diego, L-T. You can bet on that."

They all laughed and Murdock could feel the tension of the mission start to fade away. He smiled. It was good to be alive, to be back in friendly hands. He watched Jaybird and saw the dedication there. It stirred him. To hell with D.C. He was a SEAL. That got him to wondering about the next mission. Murdock was looking forward to it. As he lay there, he began to wonder just what their next assignment would be and where it would take him and SEAL Team Seven Platoon Three.